Praise for Yiğit Turhan

"This might be the first thing you have read from Yiğit Turhan, but it won't be the last. Yiğit weaves a mesmerizing narrative in his debut gothic novel around the enchanting world of magical butterflies, creating a darkly alluring and evocative tale that will leave readers spellbound. He's a captivating new voice in literature, which is exactly where he belongs."
—Dua Lipa, Grammy Award–winning singer-songwriter

"Yiğit Turhan spreads his wings with this sizzling, intricate debut. His writing is kaleidoscopic, capturing—in vivid detail—the idiosyncrasies of characters and their experiences with family, creativity, and wealth (or the lack thereof). Yet, all the while, something dark and ominous simmers beneath the surface, with tension threatening to explode from its cocoon at any given moment. There were butterflies in my stomach as well as on the page."   —Jack Edwards, #BookTok influencer

"*Their Monstrous Hearts* is a take-no-prisoners wild ride! Creepy, cool, and fearless in equal heaping measures! Highly recommended."
—Jonathan Maberry, *New York Times* bestselling author of *NecroTek* and *Cave 13*

"I love how the mystery and the magic unfold gradually and unexpectedly, doled out to the reader in exciting scraps. The themes of inheritance and generational trauma are exquisitely handled and feel bone-real. I was floored by the cinematic explosion of monarch butterflies overtaking the home."
—Lisa Taddeo, *New York Times* bestselling author of *Three Women*, *Animal* and *Ghost Lover*

THEIR MONSTROUS HEARTS

YIĞIT TURHAN

/||MIRA

/II MIRA™

ISBN-13: 978-0-7783-6827-4

Their Monstrous Hearts

Copyright © 2025 by Yiğit Turhan

Mira
22 Adelaide St. West, 41st Floor
Toronto, Ontario M5H 4E3, Canada
MIRABooks.com

Printed in Lithuania

Recycling programs
for this product may
not exist in your area.

MIX
Paper | Supporting
responsible forestry
FSC® C021394

to Giuliano,
on this harvest moon

"I must also have a dark side if I am to be whole."

Carl Jung

"I am terrified by this dark thing
That sleeps in me.
All day I feel its soft, feathery turnings, its malignity."

Sylvia Plath, "Elm," *Ariel*

PROLOGUE

Perihan gazed at the opulent villas lined up like precious pearls on a necklace, feeling overwhelmed by their excessive beauty. The sight was almost terrifying, reminiscent of the antique pearls adorning her own necklace. As the dark clouds were illuminated by a sudden flash of lightning, she shook off her thoughts and quickened her pace along the deserted road. The gentle raindrops on her tired face felt like an ominous sign. The unexpected gust of wind, unusual for a mild November afternoon, added to her unease.

On her seventieth birthday, Perihan had indulged in a day of shopping at Milan's most luxurious stores. Despite her age, she possessed a strong physique, with firm knees, agile movements, and enough strength to carry her shopping bags from the stores to her home. The kind store managers at Cartier and Valentino had offered to send the packages to her address with a courier, but she declined, insisting she could manage on her own. Though she lacked a family to celebrate with, her small group of friends had arranged to gather at the villa, refusing to let her spend the evening alone. They had asked her to leave the house and return around seven o'clock. Glancing at her watch, Perihan realized she was already half an hour late.

Oh my… Licia must have already set the table, she thought as she turned the corner onto Via Marco de Marchi, where she resided. Just then, another lightning bolt flashed across the sky, and a large monarch butterfly appeared seemingly out of nowhere. Despite the heavy rain, Perihan could hear the faint flapping of its wings. The butterfly had bright orange and black stripes, with one wing decorated with symmetric white dots. It seemed to hover in midair.

"What a miracle," Perihan exclaimed, a smile stretching across her wrinkled face. "It's been years since I last saw this one…and on my birthday!" Hastily shifting the heavy bags onto her shoulder, she wiped the raindrops from her eyes with her long red nails and followed the butterfly. It fluttered around in circles for a few moments, before darting straight ahead. Despite the downpour, the orange-and-black wings moved swiftly. Overwhelmed with excitement, Perihan disregarded the red light—and almost got hit by an old Ford passing by. The driver, an unattractive man with numerous moles and few teeth, leaned out of the window and cursed at her in an Italian dialect she couldn't understand. Unfazed by his behavior, Perihan remained focused on following the butterfly, which flew rapidly and ascended into the sky.

"I wonder where it disappeared to," she mused with a melancholic expression on her face. The rain intensified, the drainage problems in the area turning the road into a pool of water. Perihan's bare feet were drenched as the rain seeped through the open toes of her green python slingbacks.

"You're blocking my view." The unexpected comment startled her. She looked at the stranger, hoping to recognize a friendly face, but it was no one she knew. She turned to notice the growing crowd of people with their faces hidden behind their phone screens. She wondered if they were filming her. Lacking an umbrella, her meticulously coiffed hair now wet, her makeup smudged, and her silk skirt ruined by the muddy street, Perihan was struck by the crowd's indifference. They shifted slightly to the right, attempting to remove her from their line of sight, all the while continuing to record whatever got their attention. Curious, Perihan turned around and was terrified by what she saw. In shock, she dropped her red shopping bags, causing more muddy water to splatter onto her skirt and completely destroying her shoes.

"This can't be happening," she screamed to the sky at the top of her lungs. Her knees trembled uncontrollably, left her unsure about taking another five steps to cross the road. Perihan noticed the cameras turning toward her in her peripheral vision, but she paid no mind to the desperation and terror that would eventually go viral on numerous social media networks in multiple countries. Her villa loomed in front of her, concealed by high walls covered with lush green bushes—now invaded by hundreds, if not thousands, of butterflies. They hovered over the garden, flapping their wings vigorously despite the pouring rain. The entire structure, partially visible through the bushes, seemed imprisoned within a butterfly sanctuary. When Perihan realized the creatures were all monarchs, each one so exquisite and valuable, she paused. Beauty had a threshold, and beyond it, it became a captivating terror, holding people's attention hostage to fulfill its own needs. She propelled herself into the flooded road, heading for the garden gate. With what little strength remained after the ordeal, she pushed her way through the floral Art Nouveau door.

"Licia! Where are you?" she shouted upon entering the garden. Before closing the door behind her, she turned to scream at the onlookers, "Leave! The show's over! This is my property!" Yet, the crowd remained unaffected, mesmerized by the extraordinary natural phenomenon unfolding before them.

Licia, Perihan's housekeeper and closest friend of nearly forty years, looked like a ghost. Her complexion was drained of color, her wet hair clung to her face in disheveled patches, and her shoes were ruined by dark mud. She trembled as she spoke. "Perihan... We did our best, but..." Licia glanced quickly at their small group of friends, who observed the scene from the kitchen window on the first floor of the house. Perihan brushed Licia aside with the back of her hand and made her way toward the large greenhouse on the left side of the garden. Orange butterflies continued to emerge rapidly through a broken pane in its ceiling, swarming through the air. Looking up at the vortex of butterflies resembling a brewing tornado, Perihan felt a wave of dizziness. Her bony hand reached for the intricately detailed metal handle of the greenhouse door, but fear gripped her body. She hesitated, afraid to enter, yet knowing she had no other choice. Slowly, she pushed the door open, entered, and closed it behind her.

Licia tried to conceal her sobbing behind her hands. Should she follow Perihan into the greenhouse or return to the house? The rain cascaded like a waterfall, obstructing not only her movements but her thoughts as well. She compelled herself to decide, but the sudden outburst from within the greenhouse froze her in place.

"No... No... No!" Perihan's voice echoed, growing louder with each repetition—until the world fell silent, save for the raindrops tapping against any surface they encountered. The darkness beneath the swarm of butterflies gradually gave way to a dull light as they departed from the house. Licia collapsed onto her knees and allowed herself to sink into the saturated garden soil, her tears mingling with the raindrops. Once the first monarch butterfly Perihan had witnessed a few moments earlier found its way to her villa, it hovered briefly over the garden before heading in the same direction as the others. When the last of the butterflies vanished, no trace of the miraculous event remained.

1

Assuming every city had its own anatomy, twenty-year-old Riccardo lived alone in a part of Paris that could be best described as the city's appendix: ready to explode at any moment and serving no purpose in the life of Parisians. Although it was a Sunday, Riccardo had set his alarm for seven in the morning and sat in front of his computer at half past seven to fill in the blank pages of his novel draft—that should have been submitted to his editor months ago. When he looked at the Garfield clock on the wall of this rundown rental house, he realized that he had been sitting in front of a blank screen for five straight hours.

"If only I could find the opening line... I know what comes after that," he repeated to himself without taking his eyes off the screen. He ignored the rumbling in his stomach, found an old Portishead album on Spotify, and placed his AirPods in his ears. He tried to place letters and sentences on the white page for another half hour, but when he got no results, he shut the laptop with a sudden movement and got up, wobbling as he stood. Even his chair was unstable, with one leg shorter than the others. Today didn't seem like a productive day. He walked into his mousetrap-size kitchen and opened the small refrigerator. A chunk of mold-covered cheese was waiting alone in the cold, under the dim light of the fridge. Since there was nothing else to eat, Riccardo took the cheese out and placed it on the counter. He tried to remove the moldy parts with a blunt knife, but he couldn't count on the remaining piece to quell his hunger. After throwing both the moldy and the remaining pieces into the trash can, he opened one of the kitchen drawers and found a pack of cigarettes.

I must finish this book no matter what. It's the only way out of this rundown apartment, he thought as he lit his cigarette with the fire from the gas stovetop. He took a big puff of smoke and let himself enjoy the loud music in his ears. Heading back to the living room, Riccardo grabbed his laptop and went to the sofa instead of sitting on the chair. He tried to flick the ashes of his cigarette into the ashtray, where dozens of butts were lying on top of each other, but instead he scattered them on the unopened bills on the coffee table. Although he was aware that he would not be able to pay his debts, he opened one of the bills, both out of curiosity and to kill time.

"Electricity… Let's see. One hundred and seventy euros, and two weeks overdue…" He threw it to the floor and opened another one. "Gas… I don't cook at home, and it's always freezing in here… Yet, guess what? One hundred euros…" Riccardo could not hear his own mumbling due to the Portishead song blaring in his ears. He kept opening more bills and found everything was either overdue or urgent, if not both, from gas to the annual subscription fee of the modest library twenty minutes away from the apartment to the red-letter notice from his internet provider to the monthly fee of the gym which he thought he had canceled long ago. Panic arose in him; he needed to find the opening line of his novel.

He craved another puff from his cigarette, but the fire had gone out. He was too lazy to go back to the kitchen and had no matches on the table. He reached out for the big ashtray to check if there was a lighter somewhere hidden under the cigarette butts, but as he moved the ceramic object, he saw a salmon-pink envelope with his name on it, written in letters as thin as the threads of a spiderweb. "It's definitely not a love letter…" he said as he took it in his hands and tore it open. Inside was a crumpled piece of paper, carelessly torn from an old notebook. On it, a shaky handwriting read *If you're looking for free accommodation, that's what streets are for. Or, for someone like you, animal shelters would be just fine too. Either you pay me the three months overdue rent tomorrow, or I'll be back with the police. Theodore.*

Riccardo reread the note and placed his unlit cigarette behind his ear. He slowly rolled the note, stood up, went to the kitchen, and turned on the stove. Instead of lighting the cigarette directly with the flames, he fed the rolled-up paper to the fire and, once it caught, used that to light up his cigarette. While fighting the panic taking over his whole body, he threw the flaming note into the sink and turned the tap on.

Riccardo felt trapped. Life was expecting too much from a twenty-year-old who had not heard from his family in years, who had been forced to live alone almost his entire life. He dumped the butt into the sink, filled a glass with tap water, and as he brought it to his lips, Portishead suddenly stopped singing. The transformation of the music to a ringtone startled Riccardo and caused him to drop the glass onto the floor. It shattered into a thousand pieces.

"Damn it! Where did I leave the phone?" he shouted and started searching for his cell back in the living room. When he finally found it, the name on the screen sent goose bumps down his spine. It was his literary agent, Louis.

"Hey, Louis, what's up?" Riccardo answered.

"Riccardo, you know why I'm calling. You can skip the chit chat. I already know you can't keep a promise, but I do need an answer. When are you sending me the synopsis and the first few chapters of your draft?" Louis's voice was controlled but had a nasty edge, ready to explode. He enunciated each word very slowly, as if he were requesting something from a toddler and had to make sure he was well understood.

"I'm working on it. I woke up at seven this morning," Riccardo responded defensively.

Louis interrupted. "To finish it? Or were you only starting? I hope you realize these are two different concepts. Everyone believed you were a rare talent. I'll give you that. There's no doubt you are talented. The award you won in that short story competition is a big deal for France, and you're the youngest talent to ever win it. Otherwise, no one gives free advances to anyone, Riccardo. There have been such high expectations for your first novel. We've sold it without even submitting the complete manuscript. But this does not mean we get to keep the money if you don't submit the work…"

Riccardo had already spent the small advance he had received, though he avoided sharing this detail with Louis. "I just need more time!" he protested.

"Time? Months have passed. There is no time left," Louis said with a raised voice.

"Haven't you ever heard of writer's block? I keep staring at this blank page every morning. Besides, why didn't they accept those chapters I sent months ago? Have you asked them that?"

"You don't have writer's block. Get that out of your head! Nobody was excited by the boring pages you sent. The character was ordinary, the catalyst banal, and there was nothing interesting, no moments to get people excited and talking.

How do I put it? There was no…life to what you wrote!"
Louis was shouting now; his initial kindness had turned into
ashes.

"You are my agent. You have to help me," Riccardo
pleaded weakly.

"Only you can help yourself. You must go out and live.
Get lost in the flow of life, let life happen to you, good or
bad! Tell that story. When was the last time you interacted
with people? You never go out, Riccardo…" Louis lowered
his voice and continued, "You have one week. Send me the
synopsis of something that will thrill these people, or we will
both be in deep trouble." Then he hung up.

Riccardo took out his earbuds and thought about what
Louis had said. He hadn't seen anyone for about a month;
he got up very early every morning and sat in front of the
screen without writing a single word. Maybe his agent was
right. He had to get out and live his life, even though he had
no idea where to start. He was lost in this train of thought
when a knock on the door distracted him. He wasn't expecting anyone. He walked toward the door with hesitant steps.

2

Riccardo looked through the peephole to see who was on the other side. He caught a glimpse of a tall skinny man wrapped in an old navy coat. The man seemed to be lost deep in thought, his right hand slowly scratching his chin while his eyes were fixed on the old doormat. As Riccardo was not expecting any guests, he thought the man had perhaps knocked on the wrong door and would leave if Riccardo stood silent on the other side, holding his breath. *Could he be someone sent by the landlord to collect the overdue rent?* he wondered, but then remembered how the landlord himself would come banging on the door when he really wanted the money. It had happened a couple of times in the past year, and Riccardo had always felt embarrassed at how the situation must have looked to his neighbors, who loved watching these scenes through their own little peepholes.

When the man knocked on the door once more, Riccardo let go of his deep breath. There was no way of avoiding this unexpected guest; whether meant for someone else in the building or specifically for Riccardo, he was going to have to interact with him. He looked through the peephole again to better evaluate the man's physical attributes. Due to the fish-eye nature of the lens, the man's head looked huge compared to his thin frame. His face, framed by thinning hair tied loosely behind his head, was very close to the door now. Suddenly, the man looked directly into the peephole with bloodshot eyes and said, "I know you're in there. Will you please open the door?"

Riccardo, startled by the sound of his voice, answered, "Who is it?"

"My name is Maurizio. I have to talk to you."

"I don't know any Maurizio," Riccardo snapped back defensively. He crossed his arms as he brought his right ear closer to the door. Mentally, he scanned through his twenty years of life—of which the first three brought back no memories, the following seven were all blurry, and anything after the age of ten included minimum social interaction. He'd spent years locked away in a boarding school, far away from home.

"It's about your grandmother, Perihan."

The name of Riccardo's grandmother was the magic word that relaxed Riccardo's crossed arms, moved him away from the door, and got him to open it just enough to break the barrier between him and this mysterious man, who apparently had come with news from a world Riccardo had long forgotten.

Through the narrow space between the door and the wall, Riccardo could better see Maurizio's face. He was probably in his early fifties; his skin wrinkled but wrapped around his head so tight, one could make out the shape of his skull underneath. His olive-green bloodshot eyes spoke of sleepless nights, while his plump lips looked like they had been recently stung by a bee.

"How do you know Perihan?" Riccardo asked, avoiding the word *grandmother*.

"Can I come in?" Maurizio checked both sides of the corridor with a worried look on his tired face. His restless attitude hinted at confidential information he wanted to share with Riccardo.

Riccardo wanted to end this interaction as quickly as possible, but he thought it would take much longer if they kept going back and forth like this. He gave up, opened the door wide, and showed Maurizio inside.

When Maurizio entered the small studio, Riccardo knew he was taken aback by the chaos. The messy apartment gave the false impression that Riccardo was moving out. There were big boxes right behind the sofa with random objects thrown in them, enough crumpled papers on the floor to burn the whole building down in seconds if they ever caught on fire, a big lump of worn clothes on the sofa waiting to be hung up, and a very subtle smell of foul cheese. It seemed as if there could be movers coming in any second to take away every object while Riccardo packed the crumpled clothes into his suitcase.

"Can I sit?" Maurizio pointed at the wooden chair by the table. Riccardo nodded, crossing his arms again in silent defense.

As soon as he sat down, Maurizio made a move to check the inner pocket of his navy coat, and that was when Riccardo noticed the serious burn marks on his right arm. There were patches of shiny skin that seemed to be stretched so thin in some spots that the skin looked translucent. Riccardo shuddered at the sight. "Can't help but ask...what happened to your arm?"

The question seemed to catch Maurizio off guard. He first looked at Riccardo, then to his right arm. Embarrassed, or simply bothered by this detail of his physical attributes, he pushed the sleeve of his jacket down to his wrist to cover the burns. "Nothing."

"It definitely looks like something…"

"It was such a long time ago, I have no memory of it anymore," Maurizio said, pulling a yellow envelope out of his inner pocket. He unfolded and read briefly what was written on its back before concentrating all his attention on Riccardo. "Your grandmother is dead, and she left you a collection of butterflies—"

Riccardo's initial response was a burst of laughter. "A collection of what?"

Maurizio slapped both of his legs to push himself up from the chair. He took a few steps toward Riccardo, whose laughter had already died down. Their faces were so close, they would look like a couple about to kiss if their body language were not so tense.

"A collection of butterflies," Maurizio repeated, the words punctuated by his heavy breath, smelling like cigarettes and bubble gum.

"Look, I'm sorry she's dead. I'm grateful she left me some dead insects, but I haven't heard from her in years, and we've had no relationship for a long time. I was expelled from home at a very young age. My only memories of Perihan are from my childhood—and let me tell you, these are all blurry pieces of flashbacks. So thank you very much, but you shouldn't have bothered to come all the way here to break this news," Riccardo said. He hadn't expected to feel any anger toward a dead woman, but the whole situation seemed like a bad joke to him. No matter how desperate his current living conditions were, a collection of butterflies would not help. He walked to the door, which was still unlocked, opened it wide, then showed Maurizio the corridor.

"I can't leave without you."

"Do you want me to call the police, then?"

"They can escort us both out, then. Your doorman wasn't optimistic about your future here," Maurizio said, hinting at the collection of overdue bills on the table behind them.

"Leave now."

"I told you, I can't leave without you. Her funeral is tomorrow. She wanted you to be there."

"She hasn't talked to me in years! She hasn't called, written, visited, searched… She hasn't shown any sign of interest! Honestly, I don't even know if she was still living in the same house!" Riccardo's shouting had attracted the interest of his next-door neighbor, who tapped on the plaster and voiced some sort of grumpy complaint, unclear through the thick wall.

"She passed away in Milan, in the very house you were born in. Perihan had her own way of caring for people. You were precious to her. If you did not hear from her, there might have been reasons that you were not aware of—"

"Reasons like what?" Riccardo said in a lowered voice. He didn't want to attract more attention to the scene through the open door.

"Her funeral is tomorrow, Riccardo. Maybe it's time you came back home."

"Who the fuck *are* you?" Riccardo snapped. It dawned on him that he had no idea who this Maurizio was.

"Maurizio. I worked for your grandmother for many years. I was her right hand. You don't remember?" He passed the yellow envelope from one hand to another. "She died on her seventieth birthday, just yesterday. As soon as I heard the news, I made my way here. I didn't even have time to grieve the passing of someone so dear to me…" He turned his head, looking at various angles of the room, and dramatically raised his hands over his head. "What do you even do here? This is a mess. You deserve to live better!"

"And a collection of butterflies won't help that. Now, you

must leave. I have things to do," Riccardo said, reaching for his sneakers by the door. He thought he could get rid of Maurizio faster if they left the apartment together. His empty fridge could benefit from a short trip to the nearby supermarket. He checked the back pocket of his jeans for some cash, but ten euros was all he could find. He shrugged, squeezed it back into his tight pocket, and went out the door. He made a move with his hands to show Maurizio out.

"Where are you going now?"

"Supermarket," Riccardo responded while locking the door behind them.

"I'll accompany you," Maurizio said.

Riccardo did not object.

On their way to the supermarket, they did not say a word. Riccardo's pace was slightly faster than that of Maurizio who, for a man his age, was quite fit and did not show any signs of distress walking up the bumpy road that led to the only supermarket in the area. Riccardo was oblivious by now to the area's many supposed charms, such as the quantity of rats nonchalantly roaming the neighborhood, the barefoot children of different ages playing games on the dirty streets, and the evident lack of taste in the architecture of the neighborhood. The two women walking in front of them looked like they were not victims of any crime in particular, but of life in general. Their frizzy hair went in all directions, their clothes had food stains or big blotches of bleach, their hands carried ugly empty plastic bags, while their pace gave away a general sense of desperation. The two women stopped abruptly in front of the two men, as they saw a big trash bin on the side of the road. "They are dumpster diving...nothing to be ashamed of," explained Riccardo when he noticed Maurizio staring.

A few steps farther, Riccardo stopped briefly in front of

a tiny bookstore, whose only window faced the main road. Despite the small space, the window was decorated nicely, with several copies of a new novel hanging by invisible threads from the ceiling, creating the illusion of rainfall. Riccardo moved his face closer to the window to check the name of the novel. *Tears of the Dragon*, a sci-fi work from a brand-new author. The two blurbs on the back cover from acclaimed authors, as well as the note about the book being included as a Belletrist Book Club selection, triggered a certain amount of envy in Riccardo. The author, Cecilia della Valle, was someone Riccardo had met briefly at one of his literary events; she was represented by the same agent as Riccardo.

You must go out and live! Let life happen to you... Riccardo remembered his agent's advice from the morning's tough call. *One week...or we will both be in deep trouble*, the agent's voice echoed in his ears. Riccardo had no idea what he could write about. He was about to lose himself in his thoughts again when he felt Maurizio's hand on his left shoulder.

"Are you okay?" Maurizio asked, looking at the window Riccardo had been staring at.

"Sure," Riccardo said, taking a step back from the window.

"Is this someone you know?" Maurizio pointed at the colorful cover of *Tears of the Dragon*.

"No. Let's go."

Riccardo realized that, for the first time in the last half hour, he had included Maurizio in his plans. He shouldn't give the old man any ideas. Thankfully, they soon arrived at the supermarket. "You can leave now. I need to buy some groceries," Riccardo said. He gave Maurizio a pat on the shoulder and entered through the sliding doors of the market. He did not notice the tiny monarch butterfly that had appeared out of nowhere in the parking lot of the supermarket, flapping its wings toward them.

3

With only ten euros in his pocket and two more weeks until the end of the month, Riccardo did not spend much time in the supermarket. He used the self-checkout to avoid embarrassment, since both cashiers knew him well—one had even paid for his groceries the last time his card was declined. With only a piece of cheese, a loaf of sliced bread, and a pack of cigarettes, he did not need a shopping bag. When he exited the building, he saw Maurizio waiting for him on the other side of the street.

"That was fast," Maurizio shouted to him.

"Why are you still here?"

"Riccardo," Maurizio said, walking toward him, "you are only twenty years old. You're being given a golden opportunity. Do you really want to live like this?" He pointed at the few things Riccardo could afford from the supermarket, then looked at him from head to toe with a worried expression on his face. Riccardo was aware of his thin and undernourished frame.

"Maybe you should see this before you make up your

mind." Maurizio reached into his pocket, pulled out his phone, and seemed to be searching for something. When he found whatever he was about to show Riccardo, he spent a few seconds looking at it himself, with a satisfied smile on his face. "Look!" he shouted with excitement as he passed his cell to Riccardo.

On the old iPhone's screen, Riccardo saw a large two-story villa, with three balconies on the front, a cozy patio, and endless windows all around. The building stood in the middle of a very large garden with lush green trees, and Riccardo could also see a greenhouse covered in white flowers. Despite the low resolution, the house looked dreamy.

"Don't you remember this place? Maybe look closer..."

Riccardo took the phone in his hand, zoomed in on the image, and looked around the garden. When he found the wooden swing behind the greenhouse, he raised his head and matched Maurizio's eyes. "This is where I was born. It's her house."

"It *was* her house. Now it is yours," Maurizio corrected him.

"What do you mean?" Riccardo seemed baffled. Maurizio had mentioned a collection of butterflies, not a piece of real estate of this level of luxury in the heart of an expensive city like Milan.

"You're Perihan's only living relative."

"What about my mother?" Riccardo snapped back.

"Who has ever heard from her? All I know is she left a long time ago. Everything Perihan once owned will now be yours..." A tiny monarch butterfly appeared from behind his back, flapping its wings toward Maurizio's head. It briefly paused, changed its mind, and landed on his right shoulder. "Serendipity." Maurizio winked at Riccardo.

Riccardo's hidden anger for his lost childhood suddenly

boiled over and exited through his mouth as a snarky comment. "I've survived without her all these years. I don't need her now. Have a nice trip back to Milan." He took a step, but Maurizio's burned hand squeezed his left arm, blocking his movement.

"Fine. But take this before you leave." Maurizio extended the folded yellow envelope he had been playing with back at Riccardo's flat. Without waiting for a response, he placed the envelope on top of the pack of sliced bread. "See you soon," he said as he walked off in the opposite direction. The butterfly seemed suspended in the air for a brief second, then went off in the same direction as Maurizio.

Riccardo looked at the crinkled yellow envelope but saw it had no stamp, no specific message, or any symbol on it. His opposition to acting according to Perihan's wishes was more important than his curiosity, and he walked back home, accompanied by the sound of his rumbling stomach.

4

Riccardo tore open the pack of cigarettes in front of his building, after placing the bread and the cheese on the short side wall at the entrance. He saw the doorman was busy cleaning the main entrance of the apartment with a broom that could have previously belonged to a witch. He wanted to avoid the man at all costs, so that he wouldn't have to face any threats briefed specifically by the landlord himself.

Nothing Riccardo did ever sat well with the doorman. If he took the trash out late at night, the man complained about the rats Riccardo attracted; if he turned up the volume of some classical music a tiny bit, the doorman came knocking on his door to ask if he were hosting a rave. Riccardo checked his pockets but found no lighter. "I guess no smoking for me, then…" he mumbled. He put the cigarettes into his back pocket, picked up his things from the wall, and snuck inside the minute the doorman disappeared into the garden.

Back in his apartment, he kicked his shoes off and went into the kitchen to light his cigarette. He had too much to think about. Seeing *Tears of the Dragon* by Cecilia all over the bookstore had not only triggered a certain anxiety in him but had also reminded him once again of how much time he had lost trying to overcome his writer's block. Time Cecilia had obviously spent writing, editing, rewriting, and finally publishing her first novel. He snorted at the sudden flashback of her telling him, "Imagine if we get to have our books out at the same time! We could maybe tour the bookstores together. Wouldn't it be fun?" It would've been fun…if only Riccardo had had a book to tour with.

The sight of his laptop on the sofa irritated him. He took another puff from his cigarette, stubbed it out in the ashtray, then went to hide the laptop on top of the cupboard where he wouldn't have to see it.

He buried himself in the soft cushions of the sofa. *It's not true that I'm not living my life*, he thought. *I was prioritizing my novel… That's why I haven't seen my friends lately.* He tried, unsuccessfully, to convince himself. He took his phone out to go through the list of contacts. His eyes wandered over a hundred names, but he didn't once stop to consider a quick text, let alone a call. He scrolled up and down the list a few more times, but there was nobody he felt he could call on a whim. These were either acquaintances he'd had a few creative writing classes with or handymen coming to fix various things in the apartment. Cecilia was probably the only person on the list that he could consider a friend, even though that would still be a stretch. Frustrated, he pushed his phone away.

I'd better write, he thought, since there seemed to be no way out. A week was not enough time to fix his problems, but if he could send an interesting synopsis to his agent, he would have one less thing to deal with. Before taking his laptop back from the top of the cupboard, he made himself a quick sandwich to quiet the annoying noise coming from his stomach. He went back to the table, sat on the rickety chair, and opened his laptop. Thanks to the white light of the document, he could not catch his reflection or see the dark circles under his eyes. He tried a few combinations of words to create an exciting introduction, but nothing sparked an emotion. He shut the laptop out of frustration, took the overdue bills in his hands, and went through each one again. Like a well-practiced choreography, he reopened the laptop, pressed some keys on the keyboard, got frustrated, made a sullen face, shut it down, and went through the bills again.

After all the effort, he returned to his favorite excuse. *I'm probably tired. I should set the alarm early and start first thing tomorrow.* The moment these familiar words passed through his mind, the lights went off. He was left with the gloomy faint light coming in through the window.

"What the fuck," he cursed. He tried flipping the light switch, but there was no electricity. He opened the door to check the corridor to see whether the rest of the building had any power. As soon as he clicked on the round button next to his door, the lights of the corridor came on. Riccardo went back in, tried his own lights again, but nothing happened. He left the corridor to check whether the main switch of his apartment had been turned off.

"It all looks fine," he whispered to himself as he checked the central power line on his floor with the flashlight of his phone. He called the electricity company, only to find out they had finally cut his power due to overdue payments. No matter how much he tried to negotiate with the operator, she explained to him that there was not much she could do unless he paid what he owed.

Devastated, he went back inside, lay down on the sofa, and started crying. He had never felt so low in his twenty years in this world. He had nobody to call, no money to survive on, and no novel draft to save him out of this dark hole. As he kept on sobbing like a wounded animal on the old sofa, a mix of mucus and saliva dropped lazily onto the parquet floor. He wiped his nose with his right sleeve, and in the process, he remembered the envelope Maurizio had left him. He arched his back to squeeze his hand into his back pocket. He cut the envelope open with his teeth, while wondering whether there would be some money in it.

He slid his finger inside the slit and took out the only piece of paper it contained.

Paris–Milan, 12 a.m.

It was a one-way train ticket to Milan, departing at midnight the same day. Maurizio had given him just a couple of hours to decide—apparently, he'd known this would be a now-or-never situation for Riccardo, since there was no way he could afford another ticket on his own. He pushed himself back up into a sitting position.

So now what? he thought, even though he knew he didn't have much choice. The train ticket was a long rope thrown into this well of desperation; if Riccardo decided to give it a go, he could try to climb back up to the light, and if he didn't, there was no farther down he could fall. Pushing himself back on his feet, he wondered where his luggage was. It had been years since he last took a train anywhere.

5

Just half an hour to midnight, amid the shadows, Riccardo made his way to the train station in Paris. Clutching his backpack tightly against his chest, his eyes darted nervously, filled with worry. Rumblings of belligerent people engaged in a fight at the entrance had reached his ears, leaving him on edge.

As he entered the dimly lit building, a gloom engulfed him, underlined by the many broken lights; the remaining bulbs cast only a feeble glow. The sinister darkness played tricks on his mind, intensifying his fear. Was he doing the right thing leaving Paris behind, despite all the hardships? He wished he had a friend whom he could inform before leaving, someone who would be worried for him if they never got a text when he arrived in Milan. Once inside the station, Riccardo found the place almost deserted. Each one of his steps echoed through the empty corridors, increasing his feeling of loneliness.

He hurried up the grand staircase to find his train. As he reached the platform, he scanned the area. A handful of fellow travelers huddled in quiet anticipation, their faces etched with weariness. The rhythmic hum of the distant train approaching offered a glimmer of hope for a better future. He was happy to find that he wasn't alone in this midnight journey; the comforting presence of a few passengers offered some reassurance.

As the train's headlights pierced through the night, illuminating the station, his heart skipped a beat. With a surge of courage, he boarded the train, leaving the haunting darkness behind. Once inside, Riccardo discovered Maurizio had bought him a business class ticket, perhaps in anticipation of the comforts that were waiting for him in Milan. Still, he held on to his backpack tightly, not willing to let go of his few belongings. He had packed just some clothes, his laptop, and a few other small things.

Leaning his head against the cool window, he watched as the train started moving. The rhythmic sound of the wheels on the tracks acted like a lullaby, making him feel calm. Eventually, exhaustion took over, and he fell asleep with his head against the window.

6

Riccardo was six. He was in his grandparents' bedroom in Milan, in their private villa with the massive green-house in the garden. Perihan was busy spraying her short blond hair from all angles for extra volume. A part of him was eager to run down the stairs and spend some time with his grandfather, who was patiently waiting for them at the door, but Perihan's expensive silk caftan had colors he had never seen before. His hungry eyes were held hostage by their beauty.

"Let's go," she said with a smile, extending her hand with her long red nails. His grandfather opened the door, and they followed him outside. Licia was right by the entrance, but Riccardo paid no attention to her. Any woman would lose importance in the presence of Perihan.

"Marco, I'm happy we didn't invite anyone else. I like spending quality time with just you and our precious Ric-cardo," he heard his grandmother say. She was probably re-ferring to his grandfather's childhood friends, who enjoyed eating all together at big round tables, talking very often of the past. Perihan seemed to hate the past. The past was static, the past could not be changed, the past meant nostalgia. Instead, she spent all her time daydreaming about the future. She was also a master at adjusting the tone of her voice depending on the audience: steel cold with Licia the maid, courteous but never too intimate with friends of the family, and extremely affectionate with Riccardo and her husband, Marco. Riccardo always imagined thick honey dripping from her words when she spoke to him.

The three of them walked along the busy Milan streets. Riccardo was wearing a toy watch in the shape of an airplane Perihan had brought from one of her trips to the US. She traveled a lot, often alone. Nobody ever told him where she was going, but every time she came back, she brought a suitcase full of presents. The airplane on his wrist reminded him that it was time she got him another present. He let go of Perihan's hand and ran to the little toy store right around the corner from the restaurant. He placed his palms on the shop's window and eyed each toy attentively despite the darkness.

"Let's get whatever you like, my dear Riccardo."

"That red car! It lights up, too. I saw it on TV!" he shouted with enthusiasm. He walked up to the door and pushed it with both hands. No luck. It didn't move an inch.

"It's closed," Riccardo said sulkily. He was accustomed to being spoiled by Perihan, and thus he had become fluent over time in the secret body language between them. He knew exactly which expression to wear on his face to get what he wanted. Imagining how all the other kids would die of envy as he played with his new toy in the middle of the restaurant, he put on his angelic mask.

"What do you mean it's closed? At this hour?" she complained in a high-pitched voice to be heard by Riccardo's grandfather. Just as Riccardo got better and better at picking the right facial expressions, she had shown great progress in choosing the right tone to obtain power.

"I want that toy," he begged, clinging onto the skirt of her caftan.

Marco did not comment, so she turned to him and asked, "Do you have a piece of paper?"

He took out his gold pen and a little notebook from the inner pocket of his navy blazer. Perihan tore a page off, wrote something on it, then said, "My dear Riccardo, can you get me a rock? A big rock? And, Marco, I will leave a note for the store's owner." She was pointing at the piece of paper in her hand.

He was so excited. He didn't know what she had in mind, but he could feel he would benefit from it in the end. He found a rock the size of his hand and gave it to her. She grabbed it with such aggression that, for a moment, he mistook her red nails for bloody claws. Perihan took a strong swing with her right arm and threw the rock into the window of the shop. Riccardo heard her gold bracelets jangle. Suddenly, the whole pane shattered into thousands of pieces, like an explosion of fireworks celebrating the bond between the two of them. Marco remained silent. He was probably used to these extreme spectacles with her. She walked slowly toward the store and kneeled to take the car Riccardo was crazy for, leaving the handwritten note in its place. He watched his glamorous grandmother transform herself into a strong hero in the blink of an eye. Some people came out onto their balconies to see what was happening in their street, but nobody dared ask.

"Marco, we can go now. We got our little Riccardo the toy he wanted."

"Riccardo, can you come here for a second?" The voice of his grandfather was always authoritative, even when he tried to soften it. Riccardo walked toward him and stood right next to the tree, trying to find where his grandfather's concentration was focused. He was too short to see what Marco was looking at. Marco noticed this and took his grandson in his arms. In total silence, they looked at a sort of shell hanging from a branch. "This is a pupa. There's a sleeping caterpillar inside. Do you know what will happen to it?"

"Caterpillars turn into butterflies," Riccardo responded. Marco had taught him this himself a few months ago, while they were watching a boring documentary on TV together.

"Exactly. The little caterpillar one day feels hungry, in fact so hungry that it starts eating whatever comes its way. It doesn't realize that there are new cells in its body that do not belong to it and that require a lot of energy. It continues eating. As these new cells take over, the caterpillar dies and turns into a pupa. This is where all the metamorphosis occurs..."

He couldn't understand every single detail at that age, but at the mention of death, he got excited and asked, "If the caterpillar is dead, why is there no one at its funeral?"

Marco responded, without taking his eyes off the pupa. "Riccardo, everybody knows the death of a caterpillar is his rebirth. This is why nobody comes to mourn for him. He will come out as a beautiful butterfly soon."

"Marco, my love... Enough with the butterflies, and the insects, and the *National Geographic*. Come on, can we please go? My Riccardo hasn't eaten anything since breakfast this morning."

Marco put Riccardo back on the ground. As they trailed toward the restaurant, an unsettling sensation gripped Riccardo. The ground beneath him cracked, revealing a zigzag pattern on the pavement. Bewildered, he scanned for signs of an earthquake, but an eerie stillness enveloped everything around them. Marco was already far ahead, walking along-side Perihan. Determined to catch up, Riccardo quickened his pace, but another tremor shattered the pavement's crooked shapes. Despite his efforts to evade a crevice growing right in front of him, his right foot slipped, and a force from the darkness below yanked his leg into the hole.

"Grandma! Help me! I'm falling, Grandma!" he shouted, but his grandparents continued walking, oblivious to his dis-tress. Desperately, Riccardo placed both hands on the ground, attempting to pull his leg free, but the crack widened, claim-ing his other leg. Something pulled him deeper into the abyss.

"Grandma! Help me! Help!" his pleas echoed, but he was left all alone. Helplessly, he plunged through gaping fractures, his body colliding with cold, damp soil. Constricting walls surrounded him, making each breath a struggle. In the dark-ness, he felt thousands of tiny creatures biting at his skin, and blood oozed from his wounds.

After what seemed like hours, the walls briefly expanded, and he crashed onto the bottom of a well, losing conscious-ness from the immense pain.

Upon awakening, he found himself in a pool of squirming caterpillars, bathed in a red light from an unknown source. The creepy-crawlies, in various shapes and colors, covered his wounded body, their slimy touch inducing terror. Desperately trying to free himself, he realized the floor was slick with a blend of his blood and the caterpillars' disgusting slime. Amid the chaos, a giant caterpillar moved unexpectedly, turning its tail toward Riccardo, and squirting what seemed to be a rain of poison. The drops burned through his flesh, prompt-ing agonized howls as he fell to his knees, his face hitting the bloody floor.

As he attempted to draw breath, a monarch butterfly appeared. The red light illuminated its orange-and-black-striped wings. In a last attempt for survival, Riccardo stretched his hands toward the butterfly and jolted awake, beads of sweat lining his forehead.

To his relief, Riccardo found out he was still on the train. He glanced out the window, and his eyes locked onto a sign that read Stazione Centrale. It hit him—Milan. Relief flooded over him. It was all just a haunting dream, a reminder of the family he once had, but also of the difficult times now left behind. With a renewed sense of hope, he embraced the arrival, ready to leave his misery behind, and got out of his seat to disembark the train.

7

As Riccardo stepped off the train, he was greeted by a wave of confusion, uncertain about where to go next. He glanced around the bustling station, searching for a familiar face. Apprehension filled his thoughts as he wondered if someone might be waiting for him, ready to accompany him back to his new home. His eyes scanned the sea of strangers, observing the numerous people with name tags, clutching bouquets of flowers and signs of welcome. Yet none of the faces seemed familiar to him. The realization weighed on his heart, creating a tinge of disappointment and solitude.

The sky hung heavy with gray clouds, and a chill permeated the air, causing Riccardo to shiver involuntarily. Seeking warmth, he reached into his backpack and pulled out a windbreaker. He slipped it on, a shield against the frosty weather that matched his inner uncertainty.

He flipped over his train ticket, searching for any clue that might lead him in the right direction. Perhaps Maurizio had written the address there. With a glimmer of hope, he studied the ticket's back, examining every detail, but found no written guidance.

As Riccardo took a deep breath, a voice sliced through the air, calling his name. Startled, he turned toward the source, and his eyes widened in surprise. There stood Licia, his grandmother's devoted maid, wearing a warm smile that radiated genuine affection. But what caught Riccardo off guard was the fact that Licia appeared unchanged, as if time had stood still for her.

Licia's sparkling, emerald-green eyes locked onto Riccardo's, holding a depth of emotion that transcended mere words. Her petite frame, draped in simple yet elegant gray attire, also seemed untouched by the passage of years.

As Riccardo approached her, a mix of emotions washed over him: relief, familiarity, but also a lingering sense of unease. Stepping into this new life in Milan felt like traversing unfamiliar terrain, viewing the world through someone else's eyes. Was this just a new chapter in his own story or the beginning of an entirely new tale altogether? It had been a very long time since Riccardo had last seen Licia or heard news of her. While he often thought that people remained unchanged over time, as a writer himself he knew that every hero's journey brought transformation.

Questions lingered in his mind. After the passage of so many years, was Licia still the person he fondly remembered? How would those who knew of him—friends and acquaintances of a grandmother with whom he'd shared a brief connection when he was only a child—perceive him now, suddenly appearing for a funeral and to claim her accumulated wealth?

As Licia embraced him, her affection offered momentary relief, yet Riccardo couldn't shake the feeling that this comfort was fleeting. Everything about this situation represented new and risky territory for him. He tried to shake off the impostor syndrome as Licia let him go.

"It's been years since I last saw you! Look at how handsome you've become," Licia said.

"And you... You haven't changed at all!"

"Riccardo, I thought you would not come in the end. I waited until the last passenger left the train but could not see you," she confessed. "But now you're here, and that is all that matters. We will get through this together. Your grandmother's death is hard on all of us... Where is your suitcase?" she asked, raising her eyebrows.

"I only have my backpack. I came for the funeral, then I need to go back to Paris for school," he lied, so that he could have an excuse to leave in case things didn't seem to work out the way Maurizio had promised. Licia made a wry face to communicate her disapproval but did not voice her opinion. Instead, she walked outside. The cold wind cut their faces like a sharp knife. The weather was much harsher than he'd expected, and his initial thought of walking to Perihan's home did not seem so attractive anymore.

"Should we call a cab to go back home? I wanted to come with the driver, but we let him go three weeks ago because your grandmother had stopped using him..."

"You could've used him," Riccardo protested.

"The farthest place I ever go is the supermarket, dear. I don't need a driver to take me where I can easily walk myself," Licia said, then added, "So cab, or are we walking?" Riccardo gave Licia a strained smile, and they walked off Repubblica toward the house arm in arm, like two old friends. As they turned the corner onto Via Marco de Marchi, he suddenly stopped, searching for something he vaguely remembered from when he was very young.

What he found was unimpressive at first glance. It was just

messy, faded red paint splashed over bits of broken mosaics in the wall running along the street. These remnants triggered memories he thought he had forgotten. A distant, misty recollection rushed back to an autumn day long ago, a day he had tried to keep buried in the depths of his mind.

Riccardo, just a young child not even in elementary school, strolled hand in hand with the blind twins, Greta and Berta, through the gloomy Milan streets. Their fingers were interlaced, a peculiar yet gentle chain that allowed them to navigate the world together. It was one of those overcast days when the gray clouds threatened rain, and a perpetual chill seemed to linger in the air. The twins' white canes tapped rhythmically on the pavement, creating a steady beat that harmonized with their steps.

As they walked, Riccardo couldn't help but ponder whether they were guiding him to ensure his safety among the city's treacherous cars, or if, in their own way, they relied on him for some form of silent assistance. The scent of his grandmother Perihan's heavy tuberose perfume clung to the air, leaving an indelible mark on the path they trod.

Perihan, with her diminutive head nearly engulfed by the voluminous fur coat she wore, seemed to be in a rush, her hurried pace so pronounced that she hardly registered the twins' excited chatter. They seemed engrossed in a private dialogue, discussing an upcoming theater performance that promised to be the highlight of their weekend.

But it was Perihan who first turned the corner onto Via Marco de Marchi and came to an abrupt halt. Riccardo, his senses tuned to her sudden pause, managed to slow his pace in time. The twins, however, oblivious to the change, collided with his grandmother. She paid no heed to their presence as her attention was riveted by a strange sight.

She stared at the brick wall, a fixture that ran the entire length of the street and seemed to merge with every building in its path. On this particular corner, where Via Marco de Marchi met Via Montebello, her gaze was captured by a small square of mosaics.

The mosaics glistened, their beauty radiant even in the gray gloom of the afternoon. The square, not larger than twenty by twenty centimeters, artfully composed a delicate monarch butterfly. With its intricate mosaic tiles, it was a stunning blend of vibrant oranges and velvety blacks that defined the edges of its wings. Riccardo was too young to read, but he recognized the letters below the butterfly. They spelled his grandmother's name, *Perihan*.

Perihan spun around to face the women and, in a tone laced with anger, inquired, "What is this nonsense? They've erected some sort of artwork, a public tribute to my name right here in my street. Can you believe it? They've fashioned it with the symbol of a monarch butterfly, created with tiny mosaics! This is unacceptable! Who conceived of this? Who executed it? Why wasn't I informed?"

The twins, however, bore serene smiles, unperturbed by Perihan's fury. Greta leaned in closer, her fingers brushing the mosaic, as if she could somehow decipher its shape through touch. Her hair inadvertently swept over the artwork. Berta, her fingers adorned with an array of peculiar rings, began to caress the mosaics, her touch gentle yet oddly intimate.

As they interacted with the unseen butterfly, their grins widened.

Riccardo, overwhelmed by the scene, felt a sudden surge of fear welling up. He began to cry, and his sobs only served to further irritate Perihan. Her patience reached its breaking point as she tightened her grip on Riccardo's arm, scolding him, commanding him to stop his whining.

With a rough shove, Perihan pushed the twins aside and took it upon herself to pluck each mosaic piece from the wall. Her bare fingers proved ineffective, and she broke a nail, which elicited a burst of colorful curses. Determined, she reached into her purse, extracting the metal keys for the villa's greenhouse.

Utilizing the keys as makeshift tools, she succeeded in dislodging a few of the mosaic tiles. Her eyes darted around in her bag, searching for her red nail polish, and, upon its discovery, she fervently began painting over the remnants of the butterfly symbol and the letters of her name. The result was a chaotic, haphazard mess, a far cry from the intended homage.

Satisfied with the disarray she had created on what was supposed to be a dignified tribute, she carelessly tossed the nail polish and keys back into her tiny purse. Without waiting for anyone, she turned and stormed away, her fur coat swaying with every stride.

The twins, now pouting, stared forlornly at the ground, their white canes tapping hesitantly as they walked in Perihan's shadow. Riccardo, his eyes still blurred with tears, watched as Perihan stormed away, the women trailing behind her. A sense of foreboding enveloped him, and he couldn't quite comprehend the gravity of the situation. In the midst of the confusion, a glimmer of curiosity flickered in his young heart. Riccardo's focus fell upon one of the golden tiles. A solitary piece, it bore the letter *P*, and it had fallen to the ground during Perihan's destructive frenzy. He bent down and gently picked it up, cradling it in his small hand, an unintended memento of that chaotic afternoon.

With the golden mosaic clenched in his hand, Riccardo followed the twins down the street, their white canes tapping away, while the tuberose scent lingered in the air, a spectral trace of his enigmatic grandmother's passage. The memory of that gloomy day became a forgotten fragment of the past, one that Riccardo, years later, would unlock and recall with nostalgia.

Licia noticed Riccardo's perplexed expression as he stared at the wall. She gently shook him, asking if he was all right. Riccardo nodded.

"I thought I remembered something... Never mind." He shifted the conversation to another topic. "Licia, you don't need to answer this question, but...did my mother ever come back? Maurizio mentioned I'm the only living relative... Does that mean you got news from my mother? Does she know that my grandmother has passed away? Is Grandfather dead too?" he asked. He wanted to see if the lines on her forehead would deepen further, but she answered rather calmly.

"Unfortunately, your grandfather did pass away. Yet your mother must be alive and happy somewhere. She left and never looked back. Not everyone who leaves us needs to suffer in our absence, you know that. Some of us are better off away from the people who brought us into the world."

"Or from the ones who they brought into the world," Riccardo added, referring to himself.

"It is not about you. Don't delve into the past when we are already going through such difficult times with the sudden news of my precious Perihan. Stay strong, and concentrate on one problem at a time," Licia suggested.

Recognizing the streets of Milan was a hard task for him. Some of what he remembered and cherished from his childhood, like the pastry shop with its delicious desserts, was still there on Via Marco dei Marchi. The vintage store a few blocks down was also open, selling everything from unusual knick-knacks to big, modern furniture. He wondered what Licia was seeing on that street that his conscience was not registering.

"My grandmother loved this place," he mentioned as they walked past the patisserie. Licia seemed burrowed deep in her thoughts. They quickened their steps in synchrony with one another, as they both realized the weather was too cold for a slow two-kilometer stroll.

A few feet away from them, there was what seemed to be the longest queue Riccardo had ever seen. There were families with a couple of children, beautiful young girls, Black women with anxious expressions, and men with serious faces.

"What is that queue?" he asked curiously.

"The local police station. I believe it is the immigration department. They must all be immigrants, you know, waiting to get their official residence permits. Your grandmother used to work closely with them."

"What did my grandmother really do? I've never understood."

He thought he saw the expression on Licia's face shift for a second, but she answered quickly. "She was a fundraiser before disease knocked on her door. After a while, it was too difficult for her to work…" He could see that Licia was choosing her words carefully, in order not to sound disrespectful behind Perihan's back.

"It is really hard for me to imagine her being sick. I was accustomed to seeing her always so strong, in control of any situation when I was a kid," he said.

"I have to say, she must be happy you never saw her in the last stage of her illness."

He nodded in agreement. Riccardo thought his grandmother would never have wanted him to see her in less than perfect condition anyway. This was the woman who refused to sit at the breakfast table before fixing her hair and putting on her makeup in the morning.

At the end of the road, a small black poster got Riccardo's

attention. It was stuck on the wall of a church around the corner. He read it out loud.

"Sometimes,
when you find yourself in a dark place,
you think you've been buried,
but actually, you've been planted."

"Not all of us bloom in the dark," Licia murmured.

"Motivational church quotes," he mocked Licia as they walked toward the villa. They arrived at the villa's entrance, enclosed by tall walls of withered bushes. From the outside, the garden appeared lifeless and devoid of any magical charm. Licia held the keys to the floral-patterned Art Nouveau door leading to the garden. Riccardo's surprise grew as he realized that the actual scene bore no resemblance to the picture Maurizio had shown him on his phone.

Riccardo's eyes swept across the garden as his eyes widened with tension. He took in the transformed landscape. Something had drastically changed, and an uneasy feeling tugged at his heart. With a hushed tone, he whispered, "What happened?" The question hung in the air like a wounded bird about to fall to the ground.

8

R iccardo's excitement quickly turned to disappointment, and a sense of unease settled within him. This was not the vibrant and meticulously maintained paradise that Maurizio's phone had revealed. Instead, the unkempt nature of the garden struck him with a profound sadness. In the heart of the desolate garden stood Perihan's villa, a once-grand structure that now appeared weathered and worn. Its two main floors stood solemnly, adorned with three balconies that seemed to hang on the brink of decay. The windows, once shining with life, now gazed emptily into the forgotten expanse surrounding them.

To the right of the villa, the greenhouse loomed abandoned, its glass windows smeared with dirt and choked by intertwining, lifeless branches of plants long gone. The sight of a shattered glass roof added a sinister touch to the scene. Riccardo couldn't help but wonder what had caused the fracture—was it a force from within, clawing its way out? Or had an external entity breached the greenhouse, leaving its mark behind? Memories flooded his mind of all the times he had tried to approach the greenhouse as a child, only to be stopped by Perihan. She would grab his arm tightly and call one of the maids to make sure he didn't go any closer. Perihan was obsessed with keeping him away from the structure, and Riccardo had always wondered why. He thought maybe she was trying to protect the beautiful flowers and precious plants inside from a curious child like him.

Every time he had tried to get closer, Perihan would pull him back and make sure he stayed away. It had made him even more curious about what secrets the building held. He had imagined there must be something very special inside that Perihan wanted to keep safe, but looking at it now, years later, all he felt was a deep sadness. Curiosity and childlike wonder were long gone.

"It's nothing like I remember," Riccardo remarked to Licia, his disappointment palpable in his voice. She paused for a moment, her eyes scanning the scene before her. It was as though she had been awakened from a trance, finally noticing the state of decay and ruin that had befallen the once-vibrant garden. Her gaze met Riccardo's, reflecting a shared understanding of the grim reality.

"Now that you mention it, it has changed so much," she responded, her tone tinged with a hint of sadness. Her gray outfit seemed to mirror the subdued atmosphere of the surroundings. "The entire garden suffered after your grandfather's passing. He used to pour his heart into its upkeep. And, just a few weeks ago, we had to dismantle the old wooden swing you used to enjoy as a child."

Riccardo felt a pang of nostalgia as she mentioned the swing. "What happened to it?" he asked.

Licia's expression turned grim, her eyes reflecting nostalgia. "It had become weak, loose, and old, to the point where Perihan deemed it unsafe. She was concerned about anyone getting hurt, so she made the difficult decision to have it destroyed."

A mix of emotions washed over Riccardo: sadness for the loss of a cherished childhood memory and an understanding of Perihan's concerns for safety. The image of the swing, once a source of joy and laughter, now faded and dismantled, added to the uncanny ambience of the garden.

Riccardo nodded in acceptance, though a tinge of longing remained in his eyes. As they continued their walk toward the house, Licia's footsteps echoing against the path, he couldn't help but wonder what other changes awaited him within the confines of those walls. Right before they entered the house, Riccardo reached into his backpack to search for his pack of cigarettes and realized he had no lighter. Turning to Licia, he asked hesitantly, "Do you happen to have a light?"

Licia's disapproving look met his. "Riccardo, you know Perihan wouldn't have approved…"

Undeterred, Riccardo insisted, "I just need a quick smoke to calm my nerves. It's been a long journey."

With a sigh, Licia nodded and disappeared into the house. Moments later, she returned, clutching a small box of matches. Handing them to Riccardo, she cautioned, "Please be careful. Don't let this become a habit."

Riccardo struck one and lit his cigarette, taking a few quick puffs to soothe his frayed nerves. The nicotine offered momentary pleasure as Licia began to speak.

"Our hearts were filled with a whirlwind of emotions," she began, her voice carrying a touch of melancholy. "Two days ago, we were busily preparing a surprise birthday celebration for Perihan, and now we find ourselves arranging her funeral. It's been a challenging transition, to say the least."

Riccardo listened attentively, his mind still reeling from

the sudden shift in atmosphere. The cigarette's smoke curled around him, veiling the weight of his thoughts.

Licia gently urged, "We should go inside now, Riccardo. There's much to be done. Let me guide you to the guest bedroom, so you can change into more formal attire. We need to get on with the rest of the day."

Riccardo asked, "What is the plan for the rest of the day?" Meeting his eyes with a touch of sorrow, Licia responded. "We've got the funeral," she began, her words carrying a certain gravity. "All of Perihan's closest friends have gathered, eagerly awaiting our arrival. It's a small affair, but the support from those who cared deeply for her will hopefully provide some consolation."

Riccardo nodded and reluctantly extinguished his cigarette, flicking the ashes onto the ground. He followed Licia to the house, the click of her heels echoing in the silence. As they ascended the stairs, she turned to him, her voice firm yet compassionate. "Come downstairs as soon as you are ready, then we'll get started."

Nodding again in agreement, Riccardo quickened his pace.

9

Riccardo stepped into the guest bedroom, greeted by the walls full of books of various sizes and subjects. The room featured a cozy bed with a white pillow and duvet, while the polished parquet floors added a touch of elegance. From the window, he caught a glimpse of the neglected greenhouse in the garden. Placing his backpack gently on the bed, he rummaged through its contents, searching for something suitable to wear. He hadn't packed much. Finally, he pulled out a crisp white cotton shirt and proceeded to change into it.

Once dressed, he exited the room and found himself facing a narrow corridor. It was there, hanging on the wall, that he noticed a striking black frame with a delicate morpho butterfly encased within. The butterfly's iridescent wings shimmered with mesmerizing blue hues. The feeble light from the guest room softly illuminated the insect, accentuating its ethereal beauty. For a moment, Riccardo was transported back in time, recalling a moment from his childhood.

★ ★ ★

"This is a morpho butterfly," Perihan whispered, her voice filled with a sense of wonder. Riccardo held his breath, observing the large brown insect closely, eagerly awaiting the magical moment when it would unveil its vibrant wings. Just as he was about to exhale, the butterfly began to move. Its wings fluttered open and closed with incredible speed, creating a breathtaking display. After a few more rapid flutters, it settled on a long branch, its wings gracefully spread wide.

Riccardo gasped in astonishment, captivated by the breathtaking sight before him. The luminescent blue of the wings seemed to shift and change with each movement. The intensity of the color varied as the light hit it from different angles, creating a captivating play of shades.

"What color is it really?" Riccardo asked, his eyes sparkling with curiosity.

"It's brown, but then it transforms into an electric blue," Perihan replied, utterly fascinated by its beauty. "The brown serves to help the butterfly blend into its surroundings, granting it a sense of invisibility. But when it takes flight, the shiny blue confuses predators, as its colors continuously shift. The morpho appears in a flash, only to vanish once again."

"Like the magician we saw on TV!" Riccardo exclaimed, recalling a performance where the illusionist seemed to magically disappear and reappear elsewhere.

"Indeed, the butterfly is an illusionist," Perihan agreed, a smile gracing her lips. "Did you know that it doesn't possess actual colors? What you see as shades of blue on its wings are reflections of light from different angles. The wings are made up of translucent membrane with layers of scales, much like the tiles on the building across from our balcony. These scales overlap, covering the entire wing surface. And when the sunlight hits…" she tried to explain, simplifying the intricate beauty of the butterfly's structural color.

"When the sun shines, it illuminates its wings, and they turn blue," Riccardo finished her sentence, feeling pride in his understanding.

"You're absolutely right. In the end, the butterfly uses illusion to survive in a world full of predators," Perihan replied, her smile growing as she gently caressed her butterfly necklace, the realistic-looking insect with orange and black scales.

Shaking off the nostalgic reverie, Riccardo continued down the corridor and smelled a faint yet familiar fragrance lingering in the air. It was the unmistakable scent of tuberose, reminiscent of Perihan's beloved perfume, Fracas. The fragrance filled the corridor, seeping into the very walls of the house, as if it had become part of their very essence.

Perihan had always adored the scent of tuberose, often applying it with a heavy hand, indulging in its allure. The fragrance had become synonymous with her, an extension of her presence in the house. Riccardo could almost imagine her walking through the corridors, her elegant figure trailing the scent in her wake.

Curious, Riccardo followed the hallway, his steps guided toward a closed door at the end of it. The scent grew stronger, enveloping him in a cloud of memories and nostalgia. "I should not be here exploring rooms. Licia is waiting for me downstairs… I should go to her now," he said, trying to convince himself, but nevertheless, he turned the doorknob and entered the room, his heart pounding in his chest. *I just want to inhale my grandmother's perfume again, then I'll leave,* he thought, as he closed the door softly behind him.

Riccardo's heart ached with longing as he entered the bedroom, yearning to see his once-beloved grandmother seated in her antique chair in front of the vanity table. There was a flicker of hope in his mind, a desperate wish that perhaps this was all just a cruel joke and Perihan was still alive and well. But deep down, he knew the truth, and it weighed heavily upon him.

As he stepped farther into the room, a multitude of scents mingled in the air, creating an olfactory world that told the story of a life lived. The fragrance of clean bedsheets, vintage leather bags, talc powder, lipstick, and old age danced around him, intermingling with a heady dose of tuberose flowers. Perihan's signature scent permeated every corner of the room.

The sight that greeted Riccardo was one of eerie perfection. The room seemed frozen in time, as though it had never been touched. The bed was flawlessly made, the curtains meticulously ironed, and the top of the vanity table presented a symmetrical arrangement. On one side, an extravagant quantity of crystal bottles of different shapes and sizes stood proudly, each one reflecting the soft glow of the room. It was as if they were treasures collected over a lifetime, a testament to Perihan's refined taste and perhaps even her obsession with their delicate beauty.

Thoughts swirled through Riccardo's mind as he took in the immaculate orderliness of the room. Sudden deaths, he realized, left behind a trail of intimate details, exposing the hidden aspects of one's private life. The history of our digital explorations, the remnants of unfinished conversations, the accumulation of unwashed dishes in the kitchen sink, the presence of worn socks strewn about—all told a tale of the person we were when no one was watching. But Perihan would never allow such vulnerabilities to be exposed. Even in death, she remained an enigma, preserving her public image with unwavering dedication. In that moment, Riccardo couldn't help but feel a strange understanding for her ultimate choice.

Sinking into the antique chair, Riccardo turned his attention to the mirror before him. His gaze lingered on his own reflection, his eyes searching for any resemblance to his grandmother. With tender care, he examined his nose, lips, eyebrows, and cheekbones, tracing the contours of his face.

Amid his reflection, a familiar painting caught his eye. Picasso's *Maya in a Sailor Suit* was on display, its deformed and fragmented depiction of his own daughter serving as a visual metaphor for the intricate complexities of human connection. Riccardo couldn't help but wonder if Picasso, too, had searched for traces of someone within his daughter's face, just as he was doing now.

Adjacent to the Picasso painting, an old photograph hung on the wall, a portrait of his grandmother alongside her friend Eva, draped in a black veil adorned with spider brooches.

Focusing his interest back to the vanity, Riccardo's eyes were drawn again to the assortment of crystal bottles, glistening in an array of sizes and colors. The sight was beguiling, as if he had stumbled upon a hidden treasure trove of exquisite craftsmanship. Each bottle possessed its own unique charm, and had delicate, butterfly-shaped stoppers that sparkled with ethereal beauty. Riccardo couldn't recall the brand, but he knew they held great value, a testament to his grandmother's discerning taste and her willingness to invest in the allure of these prestigious crystals. Curious, he reached for one of the bottles and unscrewed the cap, only to find it empty. Disappointed, he tried a few others, only to discover the same emptiness. With a tinge of sadness, he carefully placed them back on the table, their magnificence momentarily overshadowed by the void within.

Riccardo turned his attention to the books stacked beside the crystal bottles. The titles revealed glimpses into Perihan's intellectual pursuits and inner world. Among them were

Nietzsche's *Thus Spoke Zarathustra*, Vladimir Nabokov's *Letters to Véra*, Carl Jung's *The Red Book*, and Ram Dass's *Be Here Now*. Riccardo reached for the latter, opening it to a page marked by his grandmother with a vibrant red underline. *You can't rip the skin off the snake. The snake must molt the skin. That's the rate it happens.*

Delving deeper into the collection of books, Riccardo stumbled upon a series of aged printouts, their edges worn and nibbled. The centerpiece of one page was a photograph of an old woman, her face heavily made-up and framed by her hands, adorned with pink nails that seemed longer than her plump fingers. A bittersweet smile played on Riccardo's lips, momentarily distracted by the comical nature of the image. However, his amusement quickly faded as he read the headline of the news article.

THE QUEEN OF CIRCUS, ELETTRA, COMMITS SUICIDE

Maria Prandini dell'Orto, known to the public as Elettra, allegedly committed suicide on her sixtieth birthday in the outskirts of Turin, where she was supposed to broadcast her new show at the circus on national television the same night.

Maria Prandini dell'Orto consumed some poisonous substance at her hotel in Turin, as well as five bottles of sleeping pills, and later died in the San Lorenzo Hospital, a spokesman said.

He said the motive behind this extreme step was the event that occurred earlier that afternoon at the circus, where animals ran wild and killed sixty elementary school children who were attending the rehearsals with their teacher. Even though the reason for the mass frenzy of the animals, none of which were new to Il Circo di Elettra, is still unclear, the police department is working with a group of veterinarians to investigate further.

Startled by the unsettling story, Riccardo felt a shiver race down his spine. *Why would she keep such a dark article? Was Elettra perhaps her friend?* he wondered, while dread settled within him. He instinctively brushed his hands against his pants, hoping to rid himself of the unnerving energy that clung to him. He put the worn printouts back in their original order. He wanted to preserve the arrangement his grandmother had left behind, so that nobody would notice he had visited this room.

As he stood in the room, a sense of curiosity tugged at him, drawing his attention to the concealed space hidden behind the silk screen next to Picasso's painting. Intrigued, Riccardo approached, and a flicker of anticipation ran through him as he discovered a wall with wooden shelves. Each shelf held a glass dome, safeguarding delicate butterflies within.

The sight was breathtaking, each dome a masterpiece. A tiny butterfly with transparent wings sat beneath one dome, while two magnificent morphos graced another. Yet, it was a display showcasing a large black butterfly with a massive wingspan that truly captivated Riccardo's imagination. "Are you even real? Look at those wings!" He marveled at the intricate patterns and delicate beauty of these preserved creatures, his eyes moving from one dome to another, each holding its own captivating allure. Riccardo's early, and perhaps only, memories with his grandmother were always mixed with the presence of butterflies. However, the discovery of this collection that must surely be the one Maurizio had described surpassed his expectations in both size and importance. Rather than envisioning a mere drawer of lifeless insects pinned to dusty foam boards, he was met with this beautiful assortment.

As Riccardo observed the grouping, contemplation set in regarding its potential value beyond aesthetic appeal. Could these butterflies hold economic significance? After all, he had to find a way out of his current situation.

"Riccardo, choose one. Today, we shall learn something new," Perihan declared, pointing at the small white packs arranged atop her desk. She settled him comfortably on her lap. The room exuded a combination of damp cotton, decay, and a potent chemical odor that eluded his limited seven-year-old vocabulary. Riccardo had been away in Paris for school, but his grandmother had decided to whisk him away for a weekend in Fontainebleau.

An assortment of triangles, each of varying sizes, captivated Riccardo's curiosity. He had no inkling of what lay concealed within, yet he eagerly embraced the game his grandmother proposed. She would often impart new knowledge, which he would later boast about to his friends at school. With his slender hands, he selected three different packs, feeling a tinge of confusion as to which one to choose. Sensing his uncertainty, his grandmother intervened and chose the largest triangle, stating, "It's better to begin with a big one for the first time, as it will be easier to handle. Which color appeals to you most?"

"Purple," Riccardo replied.

"Very well. Now, gather an abundance of purple sewing needles," she commanded.

Riccardo's gaze fell upon the profusion of colorful needles on the plush pincushion. He momentarily contemplated changing his selection but swiftly dismissed the idea, instead collecting a handful of purple needles before him.

With utmost care, his grandmother gingerly unfurled one of the small triangles, unveiling a lifeless butterfly with ebony wings.

"Riccardo, touch its wings gently," she instructed, her voice a soothing melody.

Riccardo gingerly extended the tip of his index finger, allowing it to graze the velvety texture of the insect's black wing. A subtle, tingling sensation coursed through him.

"Remember, butterflies are delicate creatures. We must handle them with great care. Observe what transpires when we apply excessive force between their wings and our fingers," she remarked, gracefully swinging the lifeless insect through the air. Riccardo's astonishment peaked as he witnessed a sprinkling of shimmering dust slowly descend from the wings, leaving a delicate residue upon his grandmother's blood-red nails. In hushed tones, he whispered to his grandmother, "Fairy dust."

"Fairy dust? Let us embrace that term. Fear not, young apprentice, for today is a day of learning. Now, observe closely," his grandmother continued, deftly maneuvering the butterfly to reveal the hidden kaleidoscope of colors nestled within its dark wings.

"Behold their uniqueness. These wings harbor multiple layers through which light must pass. Consequently, when light arrives, it encounters countless opportunities for its waves to reflect and magnify one another. This is the source of their iridescence. Though seemingly minute, envision thousands of microscopic scales, meticulously arranged in intricate layers. Each layer is separated by the air, allowing the light to undergo numerous reflections, thus giving rise to the vibrant hues we behold. Do you grasp the concept?" she asked.

Riccardo nodded, his understanding awakened. His grandmother had once enlightened him on the art of invisibility, illustrating how certain butterflies possessed seemingly imperceptible wings due to their mastery of light absorption and reflection. The notion of reflecting a rainbow seemed far less intricate than the pursuit of transparency.

With delicate movements, he cradled the butterfly's fragile abdomen between his fingertips, applying gentle pressure to unfurl the wings. Skillfully, he inserted a robust purple needle between the creature's head and lower body, swiftly affixing it to a substantial foam board.

"By placing thin sheets of paper on both wings, we shall allow it to dry in our desired position. Let us begin with the wings spread wide-open. Once I position the paper, you shall secure it to the board using these purple needles, following the contour of its wings. Is that clear?" Perihan asked.

Riccardo nodded, observing his grandmother's movements attentively. As she placed the sheet parallel to the left wing, he inserted the needles one by one around the circumference. As he pushed in the last needle, it slipped from his grip and pricked his fingertip. A drop of blood emerged, staining the lower portion of the wing with a deep shade of red. The pain was momentary, but the embarrassment lingered for a couple of minutes, as Riccardo found himself unable to complete even half the task his grandmother had assigned without creating a mess.

"Let us proceed to the other side now," the woman calmly suggested, acting as though nothing had happened. Riccardo followed suit, carefully inserting more needles around the wing, ensuring the two paper sheets were neatly positioned.

"You see? It wasn't that complicated. We shall now leave it undisturbed for a day, allowing it to dry in the position we have set."

Riccardo smiled at the memory. Among the shelves, he noticed a spiral-bound book. Placed atop the highest shelf, it seemed intentionally left for someone to take notice, an easy place for anyone to find. The words *For Riccardo* appeared on the front of the book and stirred his curiosity. Cautiously, he reached out and carefully took hold of it, knowing he needed to leave before his presence was noticed. He made his way back to the guest bedroom, where he carefully hid the book in his backpack, ensuring its secrecy beneath the bed.

Taking a moment to check his reflection in the window, Riccardo observed the solemn expression on his face. He knew it was time to join the others downstairs for the funeral, yet his mind remained consumed by the mysteries he had encountered in his grandmother's room. Obsessive collection of crystal bottles, butterfly domes, newspaper articles about a circus… The book in his backpack served as a constant reminder of the enigma that awaited him.

"Riccardo? Are you there?" Licia's knock on his door saved him from his deep thoughts.

"Yes, I'm ready," he answered, opening the door. He followed Licia in the corridor, then down the stairs, prepared to pay his final respects to his grandmother. Yet he could not stop thinking about two things: Where was Maurizio? And what was the book about?

10

When Riccardo descended the master staircase, he anticipated all eyes turning toward him. However, to his surprise, the group of guests was small, and they had their backs to him as they walked toward the corridor beneath the staircase. Joining them, he reached Licia, who remained dressed in the same outfit she wore when she had picked him up from the station. The first thing that caught Riccardo's attention was the casual dress of the guests, devoid of the customary black mourning clothes.

Her tiny fingers holding his hand, Licia whispered, "She would be happy you're here." Together, they made their way to a room at the end of the hall, with an old man leading the group and opening the door wide for everyone to enter.

Inside, neat rows of chairs awaited them, with a shiny oak casket placed at the far end of the room amid drawn curtains. The dimly lit space reeked of the pungent scent of a large floral arrangement, decorated with silk ribbons bearing the words *Perihan. Forever.*

"Ahh...tuberoses," someone sighed, inhaling the heavy fragrance that permeated the room. "She loved those flowers."

An old man with a thick mustache, round glasses, and a purple blazer that strained against his belly approached Riccardo. "You might not remember us, but I met you when you were just a kid! I'm Luigi from Purple Cinema, where your grandmother used to work as a student." He seemed charming and sweet, and he extended his hand to Riccardo. Riccardo shook it, pretending to recall the past, saying, "It's been a while... Sad that our reunion had to be like this."

"Oh well, it's not like you ever came to visit us!" someone chimed in from behind. Riccardo turned to see a rather intimidating woman covered in a black veil, with spider brooches on her headscarf. It was Eva, Perihan's best friend from years ago, the one he had seen in the picture in her room. She wore cat's-eye sunglasses and red lipstick, and her porcelainlike skin seemed eternal, defying the passage of time.

"Eva, I do remember you," Riccardo said, opening his arms for a hug. She embraced him, and for a fleeting moment, he felt he belonged. However, he reminded himself that his purpose here was not to build a new family or seek a sense of home. He was here to claim what he had inherited by pure luck: a magnificent, albeit decaying, villa in the heart of the city and a considerable amount of money in the bank—or so he hoped. He tried to maintain this rational perspective. "You know...it's like she never left," Eva whispered in his ear, sending a shiver down Riccardo's spine. He scanned the room, searching for Maurizio, but he was nowhere to be found.

While everyone took their seats, Riccardo found himself positioned behind two women who also seemed frozen in time, unchanged since the last time he saw them: the blind twins, Greta and Berta. Though he had forgotten all of these names while he was in Paris, he was noticing that the more time he spent here, the more his memories of his early years were returning. Licia, acting as his shadow, sat beside him.

"Isn't Maurizio coming?" Riccardo asked. Licia simply

shrugged and replied, "He avoids all sorts of spectacles and gatherings…after the circus." Then, she quickly bit her lip, as if realizing she had revealed too much.

"Circus?" Riccardo wondered, his mind flashing back to the article he had read earlier. But his attention was diverted as the old man, Luigi, rose to take the stage. He opened the casket, unveiling Perihan's peaceful body, and turned to address the seated guests. Riccardo did not move toward the coffin. He preferred to watch everything from his chair. He had no desire to approach his grandmother's lifeless form. He had not seen her in years and didn't want to risk tarnishing the beautiful image that had been engraved in his mind since he was sent away to boarding school. He could see from where he sat that her body was dressed in a red outfit.

"Perihan… Where can I start?" Luigi began. "Today, we gather here to remember and celebrate the incredible life of our friend, Perihan. I had the pleasure of crossing paths with her back in the day, when she stumbled into my little Purple Cinema. Man, did she have a knack for those niche films! It was like she had found her calling, and she made friends left and right, leaving a lasting mark on all of us."

Luigi continued his eulogy, recounting Perihan's academic pursuits and her partnership with Marco in creating a home that became the heart of their community. He concluded with a poetic sentiment. "May Perihan's spirit forever soar, like a butterfly in the darkness, fluttering in the shadows, reminding us that, even in the afterlife, her presence lingers among us. Farewell, dear Perihan. Your light shall forever illuminate our hearts. We'll definitely miss you around here."

Applause followed as Luigi shed a few tears, approached the casket, and placed a gentle kiss on Perihan's forehead. Riccardo expected others to step forward and give their eulogies, but instead they formed a line to bid their final farewell. He hesitated for a moment until Licia took his arm and offered,

"If this is too much, we all understand. Would you like to grab a bite? There is a nice buffet after this. Perihan loved to overfeed her guests. It's a tradition."

Riccardo nodded, appreciative of Licia's kind words, and left the room with her. He wasn't in the mood to linger and mourn the loss of someone he hadn't seen in years.

As Licia led Riccardo to the kitchen, they were met with a peculiar and unsettling sight. The room was filled with an overwhelming abundance of delicacies, far exceeding the needs of the few guests present. Pistachios, reminiscent of Perihan's Turkish heritage, were scattered everywhere. Multiplying like tiny green creatures, they overflowed from bowls and covered the countertops.

The air was heavy with the tantalizing scent of spices and freshly baked goods. The table groaned under the weight of overflowing platters, brimming with an assortment of Turkish delights, baklava, and savory dishes. It seemed as though Perihan had meticulously prepared a grand feast before she died, ensuring that no guest would leave hungry.

Riccardo felt overwhelmed by the excess and struggled to choose from the array of options. He filled his plate and settled in front of Licia, who continued to pile more food onto his plate, in order to infuse him with energy. After a while, he excused himself, giving her a warm hug, and called it a night. He retreated to his room, undressed, and began reading the first chapter of the handwritten book inscribed *For Riccardo*.

PERIHAN'S MANUSCRIPT

I grew up with devoutly religious parents. The haunting melodies of my mother's voice reciting various surahs from the Qur'an filled the air of my childhood. Her favorite word, An-nar, meaning *fire* in Arabic, echoed through our humble abode. But this was long before caterpillars transformed into butterflies, dear Riccardo, long before. Day in and day out, I was immersed in tales of heaven and hell within the confines of that tiny room. Hell, a realm of blazing fires, where people melted and water boiled, became the dominant narrative. My mother instilled a constant dose of fear in me and my six sisters, warning us about the Qur'an's depiction of the seven gates of hell. It seemed fitting, for we were seven sisters, each seen as a potential gateway to trouble in our small eastern Turkish town—a place consumed by the anxieties of an extremely devout family, forever fearful of their daughters succumbing to sin. When she finished her recitations, "Ameen" would escape her lips, followed by a tender kiss upon the black leather casing of the holy book before carefully returning it to its velvet pouch on our living room wall. Curiously, my mother bestowed more kisses upon the book than she ever shared with my father. In fact, now that I reflect upon it, I cannot recall a single instance where I witnessed their lips meeting in affectionate embrace.

All of this serves to emphasize that I was mentally prepared for the metaphorical seven gates of hell when I seized the opportunity to immigrate to Italy. This chance was granted to me through a generous scholarship I had earned during my inaugural year at the Boğaziçi University in Istanbul.

However, Milan boasted a multitude of gates, far exceeding the seven. On our inaugural day at the university campus in Milan, the guide imparted an intriguing piece of information to all the international students. "Milan, throughout its history, has witnessed the construction of three distinct systems of defensive walls: the ancient Roman walls, subsequent walls from the Middle Ages, and the latest fortifications erected by the Spanish in the sixteenth century. Presently, these walls encompass a staggering count of eleven gates that serve as entryways to the city, such as Porta Romana, Porta Ticinese, and Porta Venezia..." Curiously, the revelation failed to ignite curiosity among my fellow students, but for me, it sparked a profound fascination. With seven gates believed to lead to hell, I couldn't help but contemplate what sinister forces might infiltrate a city adorned with *eleven* gates. A shiver crept down my spine at the mere thought, foreshadowing the revelation that awaited me in due course, when I would finally cross paths with her.

Riccardo, my dear, perhaps you are not aware that prior to my immigration to Milan, and even for a few years after I settled here, my name was not Perihan. No, Perihan came much later. It was a name I personally chose. Before that, I bore a different name, one that was bestowed upon me.

"Yeter!" That's how I envision my name coming into existence, uttered for the first time by my parents, with an exclamation mark at its conclusion. I remain uncertain whether it was my mother who cried it out in pain after delivering seven girls in the span of ten years, or if it was my father who bellowed it at her, burdening her with unjust blame for being unable to bear a son. But enough was enough; they believed they were justified. My mother's body had been exhausted, depleted, drained. My father carried the weight of shame. He felt publicly humiliated, incomplete with seven daughters and no son. In Turkish culture, it was not merely important but essential to have at least one son within the family. Without a male heir, our family name had no chance of perpetuation. It would not be carried forward to future generations through a brother. Seven girls could not fulfill our father's quest for immortality as a boy would have. Instead, seven girls could only open seven doors to hell.

"Yeter! That's what we shall name her."

I was born in an inconspicuous small town in the eastern part of Turkey, a place that no one cared about. It transpired within the confines of a minuscule room devoid of heating and electricity. My name was Yeter, a Turkish word embodying the notion of *enough*. Whenever I tried to explain the meaning of my name to foreigners, they invariably assumed I was joking. To me, it felt like a bitter joke. Nevertheless, I insisted on offering an explanation. "In the eastern region of Turkey, having daughters instead of sons is regarded as a form of doom. The more daughters one has, the more detrimental it becomes to their standing as a man within society. That's why, after the birth of the first daughter, subsequent girls are given names like this, serving as a subtle lament directed at Kader, the destiny in which we strongly believe." Foreigners would nod politely, as though I were discussing a local recipe or a popular tourist attraction. They couldn't empathize with me or comprehend the burden I carried with a name like Yeter weighing upon my shoulders.

As Yeter, I would ironically discover that nothing was ever enough. There was always a scarcity of money, food, warmth, illumination, love, and affection. Thankfully, I possessed the intelligence and curiosity to rescue myself from that town. I harbored an insatiable hunger for knowledge. Every book that crossed my path was devoured, consuming as much information as I could before the final flicker of candlelight faded within our cramped abode. Occasionally, my older sisters, who had never experienced formal education, would compel me to assist them with daily chores or even resort to physical aggression when I resisted. Nonetheless, I would always find moments in the candlelit room to read before retiring for the night. I delved into topics such as DNA strands, extinct creatures, chemical tables, mathematical equations, photosynthesis, religion, mythology— anything and everything. Some of my bruises would scream louder than the knowledge, diverting my focus with pain. Yet even then, I would patiently await their subsidence to resume my intellectual consumption.

My escape from that town was not immediate. "You girls are fortunate to be here. Each day, remind yourselves that there are hundreds of girls in this town who would long to be in your place," our teacher used to affirm. She had a valid point. I was the sole girl in my class, encircled by forty boys. Throughout the entire school, there were merely ten girls in total. My father did not invest much care in me, so he allowed me to continue my education without much protest, and so I took advantage of it. I remained there, anchored to the same desk until the culmination of high school. Following that, I earned a scholarship to attend Boğaziçi University and departed without ever casting a glance back. Once there, I applied for another scholarship in Italy. I yearned to distance myself physically from my past. To be away. I felt akin to a caterpillar, ceaselessly crawling toward a place where it could construct a cocoon, a protective barrier. Like Milan, a fortifying wall, although history lessons had taught me that walls could also be used to divide rather than protect. Does a caterpillar find security within the wall it builds around itself, even though it will eventually emerge, live fleetingly, and then perish?

(I wish I could pose this question to my fallen angel. Technically, I can, but I doubt she would be capable of responding. Her words are scarce now; she prefers the embrace of darkness over the illumination of light.)

However, there was a time when there was light. An unexpected abundance of it. As radiant as an unanticipated summerlike day in late November in Milan... It was then that I encountered her. I was in my early thirties, still bearing the name Yeter, and desperately searching for something specific to bring to the castle.

The castle.

That was the essence of the invitation—an invitation to a castle in Tuscany. Naturally, I was invited because of your grandfather. He had connections with influential individuals from noble Italian families, who hosted extravagant parties in their opulent estates. We had previously attended gatherings in Venice, Turin, Verona, and Naples. They seemed like ordinary get-togethers among friends, except for the unexpected guests who always added a dash of excitement: aging prostitutes claiming to have posed for Carlo Mollino's Polaroids, eccentric bouncers from the legendary Milanese club Plastic, fire-eaters, burlesque dancers, and once even a garbage man, brought along by one of the guests.

We had visited various lavish properties but never a castle. This was a first. I must confess, I had always associated castles with fairy tales, probably because the few I had ever laid eyes upon were either in cartoons on small television screens or within the colorful pages of big books. With the castle as the backdrop, I anticipated a fairy tale where there would be a prince, a princess, and some problem-solving before they lived happily ever after. However, I had forgotten about the rest of the story: the monsters always followed.

Please forgive me, but I don't recall the exact date. I do remember it was before the fall of the Berlin Wall. There were speculations, but nothing concrete. My father had already immigrated to Germany in the early sixties as a construction worker and had completely vanished from our lives. Whenever I heard about the wall, I wondered how it would impact my father, if at all. I would spend time imagining him with a German wife and one, maybe even two or three, sons if fortune favored him. In my mind, our surname, my surname before marrying your grandfather, would multiply, branch out into new families through his imaginary German sons—a tiny surname resembling amoebas under the microscope, dividing into similar yet smaller entities. Numerous new sons, carrying the same surname in different cities, marking new individuals as an extension of my father. My father, forever immortal, forever existing in the future of the world. Would he find happiness then?

"Costanza and her husband are thrilled to have us tonight. They're hosting a birthday party for Fumito Misake, the oldest living man," your grandfather informed me.

"How old is he?"

"I heard he's over a hundred. Japanese. They eat well, sleep a lot. Life must be kinder to them than it is to us," he grumbled. But how difficult was his life, really, when you think about it? Only his vices would prevent him from reaching a hundred years. With his lifestyle, he would shoot himself if he ever came close to that age.

"What should we bring?" I asked. We always brought something intriguing to these gatherings. Once, I managed to acquire a highly rare, spider-infused vodka from Thailand. Can you imagine? It was quite a spectacle. Unexpected from a religious Turkish girl with a scholarship from a prestigious Italian university...but I loved surprising people. I still do.

"Bring whatever you please. I am bringing you, and I couldn't be prouder of my choice," your grandfather replied with his devil-may-care attitude, planting a kiss on my lips. "Oh," he added, "and dress up! People will surely overdress for this castle party... Get a new dress that will make you feel good."

It was still early in the morning when I left him at home and decided to visit Eva's store in the heart of Navigli.

The concept behind Navigli fascinated me. They had tried to make Milan accessible from the sea by constructing artificial canals, starting with Naviglio Grande in 1179, and later Naviglio Martesana in the sixteenth century. These canals not only facilitated the movement of merchants but also served as transportation routes for important commodities, like the marble of Candoglia for the Duomo and rolls of paper for the typewriters of *Corriere della Sera*. Even Leonardo da Vinci had contributed to these structures at one point. There was a rich history within its narrow streets, you see. However, that was all in the past. By the time I visited, Navigli had transformed into a meeting point for artists and antique dealers. I remember asking myself, "Will I discover any-

thing magical here today?" as I strolled along, searching for something suitable to bring to the castle. If Eva
didn't have what I was looking for, I doubted anyone
else would.

On both sides of the canal, various vendors offered an
array of items, from old movie posters to antique furniture. A strong melancholy enveloped me. There was
something peculiar about the entire experience, even in
broad daylight. Everything at those stalls appeared abandoned, as if once upon a time they had been cherished
possessions that someone eventually deemed unworthy.
Perhaps I didn't appreciate antiques as much as I should.
After all, how could I determine whether those silver
spoons had fed contented children with hearty appetites
or ailing individuals battling terminal diseases? Had the
pink dress hanging desolately on a rack been worn with
love on a first date or left with a price tag inside a dark
wardrobe? But not everyone shared my perspective. Most
of the booths were already bustling with early birds,
eager to peruse the inventory.

I longed for a quick shot of espresso to revive myself,
but I decided not to waste any more time in Navigli. I
headed straight for Eva's store, tucked away in a secluded
street off the canal. Regardless of how sunny the day was,
that street never seemed to receive any light. It perpetually exuded an aura of gloom. Beside her store, there
was an old pharmacy, but nothing else.

When I finally arrived, I spotted Eva, standing tall
in front of her shop window. She had donned her usual
ensemble: a black taffeta cape, a long black dress, a black
turban, and a pair of black sunglasses. She was old, as ancient as the world itself, yet her thick ebony hair could
evoke envy in a fifteen-year-old girl. I often wondered

whether she dyed her hair, but I never dared to ask. Eva was shrouded in mysteries, and this could remain one of them.

In that moment, I had a vivid flashback to a childhood memory. Eva's attire reminded me so much of my mother.

I must have been five or six years old. We were walking toward the archaeological museum in Hatay, where my father worked as a guardian. It was a long walk, and my feet were already aching in shoes a size too small for me. All my clothes were hand-me-downs from my older sisters. In fact, the only one who ever received new things was the eldest sister. Those who came after her would inherit her belongings as we grew up.

On our way to the museum, I spotted the most exquisite rag doll in one of the store windows. She had two thick, braided strands of blond hair, just like mine, and big green eyes. She wore a striped dress and carried a pink plastic bag in her right hand. I desired her with all my heart, so I let go of my mother's hand and pressed my face against the store window.

"Mom, please! Everyone at school has toys. I have none. Just this one, please. She's the most beautiful doll ever," I implored, convinced that the doll was winking at me from the other side of the glass.

"Your father would tear us apart if he ever heard what you just said. False gods! Idolatry! Pray to Allah for forgiveness. Toys are the tools of the Devil. Pray for forgiveness!" My mother seemed possessed. Her eyes held a hint of rage I had never witnessed before. I was frightened. I didn't remember any of the prayers. I detested reciting prayers in Arabic. I resented that I couldn't communicate with Allah in my own language, that I had to mimic sounds I didn't even understand. What did I say? Did my message ever transcend the language barrier? Every night before bed, when I asked for things and made wishes, was I clear even though everything was in Turkish? She dragged me away from the store and onto the street. We didn't exchange another word for the rest of the journey to the museum, but her brisk strides betrayed her anger. I felt a painful warmth on the sides of my toes inside the tight shoes. Due to our hurried pace, my feet were bleeding. I didn't dare tell her. I knew it was better to keep my mouth shut. Nevertheless, I looked at her intently, observing her robust figure cloaked in a black sheet. I gazed at her head, concealed beneath a black scarf. I wondered, as only a little girl could, whether my mother's burka was meant to be her cocoon and, if she secretly yearned to emerge from it someday as a beautiful, dazzling, magical butterfly, ready to soar away...had she?

When we finally arrived at the museum, I don't know what came over me. Throughout the painful walk, I had convinced myself that if I could just help my mother remove her pitch-black burka, I would set her free. She would be happy again, or perhaps happy for the first time. As we caught sight of my father at the corner of the archaeological museum, I grabbed at the edge of my mother's burka and yanked it off with all my strength. I heard her scream. She was wearing just her underwear, and I had exposed her in public. There was no one around us, but the notion of intimacy outside the home spelled trouble. I had only wanted to help her, but instead I had caused even more trouble. My father sprinted toward us like a wild animal, striking my mother with his hairy fist and kicking me off the road. I lost one of my milk teeth, and my mother lost her hearing in her right ear because of that incident. She would remain a prisoner in our house for the rest of her life: my father would never allow her to go out alone again. At least, not until he left us for Berlin.

I forced myself back to the present. The past hurt me; I didn't want to dwell on any of it.

"Eva!" I called out.

She turned slowly, a smirk playing on her red lips. I noticed two large spider brooches on her turban.

"Look who's here," she said, her voice rich and deep, as if it emanated from the depths of a well. If you happen to encounter her again, and I'm certain you will, listen to what she says. It's not always easy to hear.

She held an antique wooden doll between her bony fingers, her sharp red nails contrasting against its delicate form. She lifted it up for me to examine closely. "From England. Perhaps it belonged to the queen, perhaps not. Exquisite embroidery for a doll's dress. A genuine emerald, no larger than one karat, adorns her collar. Nobody will buy it, but it creates a bella figura in my window. Makes everything else appear more expensive."

At the mention of *bella figura*, I couldn't help but smile. It was precisely what had been weighing on my mind that morning. With Italians, especially the noble ones, one always had to make a bella figura—an excellent impression, in other words. It wasn't always easy, as the social codes differed from what I was accustomed to. For instance, taking off shoes before entering someone's apartment wasn't necessarily seen as a good impression in

Milan, whereas where I came from, it would be considered rude to step inside a house with dirty shoes.

"You have to help me find something intriguing. We've been invited to the castle," I implored.

"Come on in," she whispered calmly, stepping into the darkness of her store. Her cape was so long that she appeared to be floating in the air. I followed her into the dimly lit space.

When someone gently knocked on the door, Riccardo hid the book under the duvet.

"Come on in," he said. Licia entered Riccardo's room, a photo album cradled in her arms.

"Riccardo," she began, "you asked me about your mother. Well, she never came back. She wasn't known for her responsible nature or her affectionate character, as you might remember."

Riccardo looked up, his eyes revealing a hint of sadness. "Yes, I remember. But she left without a word, just disappeared. This I remember."

Licia nodded and sat down by his bedside, her eyes warm with affection. She opened the album, revealing a collection of old letters and pictures. "Perihan was the one who truly cared about you, Riccardo. Look at this."

She handed him some letters, and he felt a wave of discomfort. Hidden beneath his duvet was Perihan's book, safely concealed. Careful not to arouse Licia's suspicion, he took one of the colorful, childish letters and glanced at the writing. It was a message from his younger self, written in basic, innocent words. *I miss you, Grandma. When will you come?* Another letter read *My grandmother lives in Italy, and I don't live in Italy. I have my grandmother, but I don't have a family.*

Riccardo's face reflected his sadness, and Licia shared in his melancholy as she read the letters with him. She then handed him a picture. It showed him and his classmates, posed together in a semiannual image. The school principal had asked them to pose for it, and these images were sent to families worldwide every six months to show how their children were integrating into a diverse group. Riccardo brought the picture closer, studying it with keen interest. There, he saw a younger version of himself, a sad, skinny child, tucked away at the end of the line. His classmates beamed with confidence and joy, but he stood apart.

Riccardo's voice trembled as he spoke. "I felt so alone. It made me withdraw, close myself off. I didn't make many friends."

Licia offered him a reassuring hug. "I'm so sorry you went through that, Riccardo. It must have been hard."

Riccardo nodded, his attention on the old photographs. "That solitude…it led me to create stories in my mind. I started writing early on. Writing just required a pen and paper. I could imagine anything and make it real on those pages. It was a way to keep myself company."

With a somber sigh, he continued. "It was easy to leave everything in Paris. I had nothing much under my name and not many friends who would look for me. Just my agent who I avoid when I can… Oh, and the landlord, of course… Probably very happy I left."

Licia hugged him again, feeling the weight of his past loneliness. "You're not alone now, Riccardo. You have us."

She stood up and said, "There's one of those images hanging in the corridor on the way to the guest bathroom. Perihan loved how cute you looked in that one. Now I'm going to leave you alone… I just thought you would enjoy looking at these."

With those words, Licia left the photo album on the table

next to the bed before leaving. As soon as she was out of the room, Riccardo returned to Perihan's manuscript, his heart still heavy with the echoes of his solitary past.

PERIHAN'S MANUSCRIPT

I met Eva while working on my thesis about movies. She used to be a well-known journalist and had connections with famous Italian movie directors. Her appearance struck me: she dressed like a mysterious witch, wearing layers of extravagant black fabrics. But as I got to know her better, I realized she was the furthest thing from a witch. I once saw a photo of her from her teenage years. She looked like a cheerleader, wearing sparkly shorts and a pink cropped sweater, and holding pompoms. She was the popular girl in high school, the one who had it all: lots of friends and the perfect boyfriend. It was like a fairy tale, but only for a while.

"One thing I've learned is that things only last as long as they do," she told me one day. We were celebrating my graduation with top honors, thanks to her help editing my thesis. We were at her store, enjoying her favorite dish—steamed broccoli—and I treated us to a bottle of champagne. She shared some advice with me. "Don't hold on to things that no longer make sense. It's important to lighten your load, not just physically, but mentally too. Anxiety brings you down faster than gravity. Once you stress less and accept the end of things, it becomes easier to navigate through life's different paths."

Little did I know then how much her words would resonate with me. They changed my perspective on relationships and the natural cycle of endings. Inspired by her wisdom, I learned to let go of the past and embrace the present. This newfound mindset allowed me to experience the thrill of transformation, witnessing the beauty of life's unpredictable journey. And little did we know that evening marked the beginning of an extraordinary adventure filled with mystery, captivating discoveries, and unexpected challenges.

I must have stared at her with a blank expression, because she decided to provide more details. "I was a cheerleader back in high school," she said with a tinge of nostalgia. "Every night was full of events, people to meet, and places to explore. My boyfriend, who later became my husband, was the captain of the rugby team. You can imagine how popular we were as a couple. We were incredibly happy, so happy that it felt like we were living in a dream. After finishing school, we got married, moved to New York, and began building our dreams together. I started working as an assistant to various movie directors on the sets of some of the most important films of the 1940s and 1950s. He pursued a career in finance..."

As she spoke, a teardrop silently rolled down her pale cheeks, concealed behind her dark glasses. I held one of her hands in mine, offering comfort. "Then, everything changed in an instant due to a tragic accident," she continued. "That life was unexpectedly taken away from me. I was alive, but I felt dead inside. He was gone, but his memory remained vivid in my mind. His smile would appear before me every morning. I could still smell his musky fragrance..."

Eva began to cry, her tears caught by a tissue she dabbed behind her glasses. "It's enough, please don't... I understand," I tried to reassure her. But when it came to love, every story longed to be told again and again.

Love was the only remedy capable of transforming darkness into something beautiful, whether it be a story or an object.

She gathered herself and continued. "His musky fragrance lingered in our wardrobe long after his passing. I would hear him commenting on things in my head as I wandered the streets of New York, feeling utterly alone. People would ask about him. I would stumble upon forgotten pictures of us in drawers, abandoned bags, and between the pages of poetry books... How could I accept his death when his memory still felt so alive? So I decided. I left everything behind and immigrated to another country. I chose Italy because I was fascinated by Fellini's movies, and I knew that grief was acknowledged and respected in Italian society. I could mourn his loss for as long as I needed. And so I started anew."

Her voice trembled with emotion. "It was even more challenging in Italy than in the United States. Not only was I a widow but I was also a sad, disheartened immigrant who would cry frequently. I struggled to make friends and often dressed in black lace. But then I met Luigi, the owner of the Purple Cinema in Milan. That's when my second life began. I never fell in love again, but I rediscovered my zest for life. I curated weekly film screenings at the small cinema and wrote reviews for a national newspaper... And that, more or less, is my story."

"I have to confess something to you," I admitted to her. "I don't think my parents ever truly loved each other. And if I'm being honest, I don't think I've ever experienced love myself. I have six sisters, but we hardly ever speak. I haven't heard from my mother since last year. Well, I did write her a letter, but she doesn't know how to read Turkish, so maybe nobody read it to her..."

When I shared these thoughts with Eva, I had yet to meet your grandfather. That would happen a few weeks later, at a university reception for new graduates.

But for the moment, we were still commiserating in Eva's store.

"They will come into your life, stay for a while, and eventually leave," Eva said. "Your task is to ensure that when a relationship ends, your love has transformed them into someone happier, more beautiful, and less broken. That should be the only way you interact with the living, like a shaman casting magical spells with the power to heal. Remember, a diamond begins as a lump of coal, and a pearl starts as a tiny grain of sand. Even dark matter knows how to receive love and metamorphose into something beautiful."

That dinner, with the steamed broccoli and the champagne, marked the beginning of our friendship.

"I have original artwork dating back to the sixteenth and seventeenth centuries. I possess antique dolls, some of which may even be haunted. Rare editions of books grace my collection, along with a variety of Victorian wedding gowns. I have a little bit of everything," Eva proudly shared as she settled into her seat behind a grand oak desk.

"There's a birthday celebration for the oldest living man. His friends have organized a party in his honor at a castle near Tuscany. We need to leave in a couple of hours to ensure we arrive on time," I informed her.

"Is he Italian?"

"No, he's apparently Japanese. It's bound to be an

eclectic gathering. They always bring together an interesting mix of people. I just don't want to feel inadequate, you know? I can't compete with the grandeur of the castle with my small treasures from Navigli—no offense," I mumbled.

"Well, don't be so quick to underestimate yourself. What are you planning to wear to the party?" she asked.

"Marco asked me to buy something I like," I said.

"Buy? Why not just choose something from his mother's closet? Didn't she give you plenty of couture gowns when you two got married?" Eva's suggestion was a practical one. She added, "There's no easier way to fit in with a group than by dressing like them. You can also share the story behind the dress you choose. Just ask Marco or call your mother-in-law."

However, I had a different desire. I wanted to wear something new, something that was exclusively mine. Something that hadn't belonged to anyone else before. Perhaps it was a way of rebelling against my childhood wardrobe or, rather, the lack thereof.

"I need something brand-new to complement these couture gowns," I explained.

Eva remained silent but quickly got up from her chair and disappeared into the small room behind the racks of Victorian gowns. When she returned, she held a velvet pink box in her hands.

"Here are a pair of gloves from 1936. They have never been worn before, completely brand new," she announced.

I slowly opened the box, revealing the gloves. I gasped. They were the most peculiar fashion accessory I had ever seen. Two long black gloves with metallic gold claws on each fingertip.

"Can I try them on?" I asked.

"Of course!" Eva replied, taking one glove from the box, and sliding it onto my hand. I put on the other glove as well and examined my reflection in the oval mirror next to her desk. I felt an immense power. It was as if I possessed claws that could protect me from any monsters that might lurk in the castle's surroundings. I moved my fingers slowly, admiring how the chandelier's light shimmered on the metallic nails.

"These gloves were designed by Elsa Schiaparelli, who passed away in the early seventies. She was great friends with Dali and always infused her designs with a touch of surrealism. I had two more pairs like these, but I sold them both to a lady a month ago. Take these. They belong to you now," Eva said.

I nodded, knowing that these gloves had to accompany me to the castle that night. They were mine, and I felt a connection to them.

I was sitting in the hair salon when it happened.

The salon welcomed wealthy Milanese ladies who resided in Corso Magenta. They were married to men with prestigious surnames and enjoyed flaunting their Chanel suits embellished with cherished brooches. It was my mother-in-law who had recommended this salon to me, even though she would never set foot in it herself, saying it was "inelegant to have one's hair done in public."

My hairdresser, Alberto, held my thick blond hair in his hands and remarked, "Farah Fawcett...again? You only have one life, make the most of it while you can. You can't be stuck in the past like this," he said, rolling his eyes. The salon smelled of hair spray, nail polish, and a blend of heavy, white floral fragrances.

"Yes, please. The new hairstyles just don't appeal to me. I prefer a timeless style that works with any outfit. I still haven't decided what to wear tonight," I responded.

"Are you going to Costanza's party in Tuscany?" asked Elena, the wife of a businessman who had made his fortune with sweet treat stores all around Milan.

"Yes, we'll be leaving in a few hours," I confirmed.

"Oh, you'll just make it in time for the aperitif. I'll be leaving in an hour myself. It's a three-hour journey to the castle from here, you know," Elena shared. There was a hint of envy laced within her words as she spoke to me. "It's going to be an intimate gathering. Apparently, the old man doesn't care for large crowds."

Just as I was about to say something, the salon door swung open, hitting the plastic bird charm hanging from the ceiling, causing it to chirp in a frenzy.

A chubby child rushed inside, calling out, "Mom! Mom, look what I found!" He was heading toward Elena, who seemed slightly embarrassed and quickly excused herself, mentioning that the nanny had the day off.

"What did you find?" someone asked.

"Look!" the child exclaimed, and we all turned to see. He was holding a metallic blue butterfly with magnificent large wings, delicately perched on his finger. The butterfly seemed unperturbed by the commotion and the salon's scents, calmly fluttering its wings. The underside of its wings displayed dark shades of brown with circular patterns, while the top surface showcased an array of blues, more shades than you could ever imagine.

"It's so beautiful, young man. Where did you find it?" asked Alberto.

"Outside. A girl gave it to me," replied the chubby child, glancing at his mother. "Can I keep it, Mom?"

"Well, first of all, lower your voice a bit. You're disturbing everyone. Yes, you can keep it," she responded. Then she looked at me and added, "I'll leave them with my mother for tonight. The nanny's off, but they won't be coming with us to the castle… I used to send them to the circus, but there's no circus anymore either." Elena seemed desperate, but I didn't understand what circus she was referring to at the time. I can't remember if I told her right then that I disliked children and doubted I would have one of my own. Nevertheless, she ended up telling Marco when they next met at a social gathering—using those exact words, whether they were true or not. I later discovered that he was upset about it.

Don't take offense on behalf of your mother, my dear Riccardo. After immigrating, I cherished my freedom and didn't want others to depend on me, let alone a newborn. I also had doubts about my capacity to love someone else.

The door swung open again, accompanied by the invisible bird's chirping within the plastic charm. This time, it was Elena's daughter, even plumper than her brother. There was no doubt they had indulged in their fair share of sweet treats… When we realized what we were witnessing, we gasped in a mix of surprise and awe.

Elena's daughter was covered in butterflies. They were a deep orange color with scattered hints of black, all fluttering their wings in synchrony. Later, I would learn that they were called monarch butterflies. The little girl seemed frightened, swatting at the butterflies on her arms, legs, and hair while crying. We all hurried to remove them from her, and although we managed to free her, the butterflies didn't leave. Instead, they found new places to perch and enjoy the salon. Some settled on the hairdryers, a few on the damp towels, while the rest continued to flit freely through the room. Initially, there was nothing alarming about it; in fact, it felt magical. I was so taken aback by the spectacle unfolding before my eyes that I started imagining my life as a musical, with the sound of blow-dryers, the plastic chirping-bird charms, the cries of the chubby children, the laughter of the wealthy women, and the jingling of gold bracelets on their arms. It was a musical, and I found myself right in the middle of it. Butterflies were everywhere… It all began with the butterflies.

11

Having read Perihan's book until he fell asleep, Riccardo woke up in the middle of the night to strange noises and thumps coming from the hallway. He was unnerved by someone rummaging through drawers and wardrobes in the room next door. He couldn't understand who could be making all that noise so late at night. Riccardo tried to get up, but his body felt strangely numb and unresponsive. He couldn't move his arms or turn around. It was as if he was trapped in his own body. His eyelids felt heavy, and he struggled to keep them open.

Suddenly, the door to his room opened, and someone entered. Riccardo strained to see who it was, but he couldn't turn his head. He tried to speak, but his voice wouldn't cooperate. The person in the room made a comment that Riccardo couldn't quite hear, and then they left, closing the door behind them. Exhaustion washed over him, pulling him back into a deep sleep. The mystery of the intruder remained as he drifted further into slumber.

★ ★ ★

The creaking door signaled Maurizio's entrance into the house. With a sense of urgency, he navigated the darkness, aware that Licia awaited him somewhere within the silent halls. Not daring to disturb Riccardo's slumber, Maurizio tiptoed toward the stairs, ascending them to reach Perihan's room.

Upon entering the room infused with the lingering scent of her perfume, Maurizio closed the door behind him and softly illuminated the space with a small table lamp. His gaze briefly grazed the multitude of crystal bottles in the room, their extravagant shapes and sizes containing only emptiness. Time was of the essence, so his focus turned to the object hidden behind the silk screen.

Walking on the plush carpet, Maurizio passed beyond the screen, entering the section with wooden shelves. A gasp escaped his lips as he beheld the breathtaking sight of domes, each housing a different butterfly within. The vibrant colors and delicate wings created an ethereal ambience, akin to a portal to another world. With reverence, he approached the dome showcasing two morpho butterflies, tenderly kissing his index finger and gently touching it to the glass in a gesture of homage.

He checked the shelves, meticulously scanning for the spiral-bound book meant for him. However, the book was nowhere in sight. Frustration welled within him, and he considered the possibility that Licia had moved it elsewhere for safekeeping. He examined each shelf once again, even inspecting behind the domes, but there was no sign of the book.

Leaving the area behind the screen, Maurizio made his way to the vanity and perched on the edge of an antique chair. He began a thorough exploration of each drawer, hoping to uncover the hidden treasure. As he ran out of places to look, he couldn't help but feel a pang of anxiety. Where could the book be?

Opening the wardrobe, the thrilling smell of Perihan's perfume enveloped him as the clothes, steeped in her signature fragrance, surrounded him. His hands searched the bottom of the wardrobe, hoping for a fortuitous discovery. When his fingers brushed against an object, hope surged within him, only to be crushed as he pulled out an old hardback copy of a Danielle Steel novel. Frustration consumed him, and he flung the book angrily across the room, its impact against the wall punctuating his exasperation.

"Where the fuck is the book?" he muttered through clenched teeth, the stress tightening its grip on him. He scoured the drawers of the dressing table once more, his gaze flickering toward the bedside table, which was devoid of any drawers and had only a lamp on top. A thought crossed his mind: Had someone stolen the journal? But why choose the book over the valuable Picasso painting on the wall?

Maurizio checked the stacks beside the crystal bottles one by one to see if the manuscript could be hidden between these titles, but that was another dead end. However, amid the collection, he noticed something he had overlooked before: an old newspaper article about Elettra's suicide now rested atop Dass's worn paperback.

Memories of their journey in Mexico flooded Maurizio's mind.

"Elettra, get down!" shouted Maurizio. Reacting swiftly, he dropped, his body pressing against the floor.

In an instant, the air was filled with a frenzy of monarch butterflies taking flight. Their wings beat aggressively, creating vibrant orange clouds that moved with astonishing speed, surpassing any bird Maurizio and Elettra had ever witnessed.

Some of the butterflies soared through the path where Elettra lay, her head sheltered between her trembling hands. The sheer intensity of their fluttering wings produced a cacophony akin to a nearby helicopter, overwhelming their senses. Maurizio was torn between shielding his head from the forceful flapping against his skin and protecting his ears, which threatened to burst with the deafening roar.

But as suddenly as it began, the chaotic spectacle subsided. The entire forest was shrouded in silence.

Elettra cautiously opened her eyes, her heart still pounding. "Fuck!" she exclaimed, shocked. Maurizio looked upward, a flicker of fear gripping his chest, dreading another onslaught of butterflies. However, his whispered words escaped in disbelief. "No way..."

Astonishingly, the trees that were once home to countless butterflies were now vacant. Not a single butterfly remained in sight. They had vanished, leaving behind an uncanny emptiness in their wake.

Maurizio snapped back to the present. Time was slipping away, and finding the essential book became his sole focus. In the corridor, he noticed Licia's small figure casting a sturdy shadow against the wall. Her hopeful eyes and faint smile revealed her anticipation.

"Did you get it?" Licia asked eagerly.

"No, it's not there," Maurizio said, his concern increasing. He avoided eye contact, his mind racing with possibilities.

"What do you mean? I saw it this morning, right where it should be," Licia insisted, pushing past Maurizio and entering the room. Moments later, her expression turned to worry.

"You're right... Where could it be?" she wondered, her gaze shifting toward the guest bedroom where Riccardo slept. Without exchanging words, they decided to check on him.

Maurizio gestured for Licia to wait outside as he entered the room. Riccardo lay peacefully on the bed, undisturbed. Maurizio searched the surroundings, including Riccardo himself, but found no trace of the book. "I thought he might have taken it."

Licia dismissed the notion, explaining that she had accompanied Riccardo to his room both before and after dinner. "He didn't have a moment alone to steal anything. It must have been someone from the funeral. I checked on Riccardo. He didn't seem able to do much in the state he was in," she concluded.

Maurizio observed Riccardo's slight movement, but Licia reassured him that the tranquilizers in his soup earlier had rendered him immobile. "He won't be able to get up. He's barely aware of us," she assured him.

Exiting the room, Maurizio and Licia faced each other, the unspoken question hanging in the air. "What about the ritual now?" Licia said.

12

The next morning arrived, casting an atmosphere of un-ease over the entire house. As Riccardo sat alone at the breakfast table, he noticed that nobody else had shown up. He had a bad headache and was feeling groggy. The absence of the usual lively chatter and clinking of cutlery was disconcert-ing. Curiosity and concern filled his mind, but no one seemed willing to share any details with him.

Licia, preoccupied with her own thoughts, delegated the task of preparing breakfast to a young maid. The older woman moved restlessly around the room, opening and closing dif-ferent drawers in search of something. Riccardo watched her from a distance, sensing her agitation but unsure of its cause. Something was clearly amiss, but no one seemed willing to disclose what had transpired.

Finishing his simple oatmeal and coffee, Riccardo decided to head to the kitchen to clear his plate. As he entered, he in-advertently stumbled upon a conversation between Licia and the maid, their hushed voices barely reaching his ears.

"Is everything all right?" Riccardo said, a note of concern in his voice.

Licia turned to face him, her eyes betraying a hint of worry. "Of course, dear Riccardo. It's just the day after the funeral... A heavy day for all of us. Do you need anything?"

Riccardo took a moment to process her words, sensing that there was more to the story than met the eye. "No, I just want to smoke," he replied, hoping to find a quiet moment amid the turmoil. Without waiting for a response from Licia, he opened the back door and stepped into the garden.

From his vantage point in the garden, Riccardo gazed upon the gloomy greenhouse with its dirty windows, a symbol of neglect in the unkempt surroundings. He let out a heavy sigh, feeling the weight of recent events pressing upon him. Lost in his thoughts, he suddenly noticed a figure emerging from the greenhouse. It was none other than Maurizio, his presence both surprising and comforting.

"Maurizio!" Riccardo called out. The man waved at him nonchalantly, a faint smile playing on his lips, and made his way toward Riccardo. With a lighter in hand, he lit Riccardo's cigarette, a small gesture of camaraderie.

Riccardo gestured toward his own pack of cigarettes, silently offering one to Maurizio. However, Maurizio shook his head, declining the offer. "Where have you been? I looked for you yesterday... You didn't come to the funeral," Riccardo said, a tinge of disappointment evident in his words.

Maurizio's expression turned serious, his eyes reflecting a mix of sorrow and guilt. "I couldn't attend. It was incredibly difficult for me to imagine seeing Perihan lying in a casket after all our years of friendship. I apologize if my absence disappointed you. How has Licia been treating you?"

"She's been taking care of me, as has everyone else. Last

night, I thought I heard your voice. When did you arrive?" Riccardo asked, trying to make sense of the timeline.

Maurizio's response was straightforward. "I arrived this morning," he said, glancing toward the house where Licia could be seen through the kitchen window. He raised a hand in a casual wave. "See you later," he said, offering no further explanation.

The morning wore on, seemingly stagnant and devoid of any significant events. The house stood eerily quiet, save for the faint sounds of muffled conversations emanating from behind closed doors. Riccardo attempted to distract himself by turning on the television, but nothing on the screen captured his interest.

Around two o'clock, someone he had seen at the funeral appeared in the garden. The woman was carrying a basket filled with an assortment of fruits. She entered the house, making her way to the kitchen to leave the basket on the counter. Catching sight of Riccardo, she announced, "Happy you're here, Riccardo. I wanted to say hi yesterday. My name is Cristina. You might not remember me, but I was one of Perihan's closest friends. Stay here. I'll bring some cherries, and we can have a chat."

When Cristina returned with a bowl of cherries, she settled down next to Riccardo, who was looking forward to their conversation as a welcome distraction from the weight of the day. "How was your night?" she asked with genuine concern.

Riccardo contemplated his response for a moment before answering. "It was okay, I suppose. I must have been incredibly tired, as I dozed off and woke up directly this morning. I had many nightmares, but I guess that's normal given the circumstances."

Cristina nodded sympathetically. "It is… It really is. Tonight, we can all have dinner together," she suggested.

Riccardo asked, "Who will be joining us?"

"Just a few of our friends," Cristina replied with a faint smile. "Perhaps you remember the blind twins? You might have seen them at the funeral or remember them from your childhood. They were always around when you were a baby."

Recognition sparked in Riccardo's eyes as he recalled the twins. "Of course I remember them. I have a number of memories of them, actually. That time when my grandmother was upset about the butterfly mosaic in our street... Or my first-ever train ride... My grandmother had taken us to Venice for a Carlo Mollino exhibition. It's strange, though. I never understood why she took two blind people all the way to Venice for a photography exhibit..." He went back to the memory that appeared in front of his eyes in a flash.

"Next to a great forest, a poor woodcutter lived with his wife and two children. The boy's name was Hansel." Perihan was reading the first page of the book they had bought from the kiosk before they all got on the train.

"Are you reading 'Hansel and Gretel' to the poor boy? Are you out of your mind, Perihan?" said one of the scary twins sitting in front of them, hitting Riccardo's grandmother on the knee with her white cane. Perihan squeezed his hand, holding the book with her other hand. Riccardo looked down.

Riccardo observed Perihan's long red nails. She wore no jewels except her favorite ring, the butterfly-engraved marble with one teardrop diamond on each side. Her invasive fragrance had taken over the compartment.

"It's a classic. There was nothing else that attracted my attention," Riccardo's grandmother said in defense of her purchase.

Riccardo saw the white cane slowly move toward him, first hitting his grandmother's pink bag between them, then tickling him on his naked legs. It was a hot summer day, and he was wearing beige shorts with a white polo.

"There you are," the twin confirmed while tapping Riccardo's leg twice with the cane. Then both moved across their seats to get closer to him, lowering themselves so that all three of them could be at the same eye level.

"Riccardo, is this your first time traveling by train?" one of them asked.

Riccardo nodded without looking up. His grandmother squeezed his hands once more, assuring him that everything was under her control. He started counting the long beads on the constellation embroidery on his grandmother's skirt. When it proved to be an impossible task, he turned his head to see the legs of the twins. They were both wearing thick beige knee socks with their swollen, twisted varicose veins sticking out.

"Oh, there is nothing to be scared of. We are just two blind women. Perihan is a very close friend of ours. We've known her since her university years," the same voice explained.

"I'd rather continue reading 'Hansel and Gretel,' girls. You scare my poor little Riccardo more than the Brothers Grimm can ever hope to!" Perihan laughed.

Riccardo did not want to offend them, so building up all his courage, he looked up to face the two women looking at him. They had bluish opaque eyes. The more he looked at their eyes, the more he saw an imaginary cloudy sky filled with hundreds of miniature shapes.

"What do you see in the dark?" Riccardo asked out of curiosity. He remembered how, when his grandfather switched off the lights every night and everything went completely black for a few minutes, his eyes would adjust themselves to the darkness. But then, bits and pieces of the world around him started appearing again. If the caterpillar came out of a cocoon as a butterfly, there must have been some magic hidden in the darkness.

"I guess our answers will be different. So first, let me introduce myself. My name is Berta," he heard one of the twins say. The train had departed in the meantime. They were on their way to Venice.

"I was blind from birth, so I have never seen anything the way you do. I know the apple by its taste, by its shape. I can't tell you about its color. I can't tell you how tall a tree grows. For me, they grow as far as I can reach with my white cane. Whatever I don't see, I fill it with my own imagination. We will never know if what I imagine is close to what it really is."

"You never saw yourself?" Riccardo asked, intrigued. He let go of his grandmother's hand, feeling more comfortable with the twins as they continued to talk to him.

"Never. Do you think I am pretty?"

It was hard for Riccardo to decide. She had a small pointy nose with thin lips right underneath. A few freckles sprinkled over her whole face. Thick gray hair. Milky blue eyes.

"You are," he lied.

"Oh, if you like her, then you'll like me as well. That is the good thing about having a twin. You get to enjoy all the compliments together. I am Greta. Perihan told me you like snakes. Is that true?"

"Only Kaa!" Riccardo exclaimed, referring to the snake from *The Jungle Book*, which he was obsessed with.

"Who is Kaa?" they asked simultaneously, wonder filling their voices.

"It is the snake with hypnotic eyes in the cartoon. I have the toy!" Riccardo exclaimed with triumph. The twins had known how to engage the young boy by talking about things that interested him.

"Does Kaa ever change his skin in this cartoon?" Greta asked. She seemed to be suffering from the heat, or rather from having picked the wrong outfit. She was wearing a mint green wool cardigan over her white top. She took it off and folded it on her lap as she waited for his answer.

"It does not. Snakes don't change their skins," Riccardo confidently confirmed.

"Well, they do. They grow. When they grow, their bodies become bigger than their skin, so they start shedding it. During this process, a liquid starts building up between their eye and the eye cap, causing them to go blind... Only temporarily, like for a week. But then they have eyes like ours. Bluish cloudy eyes," Greta said as she turned her head to the window. She held her twin's hand as she shared her story.

"Our father was a snake breeder. We had terrariums in our apartment. I remember in every corner, there was a crawling animal in a glass cage. He also had one spitting cobra, a rare breed, a special one. Like Kaa!" When she mentioned Kaa, she hissed. Riccardo's grandmother laughed, perhaps mocking her lack of acting talent. Greta continued. "One day, when my parents were busy looking elsewhere, I found myself trying to handle it, and I put my arms down in its terrarium. The spitting cobra was shedding its skin. Therefore, it had eyes like Berta's. I was curious. I wanted to see its eyes up close. I must have scared it. It spat its venom high up in the air first, and then once more from its fangs right into my eyes. I screamed as I fell on my back with the giant snake between my little hands. My last sight was its angry head. Then there was the hospital, the unsuccessful remedies..." She sighed, briefly touching the scars around her eyes.

"Kaa doesn't do this to Mowgli. Your snake was not Kaa," Riccardo protested. He was not particularly scared of snakes, so her story hadn't traumatized him. Even though, now that he thought of it, it was a bit of an exaggerated detail to share with a six-year-old. Or was he already seven?

Perihan had given up on "Hansel and Gretel." The carriage was now silent.

Riccardo suddenly thought about how he could make them see things. He had just remembered the picture book he had brought with him, hoping to entertain himself during the long trip.

"Do you want me to describe what I see in this book?"

The twins nodded.

"There is a picture of a beautiful garden with colorful flowers. And there are children playing on a swing. The sky is blue, and the sun is shining brightly. There is a big green tree with a tire swing hanging from one of its branches. The children are laughing and having so much fun. The grass feels soft under their feet."

"Keep going," Berta encouraged him.

"Now, there is a picture of a big castle. It has tall towers and a moat around it. The castle is surrounded by a beautiful forest. I can see the leaves on the trees. They are green, and some are turning yellow. There are birds flying in the sky and squirrels running around."

Riccardo continued describing each page of the book, painting vivid images with his words. The twins listened attentively, their faces serene and peaceful, as if they could see everything he was describing.

The train finally arrived at the station, and they all disembarked. Riccardo's grandmother held his hand tightly as they made their way through the crowd. Berta and Greta bid them farewell, their white canes tapping lightly on the ground, guiding them forward.

Riccardo waved goodbye, feeling warmth and appreciation for the encounter with the twins.

Cristina's voice softened, her words tinged with nostalgia. "I remember that trip. I was supposed to go with you, but Perihan decided at the last minute that it was better if I stayed here. The twins didn't go to the exhibition. Perihan

had arranged an appointment with a renowned eye special-
ist in Venice. She wanted to find out if there was any hope
for restoring their sight. She probably took you to the exhibition alone that day."

Riccardo listened intently, absorbing the pieces of his past
that had remained hidden from him. He couldn't help but feel
a variety of emotions: confusion, sadness, and a growing desire
to uncover the truth about the elusive character of his grandmother. He finally mustered the courage to ask the question
that had been bothering him. "Right… How did she die?"

Cristina's hands gently rested on Riccardo's shoulders, her
touch offering comfort. With a heavy sigh, she said, "She
took pills. Lots of them."

The weight of the revelation crashed down upon Riccardo,
overwhelming him with a rush of emotions. Tears welled up
in his eyes, his seemingly detached manner crumbling. He
looked for comfort in Cristina's embrace.

In that vulnerable moment, Licia and Maurizio entered the
room, their presence a stark reminder of the ongoing search
for answers. "Oh no," Licia murmured as she approached
Riccardo. She tenderly patted his head, her touch offering a
soothing reassurance. "Do us a favor, Riccardo. Go upstairs,
take an hour's nap, and come back. We'll still be here when
you've rested."

Riccardo nodded in agreement, a facade of weariness mask-
ing his true intentions. As he made his way back to his room,
he caught a glimpse of Cristina in the corner, engrossed in a
task with a black notebook. She plucked cherries from a bowl
one by one, her focus undivided.

In the background, Maurizio's voice carried through the
air, impatient. "Let's go through each and every name from
the funeral. Someone must have it. It can't have disappeared
into thin air."

Cristina munched on the cherries, seeming to savor the juicy fruit as she flipped through the notebook. Her enjoyment of the detective work was evident, the red cherries adding a vibrant touch to the otherwise serious atmosphere.

As Riccardo reached the stairs, he exchanged a few more words with Licia. With a carefully crafted air of exhaustion, he attempted to assert his independence. He reminded her that he wasn't a child who needed to be guided to his room. However, Licia continued to walk with him, her true motive transparent. It was clear she wanted to ensure he entered his room and closed the door, effectively excluding him from their secretive investigation.

Riccardo, faking weariness, noticed these subtle dynamics from the corner of his eye. It was all part of his plan to gain some time alone, a precious moment to continue reading Perihan's manuscript. With a soft sigh, he stepped into his room, gently closed the door, and leaned against it. He pondered what it was they were looking for. Had something of Perihan's gone missing? He eagerly resumed his reading.

As he delved into Perihan's words, Riccardo found himself captivated by his grandmother's vivid imagination. "Wow, where did she come up with all of this?" he wondered aloud, his fascination growing with each turn of the page. He marveled at the intricate worlds she had created within the worn pages, pondering when she had found the time to nurture such creativity.

Intrigued, he reached for his phone, eager to uncover more of her story. However, a quick Google search yielded no results for other novels published by Perihan. "Strange, I thought she might have published something prior," he muttered to himself, his curiosity now tinged with disappointment. But there was no trace of any previously published works on any of the big book sites. Confusion mingled with his curiosity, and he couldn't help but entertain the idea that perhaps this book was merely a private activity, a personal pastime for Perihan.

His online search was abruptly interrupted by a buzzing notification. An SMS from his agent appeared on the screen. Any news? Time is running out. A surge of anxiety coursed through Riccardo as he read the message. *Time is running out… What if I can't deliver what he expects?* His mind swirled with doubt and insecurities.

He contemplated using his grandmother's death as an excuse, but his fingers hesitated over the keyboard. The words he considered felt feeble and inadequate, unlikely to persuade his agent. "What can I even say? Will they understand?" he mumbled. His thoughts were consumed by the fear of disappointing others. He deleted the opened text field, convinced that no one would believe his excuses. In his mind, he had become a loser, constantly putting off his dreams.

He attempted a different approach, typing Working on it… but immediately second-guessed himself, aware that such a response would only invite more frequent check-ins from his agent. "Maybe if I buy some more time, I can figure things out," he mused, desperately clinging to the hope of finding a solution.

The phone slipped from his grasp, sweat droplets trickling down his palms and smudging the screen. Noticing the low battery, Riccardo rose from the bed and located the charger near the window. He plugged in his phone, intending to address the urgent matter at hand. However, his attention was swiftly diverted by the sight of two figures emerging from the greenhouse.

"Who are they?" he murmured, squinting to discern their identities. Clad in black dresses with delicate white collars, they resembled Perihan's maids—ones he had yet to meet. Their slow, laborious movements suggested that they were struggling with the weight of two large dark green buckets they carried in each hand.

Unable to comprehend the scene unfolding before him, Riccardo observed Cristina darting out of the house and rushing toward the greenhouse. She confronted the two maids, gesticulating wildly, before hurrying to close the door. From where he was looking, Riccardo surmised that she retrieved something from her pockets—likely the keys—and secured the door. *What's going on? Why are they behaving so strangely?* he wondered, a flicker of unease creeping into his thoughts.

"Strange people," he mused, shaking his head in amusement. Setting the book aside, he positioned himself on the edge of the bed, ready to immerse himself once more in the depths of Perihan's imagination. With keen anticipation, he turned to the next page, eager to find out what happened next.

PERIHAN'S MANUSCRIPT

Due to the commotion caused by the two children in the salon, everyone had forgotten about the boy saying "A girl gave it to me." I was eager to meet that girl. Deciding that my hair looked fine, I brushed off any concerns and prepared to leave. Worst-case scenario, I could simply put it up in a chignon.

"Oh, I have to go. I completely forgot about Marco. He doesn't have the keys," I babbled. Alberto tried to say something, but instead he shrugged. It was impossible to continue working with all the butterflies fluttering about. If the blow-dryer was turned on, the poor insects would start flying en masse all over again.

I slipped a generous tip into Alberto's jeans pocket, bid farewell to Elena, and exited the salon. I had a mission to find the girl who had given the butterflies to the boy. However, the sidewalks of Via Meravigli were deserted. I glanced at the storefront of Pasticceria Marchesi, but there was no sign of her there either. I turned around, searching for any clue as to where this mysterious girl might have gone. As I gazed at the city backdrop, I spotted a large morpho butterfly with its mesmerizing, electric-blue shimmer. It disappeared into one of the intersecting streets.

Without hesitation, I quickened my pace and followed the butterfly's path. The place it led me to was more of a narrow alley between two old buildings than an actual street. But I knew the way—it would take me to Santa Maria alla Porta. Ever since I'd first arrived in Milan, I had been fascinated by the church and its intriguing story. In 1651, during the Spanish domination of Milan, a construction worker discovered a painting of the Virgin Mary and baby Jesus on one of the church's external walls. He cleaned the painting with his apron and miraculously found that his lameness had been cured. Following this extraordinary event, the painting became known as *The Lucky Virgin of Miracles*. In the early 1700s, an octagonal area was constructed in front of it, which became a place of veneration for the people of Milan.

The Lucky Virgin was believed to possess extraordinary healing powers. People with terminal illnesses, painful disabilities, and mental disorders came to her, and they left transformed. All that was required was faith. If they believed and prayed, they would be healed. Like oxygen in the air that sustains life, *The Lucky Virgin's* miracles were invisible to the eye but worked wonders. Can you believe that even during the bombings in 1943, amid the chaos of World War II, the painting survived? The butterfly seemed to be guiding me to the center of miracles. Normally, I would have felt claustrophobic in such narrow confines, but at that moment, all I felt was pure bliss. I sensed that my destiny was about to change. During the last few meters of the alley, I almost stumbled, but then I found myself standing in the small piazza.

Like Alice venturing into the rabbit hole, I had followed the butterfly into a narrow alley, stepping out of the confines of my ordinary life and immersing myself in what felt like a fairy tale. And there, in that enchanting moment, I didn't see her immediately. Instead, I was captivated by the sight of hundreds of butterflies, fluttering around the painting on the wall of Santa Maria alla Porta. One of them landed on my small bag, curiously exploring its texture. I felt as though I could be in heaven, experiencing a surreal realm. Surreal, because such magical occurrences had never happened to me before. My mother had recounted stories of the archangel Jibril's visit to Prophet Muhammad, the miraculous revelations of the Qur'an, and how Prophet Ibrahim received a sheep for sacrifice in place of his son... I had heard tales of Prophet Isa miraculously speaking as a baby. I believed in miracles, but I had never been a witness to one myself...until that moment.

Amid the fluttering butterflies, a shimmer in the dim light entered my eye. It must be her—the girl I had been searching for. I couldn't discern which gate of Milan she had entered through, nor did I know her origin. She was clad in a dirty carnival dress, the fabric shimmering with shades of pink. Her ginger hair cascaded in untamed waves before her face, and a monarch butterfly danced around her head. She lay on the floor, assuming a sleeping position, akin to an angel on the ground, at the center of the octagonal area. I approached her cautiously.

Was she unwell? Was that the reason for her presence in front of the painting?

"Hello?" I called out.

She didn't react to my words, remaining still as if in a trance. It's difficult for me to find the right words to explain this even now, years after our first encounter, but she emitted these incredibly delicate, almost imperceptible rays of rainbow hues. Picture a massive diamond reflecting faint light...

"Are you okay?" I asked, my voice filled with both concern and fascination. Despite her dress being cheap and visibly dirty, it appeared new. It was hard to determine her age, as she could have been anywhere between sixteen and twenty years old. Suddenly, another butterfly appeared out of nowhere, landing on her dress. It fluttered its wings a few times before settling down. Her wavy hair, which had obscured her face, parted like a curtain as she raised her head. At that moment, my heart skipped a beat.

She had iridescent skin.

Unable to contain myself, I uttered the first words from the Qur'an. "Bismillah..." I repeated the phrase a couple of times—Bismillah, meaning *in the name of God*. I was left speechless, unable to believe my own eyes. I was gazing upon an unearthly creature. I became convinced that I was in the presence of an angel come down from heaven.

It was as if she had captured a fragment of a rainbow or a soap bubble beneath her bronze skin. There was an iridescence to it, and upon closer inspection, her arms were the same: the luminous colors within her skin constantly shifted, depending on the angle from which I observed her. Butterflies circled above her head in a mesmerizing dance. Overwhelmed by emotion, I began to weep.

I sat down on the floor, directly in front of her, afraid to blink, afraid that she might vanish if I looked away.

My rational side desperately tried to find explanations for what I was witnessing. At first, I considered the possibility of an allergic reaction. Then, I imagined her being subjected to a brutal assault, resulting in the bruises and anomalies on her skin. But none of these explanations made sense. I had to let go of the reality I was accustomed to and embrace the unfolding of this extraordinary and natural miracle before my eyes.

She smiled. Every aspect of her being exuded a beauty defined by golden proportions and perfect symmetry. "You are the most beautiful girl I've ever seen!" I exclaimed, unable to contain my awe. She seemed to appreciate my compliment, extending her hand toward me. Unsure of what to do, I squeezed her hand gently. While others might have been concerned about the possibility of contracting some syndrome from her iridescent skin, all I wished for was to be marked by the magic she brought from the heavens above. Squeezing her hand was my way of testing if I could somehow resemble her, if her enchantment could touch me. My thoughts turned to my father. I often saw him kiss the hand of the imam at our local mosque as a sign of respect, but also as a means of seeking closeness to Allah through someone who worked tirelessly for Him. Similarly, my mother kissed the leather case of the Qur'an before placing it back into its velvet pouch. If only my father could see me now, in the presence of this miraculous being… What would he think? If Allah had blessed me with this miracle, even though I was the last of seven daughters, how would he interpret it?

"We saw the children with the butterflies. They were

so happy… Well, the boy was happier than the girl. He asked his mother if he could keep it. I wanted to come and see you. I was curious. Are you an angel? I have never seen an angel before, so forgive my excitement. How is it that all these butterflies surround you? It's like Eve before she ate the apple. She had all these butterflies and birds around her, didn't she?" I lay down beside her and gazed up at the sky. From the corner of my eye, I noticed that she continued to smile without uttering a word. I wondered if she was deaf.

"Can you hear me?" I asked, accompanying my question with hand gestures. Her smile grew even wider. It was evident that she relished my attention. The more I spoke to her, the more her beauty seemed to intensify, or perhaps it was just my impression.

"Well, I suppose you don't speak much. Would you like to walk with me?" I offered, rising to my feet. "Can angels walk?" I asked, feeling foolish. Maybe they could only fly. But she didn't seem to mind my questions. I took a couple of steps away and turned around, only to find her still lying on the ground amid the radiant rainbow emanating from her body. I gestured for her to follow me. Like an eager puppy yearning for affection, her face lit up. She stood and began walking slowly toward me, her bare feet taking brisk steps.

"You truly are an angel! I can't believe this is happening. Of all the people in Milan, you chose me! Right in front of The Lucky Virgin of Miracles, the one who heals all afflictions." She simply smiled. Nothing more, nothing less.

"We need to find you some shoes," I murmured, observing her feet blackened with dust and dirt. Would it be offensive to put shoes on an angel? After all, she was wearing a pink dress that didn't look particularly heavenly. Someone must have given it to her before we met.

I retraced my steps back into the narrow alley, with her following closely behind and various types of butterflies hovering above our heads. Was I becoming like Alice, taking the rabbit out of the hole? What would happen if you extracted something from a fairy tale and placed it outside its original context? Dragged it back into the center of reality?

As we set foot on Corso Magenta, an idea sparked in my mind. You can probably imagine what I had decided to do. Without a new dress or perfectly styled hair, this could be my chance to impress the people at the castle. It was my attempt to belong in a place where I would not be truly welcome if it weren't for my husband. I no longer needed the dress or the perfect hair. No, it was her—the special guest, the angelic girl with iridescent skin and her entourage of pet butterflies. It was her.

Initially, I had contemplated walking back home with her, but I hadn't anticipated the fluttering army that accompanied us. Instead, I hailed a cab, gently guided her inside, and closed the door. I sat in the front seat, even though it wasn't considered very ladylike to sit next to the taxi driver. But at that moment, I couldn't care less about social norms. My main objective was to distract him from her by purposely acting out of the ordinary. The driver was a grumpy old man who had long closed himself off to wonder. He might have noticed a few butterflies landing on his side mirror, but he didn't seem impressed.

"Via Marco de Marchi, please," I requested.

And off we went, embarking on the next chapter of my life.

★ ★ ★

Riccardo paused in his reading, the intricate words of Perihan's manuscript still fresh in his mind. He couldn't help but dwell on his grandmother's enigmatic life. Her obsession with butterflies, her glamorous lifestyle, and the allure of her persona had always hinted at a woman with a wild imagination. It must have been this trait that had led her to craft this piece of compelling fiction, he thought.

He remembered her friend relating Perihan's pill consumption and the tragic end of her life. Cristina had told him it was suicide, but Riccardo found it difficult to accept. With a life as opulent as hers, so few responsibilities to weigh her down, and this hidden talent for writing that he had only recently discovered, it seemed unlikely that she would choose to end it all.

As he sat in his room, lost in thought, he couldn't help but wonder if there was more to the story. Could it have been an accident, a twist of fate that had taken her from this world? Or was there something darker, something concealed in the depths of Perihan's past? The unease he felt around her circle only fueled his curiosity. They all seemed to be guarding a secret, one that hung in the air whenever he was in their presence. It was a puzzle he intended to solve, if only to uncover the truth behind his grandmother's mysterious end. His eyes returned to the page in front of him and he continued reading.

PERIHAN'S MANUSCRIPT

If only I had been more attentive to the signs, I would have realized that things were not as perfect as they seemed. But I was mesmerized by her beauty or, rather, by the enchantment of it all. It was all too good to be true for a girl named Yeter, an immigrant from a small town in Turkey. I wanted to enjoy every moment of this magic, to immerse myself in it, to dance with it, and to let it consume me. I couldn't help but think of my mother's Qur'an. I recalled the Arabic verses she would recite day and night, the stories of heaven and hell, angels and demons, Adam and Eve, Prophet Ibrahim's sacrifice, and Noah's ark. I felt so close to the surahs my mother had taught me as a child.

I had witnessed the suffering of so many women in the harsh reality of life, starting with my own mother and then my six unhappy sisters. Reality seemed to be a burden for us. My mother used these stories to shield herself from it, but why couldn't I experience one of those tales? Why not delve into the surreal? I decided to give it a try.

The cab driver turned out to be aggressive. After five minutes, he turned on the radio, blasting the volume so high that the girl became frightened, tightly clenching her fists, and hitting the window. The driver shouted at her in anger, threatening to charge us if she broke the window. I was disgusted by the yellow stains on his white shirt and his choice of music, so I quickly turned off the radio. The blaring voice of Loredana Bertè proclaiming she was not a signora was certainly not the appropriate soundtrack for the scene.

"That's okay, dear. It was just very loud music," I reassured her, hoping to calm her down. She gradually relaxed and rested her head on the windowpane.

As we stopped at a red light, I noticed that the butterflies had disappeared. I expected some of them to land on the windshield wipers as soon as we stopped, but there were none in sight. Curious, I lowered my head to look at the sky but couldn't spot any butterflies. To get a better view, I rolled down my window and stuck my head outside.

"Lady, if you need to vomit, tell me in advance," the grumpy man said. If I were alone, I would have left the car right then and there. I couldn't stand his attitude.

"No, I'm fine... The butterflies are gone," I commented, but he wasn't interested. As the traffic light turned green, he accelerated, and we continued our way, both of us silent. However, he made a wrong turn near Moscova and had to go around the block twice before finding the correct route. Impatiently, I glanced at my watch, wondering if Marco was already home. If he was, I would have to come up with a story about the girl, or maybe I would simply tell him the truth. He always seemed to enjoy the raw and unfiltered versions of stories, with his devil-may-care attitude toward life.

The driver didn't see the other car approaching at full speed from the intersecting road around the corner of Via Marco de Marchi. By the time he noticed it, it was too late. He slammed on the brakes in a desperate attempt to avoid a collision. Both the girl and I were wearing our safety belts, which locked us in place, but the impact caused her head to hit the back of the driver's leather seat. She let out whimpering sounds, and I couldn't tell if she was crying or not.

"You could have got us killed!" I screamed at the driver, my anger and fear overwhelming me.

Realizing the severity of the situation, he seemed scared too. He apologized repeatedly for the grave mistake he had made.

I turned around to face my companion, wanting to ensure she was all right. She appeared scared but unhurt. With affection, I extended my hand to touch her knee and reassured her that everything would be fine. "I hope you won't have a bruise on your forehead. Did it hurt a lot?" I said, but she remained silent. To my surprise, I no longer saw the iridescent glow or the purplish-blue sheen to her skin. It appeared ordinary, resembling my own. Was I losing my mind? Had I imagined everything that had transpired just half an hour ago? I let go of her hand, perplexed by the sudden change.

Upon arriving at the house, the driver offered a small discount to prevent any potential complaints from me, which I accepted, although I had no intention of complaining. I paid him, exited the car, and opened the back door for the girl. As he saw her bare feet through his side mirror, he couldn't resist making a comment. "Not only weird but with dirty feet too…" The remark was spoken softly, but we both heard it. I could see the disappointment and shame on the girl's face as her eyes met his in the mirror. The man drove away.

I opened the metal gates of the garden and invited her inside. "Come on in. This is where I live with my husband," I said, hoping to reassure her. She hesitated for a moment, and I felt her worry. Despite our garden's inherent beauty, she seemed hesitant. With sympathy, I repeated my invitation. She took a few hesitant steps, followed by a few more, finally walking toward the house alongside me. However, I noticed that the right side of her face appeared lower than her left. Her features suddenly seemed distorted. I should have taken the time to investigate further, but instead I let it go. Just half an hour ago, she had been the most beautiful girl I had ever seen. Beauty was fragile. Beauty required rest. Beauty required happiness.

I smiled at Marco as he waved at me from the window, his eyebrows raised with curiosity when he noticed I had company. "Welcome home," I said to the girl as we entered the house, feeling a sense of belonging and comfort.

Marco had always enjoyed the company of eccentric individuals. As he saw the girl in the hallway, along with just one butterfly that had mysteriously appeared and followed us, he let out a surprised laugh from the top of the stairs. "Hi! Is that Annabelle's relative?" he teased, winking at me.

Annabelle Whitford. It had been years since I had thought of her, but Marco had a knack for remembering the most peculiar details and bringing them up at unexpected moments. He descended the staircase, sliding down the rails like a playful child before landing on the parquet floor with a thump. Extending his hand toward the girl, who had the monarch delicately perched on her left shoulder, he greeted her warmly.

Riccardo's bladder was throbbing with pain, a relentless reminder of his need to pee. He'd been holding it for so long, unable to tear himself away from Perihan's manuscript. At times, deciphering her handwritten pages proved challenging. Her elegant script was clear for someone of her age, yet some of the pages appeared rushed, with sections deleted and rewritten, making them difficult to read. Despite his discomfort, he was reluctant to leave the book unattended on his bed, and his paranoid mind dismissed his backpack as a safe option.

With memories of his childhood in mind, he leaned over, his hand moving along the foot of the library and the wooden floor. He knew this space well; it was where he'd hidden a tiny mosaic piece years ago. His fingers found the crevice between the parquet pieces. His heart filled with joy as he retrieved the small mosaic piece, a relic from that long-ago day. The once-golden paint had faded, but the bold black letter *P* remained. He slipped it into his pocket, carefully replaced the floor piece, and slid the book into the crevice between the library and the wall.

With that task complete, Riccardo stood up and left the room for the bathroom, his need to urinate pressing him onward. The house was shrouded in silence; everyone must be asleep. He entered the bathroom and locked the door behind him, glancing at his reflection in the mirror. His normally unruly hair seemed even more disheveled. His complexion, normally far from glowing, appeared paler and more dull than usual. The stress of needing to craft a successful synopsis, manage debts, and secure new living arrangements weighed heavily on him.

He finally peed, albeit with the toilet seat down, and some urine splattered onto it. Cursing his carelessness, he grabbed some toilet paper to clean up the mess. However, when he lifted the seat, he noticed a disconcerting sight: a dark, gooey substance, reminiscent of dried jelly or perhaps blood. It was scattered in patches around the toilet bowl, as though someone had attempted to clean it but lacked precision.

A feeling of nausea welled up within him at the grotesque sight, and he quickly closed the toilet lid. After thoroughly washing his hands and splashing some water on his face, he exited the bathroom, walking the dimly lit hallway back to his room. As he lay back on his bed, he returned to the manuscript, the tiny mosaic piece clutched tightly in his hand.

PERIHAN'S MANUSCRIPT

I had the chance to encounter your grandfather during my university years, though I never envisioned him as a potential partner. Frankly, the thought of settling down with anyone had never crossed my mind. Why subject myself to the same struggles my mother had endured? After all, why would you willingly bind yourself to another cage when you've sought freedom and escaped? You understand my perspective, don't you? Despite our acquaintance, we never spent much time together. He was a charming fellow known for his extravagant escapades. Class tardiness or even absence were common for him, as he indulged in lavish parties with his privileged companions. It wasn't until that day, a few months before an alumni gathering, that our paths truly intersected.

It had been an incredibly challenging day for me. I had visited the placements office in hopes of charting my career path, only to discover that, despite being at the top of my class and poised to graduate with outstanding marks, my options were severely limited due to my Turkish passport. The concept of home had become a fleeting notion after my father left for Berlin, leaving my mother to relocate from our cramped room with my six sisters and return to live with her parents. With my grandfather lacking the will and means to support such a large family, he resorted to arranging marriages for my six sisters with men they had never even laid eyes upon, all in pursuit of monetary gain. I learned from my eldest sister that Songül, who was just a year older than me, had been traded for gold to a sixty-five-year-old man, her weight determining her worth. If I were to return, it would not be to Hatay. Instead, I clung to a glimmer of hope in starting a life of my own in Istanbul. However, even the mere contemplation of that notion stirred tears within me. Did I even truly know anyone in Istanbul? During my encounter at the placements office, the lady informed me that my visa would be extended for another six months should I secure an internship. As she remarked, "Oh, I see you're from Istanbul! What a magnificent city, bridging the gap between the East and the West. I was captivated by the vibrant colors, the enticing aromas…" These phrases echoed in my ears, repeating the same sentiments I had heard countless times whenever I disclosed my origins. They would talk to me about the Spice Bazaar's fragrant cumin and peppers, the exquisite Persian carpets and Turkish kilims at the Grand Bazaar, and the ethereal view of the Bosphorus shrouded in morning fog. Yet their enthusiasm would fade, their heads would lower in disdain, and they would proceed to interject comments about the country's political turmoil or share horrific stories they had stumbled upon in the local newspaper, all while sipping their espresso shots. Their compliments would swiftly transform into condemnations, their praise would swiftly dissolve into derision. True to form, the lady at the placements office followed a similar pattern, concluding with "but I suppose living amid such chaos and political turmoil must be hell… I understand your predicament. We'll keep an eye out for internships and contact you if we come across an opportunity that aligns with your curriculum."

Later that morning, amid the gathering organized by the university to celebrate our impending graduation, I spotted Marco.

"Are you still working at that cinema?" he asked.

"For another week. Technically, I'm not an employee there. I'm assisting Luigi and his two sisters. They, in turn, helped me with my thesis," I replied. The morning's news had dampened my spirits, leaving me disinterested in engaging in idle conversation.

"I want to come! Don't they screen a film every day?" he exclaimed.

I nodded, taken aback by his interest in Purple Cinema, which typically attracted an older and more intellectually inclined audience.

"What time should I arrive tonight?" he asked, grinning.

"The screening is actually in the early evening, at six," I informed him.

"I'll be there! So what are we watching?"

I chose not to disclose that I often struggled to find a seat in the packed theater. Additionally, I had assumed he would be accompanied by someone, not attending alone.

"We'll be exploring some of the earliest films in cinema history. The highlight will be *Annabelle's Butterfly Dance* from 1895," I said.

"Interessante!" he exclaimed, his eyes sparkling as he ran his fingers through his thick hair. "See you tonight. I need to say hello to a few people." With that, he disappeared into the sea of new graduates.

Luigi's Purple Cinema was located on Via Torino in the heart of the city. *Annabelle's Butterfly Dance* starred the renowned Annabelle Whitford, also known as Peerless Annabelle on stage. Born in 1878, Annabelle began her dancing career at a remarkably young age of eleven. By the time she was fifteen, she had already established herself as a sensation with her iconic dances: the Serpentine, the Butterfly, and the Sun Dances. Her fame soared to such heights in New York that Thomas Edison himself invited her to be one of the first subjects recorded with the Kinetoscope. The film was painstakingly hand-tinted frame by frame, creating the illusion of Annabelle dancing under vibrant, colored lights in her elegant flowing white dress, gracefully emulating a butterfly in various mesmerizing moves. It not only became a tremendous success but also marked the first-ever color film made for screen projection.

Yet, the latter part of Annabelle's life was far from glorious. There were scandals, fleeting triumphs, painful setbacks, and eventually a marriage that led her away from the entertainment industry. At the age of eighty, she found herself a widow, destitute. She passed away in Chicago. Even today, I find myself contemplating whether Annabelle's story held a deeper significance for others. Was it mere coincidence that the first color film ever produced revolved around the butterfly dance of a child prodigy whose life took a tragic turn?

That afternoon, Marco arrived at the cinema. I observed him searching for me, but I deliberately kept myself hidden. I wanted his interest to lie in the film itself, not to be drawn to me. I wanted to test whether he would stay despite my absence or simply leave upon seeing I wasn't part of the crowd. To my surprise, he chose to stay. I admired this decision, as it demonstrated his commitment to our arrangement, to engage in the activity he had promised, regardless of my presence. Eventually, I left the cinema early, satisfied with his display of devotion to our shared plan.

I resided in a rather noncentral but secure area called Viale Molise, sharing an apartment with two fellow students. The neighborhood offered safety, albeit lacking the bustling atmosphere of the city center. However, every Friday and Saturday, the surrounding streets would come alive with a vibrant mix of cross-dressers, club kids, fashion PRs, and design students clad in their most extravagant attire, drawn to the allure of Club Plastic on Viale

Umbria. From the window of my bedroom, I would observe them as they ventured out into the night, seeking a nearby tobacco shop to purchase cigarettes. Meanwhile, I remained awake, diligently studying, committed to surpass my classmates in knowledge and skill. Plastic had eluded my presence during my two years in Milan, though I would plan to visit later, accompanied by your grandfather. But I digress: that student residence was far from an ideal place for receiving guests.

However, as fate would have it, your grandfather managed to find me. Clad in my pajamas, I found myself in the living room with one of my roommates when an unexpected buzz at the front door disrupted our evening. Initially assuming it could be someone attempting to gain access to the building, we chose to ignore it. Yet, the persistent ringing of the doorbell urged me to investigate. I cautiously answered the door.

"Which floor?" I asked, trying to ascertain the identity of the visitor.

My question was met with silence on the other end.

"Who is this?" I asked, curious.

"It's Marco! I lost sight of you after the cinema, so I asked your friend Luigi for your address," he responded cheerfully.

In that moment, a peculiar sensation gripped my chest, and my stomach churned with newfound emotions. Was I suddenly perspiring? I decided to make him wait for a few moments, allowing the anticipation to build. He buzzed the intercom once again and gently implored, "If you won't let me in, at least come down. We could go for a gelato or something..."

His words lingered in the air, tempting me to venture outside, to explore the possibilities that awaited.

My roommate seemed to think it was a good idea, a way for me to shield myself from being seen in my most vulnerable state. Encouraged, I made up my mind to go down and face Marco. Before leaving, I applied a touch of pink lip balm to my lips and cheekbones, borrowing my roommate's vintage Prada coat that bestowed upon me a semblance of strength, despite feeling anything but.

As soon as I stepped out of the main door, Marco greeted me with a question I was not expecting. "Did you know she was the Gibson Girl in Ziegfeld Follies in 1907?" he said eagerly, referring to our earlier discussion about Annabelle. Confusion clouded my expression, as I struggled to place his words into context. Marco quickly understood that I was not familiar with the subject matter.

"Annabelle! I did some research before coming to the cinema tonight, hoping to see you. I discovered that the Gibson Girl was an idealized representation of physical beauty created by an illustrator named Charles Dana Gibson. He would observe women on the streets of America, capturing their most attractive and commonly shared features. Small waists, voluminous hair, ample busts… Come, let's take a walk," he said, leading the way toward the ice cream shop across from my place.

I mustered a feeble acknowledgment, murmuring, "Oh, yes, I understand now. Ziegfeld Follies…" In truth, my knowledge of such worldly and entertaining matters was severely limited. My days were spent bound to my desk, devouring pages of books to ensure the continuity of my scholarship, and to meet the lofty expectations set by my supervisor in completing my thesis. The world beyond my studies had remained largely inaccessible, leaving me yearning for the experiences I had yet to encounter.

"Yeah, the revue in New York was based on the Folies Bergère in Paris… Anyway, Annabelle was incredibly beautiful. She became the face of Ziegfeld Follies. Life was going well for her until that dreadful fire," Marco said, delving into the story. However, I interrupted him, as I was already familiar with the tragic tale. Luigi's sisters had shared the details with me when they first proposed including *Annabelle's Butterfly Dance* in our film lineup. However, they only knew of the film itself, having never actually seen it due to their visual impairment.

"She was playing Stella, Queen of the Fairies, in *Mr. Bluebeard* when the fire broke out. I can't recall if it was her dress that caught fire, but Luigi's sisters told me that five hundred and seventy-five people died, most of them children." I trailed off, the weight of the tragedy hanging heavily in the air.

"Oh, I didn't realize it was that horrific. Then I'm sorry I brought this up. I thought you might be interested…" Marco apologized, coming to a halt in front of the ice cream shop. He unrolled a poster featuring Annabelle as the face of Ziegfeld Follies. It was a sweet gesture.

"That's very thoughtful of you," I replied, touched. No man had ever done something so considerate for me before. Marco was like a breath of fresh air, offering companionship after a long and emotionally draining day filled with tears in my bedroom as I grappled with the prospect of returning to Turkey. We purchased two cones and settled on a plastic bench in front of the small store, two children seated nearby. And that was the beginning of it all—we started spending time together every day for the rest of the month.

My dear Riccardo, if you happen to enter one of the guest bedrooms—located behind the first door upstairs—you'll see Annabelle's poster hanging on the wall above the bed. It captures her at her most beautiful, perhaps the happiest moment before she became the Queen of the Fairies in that ill-fated play and witnessed the tragic demise of over five hundred souls in the fire. It was long before her own lonely and destitute end, in a cold house in Chicago.

"What a peculiar guest! Can you speak?" Marco asked when he saw my angel. I wished that the army of butterflies still surrounded us. I knew Marco would have been amused by them, but he had to be content with just this one monarch perched on her shoulder.

"I found her as I was leaving the hairdresser. I didn't want to leave her alone... Plus, just look at her beauty. I thought she would be the perfect guest for tonight's party at the castle," I explained. Her face was still not quite right, the right side lower than the left, but she was beautiful no matter what.

"Oh, we're not actually going to the castle," he responded, but I could see he was distracted by the intriguing appearance of my enchanting companion. He seemed very interested in her asymmetrical face, which I thought wasn't her best feature, so I offered a new angle to entertain his curiosity.

"You know...this beautiful new friend of mine seemed like she had captured a rainbow within the layers of her skin just half an hour ago! She was all glittery, iridescent... Almost unreal... A bit of rest and I am sure she will be back to her unmatchable glow in time for the party tonight," I suggested, marveling at the ethereal sight.

"Is that so? Could it be some kind of body makeup?" Marco wondered aloud.

"I don't think so. If it were makeup, it would still be visible," I said, running my hand over her skin and then showing my perfectly clean palms. There was no trace of rainbow, sheen, or glitter. "It's all natural and comes from her beauty within. Trust me!"

"Yeter, come with me for a moment," Marco said, leading us away from the enchanting girl toward the kitchen door. I followed him, curious about his sudden urgency.

"Should we inform the police? She's mute, wearing an unusual dress, and has no shoes... Something must have happened to her. Perhaps we should call a doctor first?" Marco whispered into my ear.

Anger surged through my veins, and I grabbed his arm, responding in an aggressive whisper. "She is the most beautiful girl you've ever laid eyes on. She will bring us boundless admiration tonight. We are not letting her go anywhere, not tonight. Tomorrow, you can do as you please."

He wasn't prepared for my reaction and gently pushed my hand away from his arm. His eyes remained fixed on her, standing in the middle of our hallway with a delicate butterfly resting on her shoulder. "Where did she come from?" Marco asked.

"Nowhere we've been, Marco, nowhere we've been... You don't understand. Just a couple of minutes ago—I told you—she was emitting this sort of rainbow glow from her skin! She's a walking diamond, pure magic. Can't you feel the enchantment in the air?" I whispered.

As she twirled around, holding the hem of her pink dress with one hand and cradling a second monarch butterfly in the other, Marco shrugged in resignation. "Okay," he said. "I guess we can figure this out tomorrow. We're not going to Tuscany. They changed the location of the birthday dinner."

"No more castle," I sighed, disappointment evident in my voice. "Where are we going, then?"

"Turin," Marco replied.

"Turin?" I repeated, surprised by the new venue.

"Trust me, the new location they've secured is much better than any castle. Costanza was quite upset when she found out that nobody would be going to her castle. Her husband sent messages to all of us, to inform us that they wouldn't be attending tonight. But that's their problem. The old man had another appointment near Milan and couldn't leave for Tuscany. Turin was a better option. Now, please go get ready. You should dress her in one of your outfits."

I nodded, agreeing with his suggestion. "I'll wear one of your mother's gowns. I didn't have time to go dress hunting. But I want something dramatic for tonight," I said, leading the mysterious girl up the stairs as she followed closely behind me. We were glowing, shimmering, and glittering together. Perhaps her beauty was coming back slowly because she felt she was in a safe environment, and we kept giving her compliments. You see, my dear Riccardo? The more she felt stressed and mistreated, the uglier she became... And at times, also dangerous. The taxi driver was to blame, otherwise Marco would have seen her unearthly beauty right from the start.

I never wore those Elsa Schiaparelli gloves I had purchased earlier from Eva. I was already adorned in magic: I didn't require artificial embellishments to capture attention.

Magic. It came in many forms, not always benevolent ones. Together, we ventured upstairs to try on clothes for Fumito Misake's birthday dinner, an occasion to celebrate the oldest man alive.

13

Riccardo's peaceful immersion in Perihan's magical world was shattered by yet another SMS from his agent, a reminder of the pressing demands of the real world. Still waiting... the message read, jolting him back to the mundane concerns of real life. He couldn't help but long for the fantastical realm he had just left behind, captivated by the vivid descriptions and the haunting image of the strange-looking girl.

Perihan's talent as a writer astonished Riccardo, but he couldn't fathom how she had kept her imagination locked away for so long without sharing it with others. The richness of the world she had created overwhelmed him, and he felt suffocated by the confines of the small guest room. It had been years since his last visit to Milan, and if he was to stay here, he should acquaint himself with his surroundings once again.

As he prepared to leave his room, his intentions were disrupted by loud and frequent thumps emanating from the attic above. Riccardo paused, his attention on the ceiling as if attempting to peer through the walls, only for the noise to abruptly cease. Intrigued, he took another step, and the thumping resumed—thump, thump, thump.

Preferring to avoid paranoia or troublesome thoughts, Riccardo attributed the sounds to Maurizio or Cristina working in the attic, engaging in the process of packaging or unboxing Perihan's belongings following her demise. Content with this explanation, he retrieved his windbreaker from his backpack and discreetly tucked Perihan's book into the crevice between the library and the wall, hiding it away.

Just as he was about to depart, a startled cry escaped him at the sight of the maid in her black dress and white collar standing at the end of the corridor, directly opposite the stairs.

Apologizing for any potential disturbance caused, the maid hurriedly passed by Riccardo, heading toward the stairs with a bulky green bucket in hand. Curious, Riccardo couldn't help but ask, "Do you need help with that?" His inquiry, however, was either ignored or unheard by the maid, who swiftly disappeared to the floor below.

Shrugging off the unanswered question, Riccardo descended the stairs as well. Instead of following the maid, he made his way out of the house.

In the garden, Riccardo's attention was drawn to Licia, who was engaged in conversation with a young woman near the main entry to the garden. The air was chilly, the morning crisp, with a gray, gloomy atmosphere hanging overhead. The house was surrounded by a high brick wall that shielded the garden from prying eyes, yet somehow this stranger had managed to breach its barriers. Riccardo couldn't help but wonder if Licia had allowed her in and what their connection might be.

As he walked over to join their conversation, Riccardo couldn't ignore the biting chill in the air, the frostiness of the weather mirroring the unease within him. He looked at the stranger, a woman in her early thirties with broad shoulders, messy hair, and clothes that appeared rather cheap. Her voice, deep and raspy like that of a heavy smoker, carried an air of affirmation rather than a genuine question. It was as if she already knew the answer.

"Are you Licia?" the woman asked.

Riccardo watched as Licia's eyebrows furrowed in confusion. "Who are you?" she asked, her voice laced with curiosity.

In a low tone, as if she wanted to keep Riccardo from overhearing, the woman replied, "I had an appointment with Perihan! I knocked on the door a couple of times, but nobody answered. You know… I'm here for my daughter."

Licia's response was firm. "I'm sorry, but Perihan's gone. We lost her, as in she's no longer with us," she said, her voice carrying the weight of grief.

The woman's face turned pale, shock rippling through her like a tidal wave. In search of support, she instinctively reached for the brick wall, her arm trembling. Riccardo wondered what the woman had wanted from his grandmother, but before he could inquire further, her attention shifted to the garden, and a look of terror washed over her features.

"What happened here? Where are all the tuberoses?" she gasped, her voice filled with disbelief. Riccardo recalled the beautiful garden Maurizio had shown him in the picture on his phone, but what he saw now was a far cry from its former glory. The woman's reaction made him question her sanity, as if the disheveled state of the garden didn't align with her memories.

Disregarding the woman's comments about the garden, Licia pressed on with her announcement. "Perihan is dead. She's gone, and there's no bringing her back," she reiterated, her voice steady.

The woman's cries intensified as she shoved Licia out of

the way and made a desperate dash toward the greenhouse, only to find it locked. Acting on instinct, Riccardo rushed to help Licia to her feet, their eyes scanning the villa for any potential onlookers who could help in escorting the distraught stranger out.

"It's locked!" the woman screamed, her voice piercing the air. She pounded on the dirty windows with relentless force. "Open the door!" Her pleas echoed through the garden as she continued to strike the glass, her hands leaving imprints of desperation. Licia, attempting to distract herself, explained the issues they had faced with the new gardener, the struggle to maintain the tuberoses. She brushed the grass and soil from her hands, attempting to regain control of the situation.

Amid the chaos, Licia firmly clasped Riccardo's arm, her touch carrying both urgency and secrecy. Riccardo understood the unspoken directive, and they approached the woman with determination.

Once more, the woman banged on the glass, her cries of desperation giving way to inconsolable sobs. She crumbled to the ground, her face buried in her hands, repeating, "I had an appointment...for my daughter..."

Riccardo's heart ached as he knelt, supporting the woman under her arms. Surprisingly, she offered no resistance, seemingly drained of all energy. "She was my grandmother," Riccardo revealed, his voice heavy with sorrow.

Together, Licia and Riccardo guided the woman outside, their movements swift and deliberate. With one final push from Licia, the woman found herself outside the garden's confines, the door closing behind her.

Taking a moment to collect themselves, Riccardo broke the silence. "Who was that?"

Licia sighed, her features full of concern. "How the hell

do I know? Some crazy woman who probably knows your grandmother from the society pages."

Riccardo's curiosity lingered. "She said she had an appointment."

Licia's response was tinged with skepticism. "She might have. You have no idea how many strangers Perihan helped throughout her life. But maybe this woman was just looking for a job or something. Did you see how she was dressed? It didn't look like she was here to discuss world politics with Perihan."

Their conversation started to veer off course. "Enough about that. Did you need me for something?" Licia asked.

"No, no. I just wanted to go out and get some air," Riccardo said.

Licia's gaze hardened, her green eyes darkening, lines deepening on her face. "You have all the fresh air you need here," Licia pointed out, gesturing toward the trees that surrounded the garden, her tone conveying a hint of disbelief.

Riccardo remained firm. "I want to see what's around," he persisted, pushing against Licia's hand to open the door. He believed that by exploring his surroundings, he could allow life to happen to him, breaking through his writer's block and finding inspiration in unexpected encounters. His agent's advice echoed in his ears, urging him to seize the opportunities that presented themselves.

Licia's hand pressed firmly against his, attempting to impede his progress. "There's not much around this area. It's very residential. Besides, Perihan was quite well-known. People will pester you for information about her death and everything."

Riccardo's resolve remained unyielding. "I don't talk to people I don't know. Don't worry about me."

With a determined push, he opened the door and stepped

out onto the street, leaving Licia behind. As he scanned his surroundings, searching for traces of the woman they had encountered, he couldn't help but embrace the uncertainty. Every experience, even unexpected ones, held the potential to enrich his life and inspire him for the draft he had to send to his agent.

As Riccardo stepped out from the villa, he found himself greeted by the refreshing shade of trees that lined both sides of the street. The vibrant greenery outside stood in stark contrast to the forlorn garden within the villa's confines. The street was lined with parked cars neatly arranged one after another, yet there was a noticeable absence of people strolling about.

Lost in thought, he pondered the captivating scenes he had encountered within Perihan's draft. The vivid imagination, the enchanting world of butterflies, magic, and intriguing characters—it made him wonder if storytelling prowess ran in his genes, passed down from Perihan. He couldn't help but reflect on his own struggles to string letters together, transforming them into living, breathing stories on the pages of his own creations.

Above him, a crow circled in repetitive patterns before cawing and flying away. Riccardo scrunched up his face, expressing his dislike for the creature, and continued along the street until he reached its end. There, a brief burst of sunlight peeked through the clouds, casting its gentle glow upon his face.

Beyond the street's end, Riccardo was happy to find a charming little bar nestled next to a grim church. A thought crossed his mind. *A coffee might do wonders...* Convinced, he made his way toward the inviting establishment.

Upon entering, his presence caught the attention of two young girls who were seated outside, exchanging notes with each other. They briefly glanced in Riccardo's direction. The interior of the bar revealed itself as a cozy haven, splashed with an assortment of little magnets from various corners of the world. The warm ambience of the bar enveloped Riccardo as he took a seat, ready to immerse himself in the comforting aroma of freshly brewed coffee.

"We're closed."

Surprised by the unexpected voice, Riccardo swiftly turned around to locate its source. He saw a strikingly handsome young man standing behind the counter. He possessed an undeniable charm, with deep blue eyes that resembled sapphires, their brilliance capturing Riccardo's attention. His dark brown hair cascaded in thick wavy locks, accentuating his captivating features. The young man's jawline was sharp and defined, adding an air of confidence to his poise.

Riccardo couldn't help but notice the man's distinctive style. He wore a vintage polo shirt and several necklaces embellished with an array of little charms dangled playfully. Leaning over the counter, he clasped his hands together and looked directly at Riccardo. Their eyes met, and in that moment, a spark of curiosity flickered between them.

"Wait. Have I ever seen you before?" the man asked.

Riccardo rose from his seat and approached the counter. "No, I don't think so. Riccardo," he replied, extending his hand for a handshake.

"Pleased to meet you. I'm Lorenzo. What can I get you?" Lorenzo asked.

Riccardo glanced at the closed bar and remarked, "I thought you were closing..."

Lorenzo grinned and said, "That'd be rude for someone who just arrived in town. Coffee?"

Riccardo nodded in agreement. "Coffee, and a lighter,

please," he requested. Lorenzo prepared a cup of coffee and handed a light to Riccardo across the counter.

"I'm going for a smoke. Want to join me outside?" Riccardo said. Lorenzo smiled and accepted the invitation, joining him at a table a short distance away from the two girls.

Riccardo took a sip of his coffee and lit his cigarette while Lorenzo asked, "What brings you here?"

Riccardo avoided direct eye contact as he responded, "Nothing fun. My grandmother passed away, and I had to come for the funeral. I just left the house for a change of pace and maybe some new inspiration for my writing."

Lorenzo expressed his condolences. Then, he said, "So you're a writer?"

Riccardo confirmed, admitting, "I've written many short stories, but now I'm working on my first novel. Lately, I've been struggling with writer's block or whatever you want to call it."

Lorenzo nodded. Shifting the conversation, Riccardo asked, "Have you worked here for long?"

Lorenzo replied, "As long as I've known myself. My mom owns the bar, and I used to come back after school to help her out here or just stay around doing my homework at one of these tables." He gestured toward the surroundings. "I studied at Belle Arti in Brera, which is close by. I paint on the weekends, and I'm currently working on my first solo show."

Riccardo smiled and quipped, "A painter and a writer meet at a bar..."

Lorenzo playfully teased him, lightly touching his shoulder. "You see? Your writer's block is cured," he said jokingly.

Their conversation was interrupted by a shout from inside the bar, as someone called out for Lorenzo, asking about their keys. Lorenzo and Riccardo turned their attention to the woman behind the counter. Lorenzo retrieved the keys from his pocket and called his mother over, suggesting that she meet his friend, Riccardo.

The older woman emerged from the bar, dressed in a long red dress that matched her vibrant red hair. She put on her coat and held out the keys, introducing herself. "Barbara, pleased to meet you." Riccardo reciprocated the greeting. Barbara possessed a classic beauty that transcended time, with high cheekbones that added a touch of refinement to her face. Her skin, fair and porcelainlike, seemed to glow with a natural radiance, hinting at a life well-lived.

Barbara seemed intrigued by Riccardo. "Do you live around here? I haven't seen you before." Her tone held a hint of skepticism, as if questioning whether he could afford to live in such a prestigious area. Lorenzo interjected, coming to Riccardo's defense. "His grandmother has passed away, Mom."

Barbara paused for a moment, processing the information she had just received. Then, she exclaimed, "Perihan was your grandmother?" Intrigued, mother and son looked to Riccardo, their eyes filled with astonishment.

Riccardo began, "Yes, she was. I left home at a very young age, when she sent me to a boarding school."

Taking a moment to reflect, Barbara nodded apprecia-tively. "Your grandmother was truly an exceptional woman," she said. "Her kindness, generosity, and boundless empathy touched the lives of many. While we were never friends, our paths crossed once, many years ago."

Riccardo felt a touch of mystery in Barbara's mention of their past encounter, but he decided to respect the unspoken boundaries. Barbara's voice softened. "I'm deeply sorry for your loss. May I ask how she died?"

Trapped in a moment of hesitation, Riccardo's thoughts raced, aware of Licia's earlier warnings about the need to pro-tect Perihan's secrets. With caution in his voice, he replied,

"She unexpectedly suffered a heart attack in her sleep." His words held a concealed truth, honoring Licia's concerns about strangers seeking information on Perihan. A faint sound escaped Barbara's lips, perhaps reflecting her dissatisfaction with such an unforeseen death.

Lorenzo said, "I was always fearful of that house while growing up," he admitted. "For years, I avoided Via Marco de Marchi."

Barbara nodded. "Yes, you were indeed afraid. The garden was magical with a multitude of butterflies, their vibrant colors and graceful wingspans captivating your gaze. It was a sight that could either fill you with wonder or send shivers down your spine."

Intrigued by the mention of butterflies, Riccardo couldn't contain his curiosity. He leaned in, his voice brimming with genuine interest. "What butterflies are you referring to?" he asked, wondering if Perihan's fascination with these creatures had been inspired by the daily spectacle she observed through her bedroom window, blurring the lines between reality and fiction.

Barbara settled on the edge of the chair, her expression pensive. "Are there no butterflies now? Perhaps the weather has turned too cold," she wondered aloud. "And what about Maurizio? Is he still present in your life?" she asked.

Riccardo's voice took on a serious tone as he responded, recounting the unexpected reconnection with Maurizio. "Maurizio is the one who brought me back to Milan. After years of silence, he appeared out of nowhere in Paris, urging me to return for my grandmother's funeral."

"Poor man. Keep him close. He has endured so much suffering."

Lorenzo, furrowing his brow, struggled to recall Maurizio's face from the depths of his memory. Suddenly, his eyes brightened, and he exclaimed, "Maurizio from the circus! Of course. I remember him. Although I wasn't even born then, I've heard countless stories over the years. That circus was a legendary phenomenon in Italian pop culture. Its demise marked the end of an era, didn't it?"

The mention of the circus triggered a cascade of memories in Riccardo's mind. In a quick flash, he recalled the newspaper article he had discovered in Perihan's room, the tragic account of Elettra's suicide, and the perpetual sorrow on Maurizio's face, haunted by the trauma of his past.

Barbara explained the story of the illustrious circus. "Italy once boasted a renowned circus, unparalleled in its magnificence. For nearly forty years, Elettra, the owner, orchestrated extraordinary performances with an unexpected cast of talented artists and majestic animals. Every show was a sold-out spectacle, an experience passed down from one generation to the next. Yet, on the eve of Elettra's sixtieth birthday, a calamity struck. A deal was signed with Italian TV to broadcast the circus nationwide for the first time, but that night, all hell broke loose. Hundreds lost their lives, and wild animals roamed free. Maurizio, I believe, emerged as the sole survivor of this tragedy. It was only later, when he began working for Perihan, that I had the chance to meet him. He would run errands for her, often stopping by this very bar for a chat with me. Lorenzo wouldn't remember, as the story of the circus had faded to a distant fairy tale by the time he was born. Poor Maurizio has burn marks all around his body—the whole thing went up in flames! Nobody really understood why."

Barbara continued. "I'm sure if you google Elettra or the circus, you can find all the information online. YouTube might even have old videos, recordings of the circus TV broadcast that night, with people sharing their ideas on what might have happened."

Before Riccardo could respond, their conversation was interrupted by the ringing of Barbara's phone. She excused herself. "Oh, forgive me, they're calling. I'm already late. It was a pleasure meeting you, and I hope to see you around," she said, blowing a kiss to her son before hastily departing. It was then that Riccardo noticed Barbara's prosthetic leg, replacing her right limb. He watched as she maneuvered with a unique gait toward the street, presumably to find her car. Lorenzo, observing Riccardo's facial expressions, offered a brief explanation. "Long story... She's grown accustomed to it now, though. It doesn't bother her."

Realizing that he should also be heading back, Riccardo said, "Perhaps I should leave as well. They might need me at the house. Can we exchange numbers?" But even as he spoke, he saw Lorenzo already extending his phone, signaling for Riccardo to enter his details into the contact list. Riccardo swiftly entered his number, rose from his seat, and made his way out.

As Riccardo walked away, Lorenzo called out, his voice trailing. "By the way, is there a greenhouse or something in your garden?"

Surprised by the question, Riccardo replied, "Yes, why do you ask?"

"Nothing in particular. It just reminded me... People used to refer to it as 'the place where the light never goes out.' Whatever that means."

"Like The Smiths song, perhaps," Riccardo chimed in.

"Like The Smiths song. Yeah, maybe," Lorenzo echoed, lost in his own musings.

With a wave goodbye to Lorenzo, Riccardo carried the weight of the day's revelations and mysteries back home.

"When's he coming back?" Maurizio asked Licia anxiously. Maurizio had initially been concerned about Riccardo venturing out alone, but as soon as he left the house, he realized it as an opportunity to search for the lost book. Maurizio was the most proactive member of the group and was driven by a strong desire to recover the precious item.

He began his quest in the living room, meticulously scouring every reachable area, trying not to leave a single corner unexplored. Maurizio's search started by examining under the pillows of the sofa, lifting them one by one and running his hands beneath, hoping to find a trace of the book. He continued his thorough investigation, shifting his focus to the inside of the cupboards. Opening each door, he meticulously inspected the shelves' contents, carefully moving objects aside in his pursuit of the missing book. His hands sifted through stacks of papers, folders, and miscellaneous items, hoping to uncover the prized possession that seemed to have vanished without a trace.

Meanwhile, Cristina rose from her crouched position and

joined Eva to search the kitchen. Other friends split up, exploring different rooms of the house, hoping to stumble upon any clue regarding the disappearance of Perihan's book. Time was running out, and Licia continued to reference the impending ritual, adding to the growing sense of urgency. "He might be back anytime now. There's not much to do in this area," Licia remarked as she entered the living room, her hands empty.

"Well, I'm telling you, if he doesn't have it, then someone must have stolen it during the funeral. Did you check his room thoroughly?" said Eva.

"I examined every single corner of that tiny room, as did Cristina. All we found was a backpack with some personal belongings. There's nothing in there… But who would steal the book, and for what purpose other than the ritual itself?" Licia pondered.

As the conversation unfolded, Cristina turned her attention to Eva. "Are you not aware that your attire and those spider brooches on your veil might only scare and raise more suspicions?"

Eva adjusted one of the brooches on her black veil and snapped back defensively, "Look after yourself, and don't worry about me." She then looked toward the garden door through the window. "He's here," she announced, anticipation glimmering in her eyes.

The group huddled together in the center of the room for a moment, before dispersing throughout the house, trying not to draw too much attention to their collective presence. They watched Riccardo stroll past the greenhouse, momentarily pausing to cast a lingering gaze upon it before continuing his stride toward the house. He rang the doorbell, and Cristina promptly went to open it.

"Lovely seeing you," she greeted him warmly.

"Oh," he responded, surprise flickering across his face. "Lovely seeing you too. I didn't know we were expecting guests." Riccardo smiled.

"Oh, I'm not a guest. You know we used to hang out with Perihan here all the time. It's like a second home to me," Cristina explained.

Upon entering the house, Riccardo was startled at seeing this group gathering, as if this were Perihan's funeral all over again. He felt no connection to these individuals, and as he caught sight of Maurizio, a wave of anxiety tinged with anger coursed through him, influenced by Lorenzo and Barbara's earlier revelations.

Maurizio, with a concerned expression, asked Riccardo, "Where have you been?"

Riccardo, feeling a bit irritated, shot back, "It's none of your business. If I feel like going outside, I have every right to do so."

Maurizio persisted. "I'm just worried about you, Riccardo. You don't know anyone in Milan. It's not safe."

Riccardo, growing impatient, suddenly asked, "Do you know why the animals went wild at that circus? The one Elettra used to run. It's been bothering me."

A heavy silence filled the room. Maurizio finally spoke, "How do you know about that circus?"

Riccardo, unwilling to reveal too much, replied, "I found some old papers today while I was exploring the city's past. And I can't help but wonder if your burned arm has something to do with what happened there."

Maurizio, avoiding the question, pressed Riccardo, "That's not an answer. Tell me where you were today, or at least who you were with."

Frustration welled up in Riccardo. He retorted, "You keep

evading my questions. What does *the place where the light never goes out* mean?"

"Pardon me?" Maurizio responded.

"I'm referring to the greenhouse. What could it mean?" Riccardo pressed, sensing a subtle change in Maurizio's attitude.

"I have no idea what you're talking about," the man replied, his body noticeably tensing.

Riccardo, increasingly angry, went for the stairs, leaving a tense atmosphere behind.

"Dinner will be at eight," Licia shouted after him.

"I'll see you then," Riccardo confirmed, taking a step up the staircase before turning around. With all eyes fixed on him, he added, "I'm sorry about what happened at the circus, by the way," before making his way upstairs.

Maurizio glanced at the two women, a puzzled expression crossing his face. "The circus? Who did he encounter outside?" he said.

Both Licia and Cristina shook their heads.

For a fleeting moment, Maurizio's eyes darkened as an old memory flashed through his mind.

Elettra struggled to keep up with Maurizio's brisk pace toward the tent, breathless as she tried to match his energy. She didn't want to spoil the surprise she had prepared for the audience that night.

"I'm God's favorite!" Elettra exclaimed at the top of her lungs when they finally reached the tent. Her eyes widened with disbelief. "I've seen it all in my life, everything! From magicians making people disappear here in Italy to old healers performing eye surgeries with kitchen knives in Mexico. But never have I witnessed such a natural miracle! This is a miracle, Maurizio!" she shouted with increasing fervor. The students, curious about the commotion, turned their attention to the door, eager to see what was happening outside.

The tent was awash with thousands of monarch butterflies, completely covering the nylon fabric that stretched over the structure. Every inch of space was occupied by these graceful creatures, their wings fluttering lazily, casting an orange hue of light upon the ground. The hum of the forest enveloped the atmosphere, creating a tranquil ambience beneath the dense fog in Turin.

"Let's go inside. I wish this could be broadcast right now. Who knows, maybe these butterflies will enter the tent?" Elettra suggested as she pushed open the curtains, leading the way into what was about to become a chaotic whirlwind.

Shaking off the remnants of the flashback, Maurizio motioned for Licia to follow Riccardo upstairs, away from the watchful eyes of the others.

Riccardo ascended to his room, softly shutting the door behind him. He lingered, giving the silence a few seconds to reveal any potential footsteps echoing his path upstairs.

Sitting on the edge of his bed, Riccardo's mind briefly wandered to Lorenzo. He imagined running his fingers through Lorenzo's thick, curly hair, the scent of his neck still fresh in his memory. It had been a long time since Riccardo had been close to anyone, lacking both friends and lovers due to his self-imposed isolation from the world. Meeting Lorenzo in Milan was an unexpected gift. His chatty and empathetic nature, coupled with his undeniable beauty, had stirred something in Riccardo.

Riccardo couldn't help but wonder if Lorenzo was thinking about him at that very moment. It was a strange and new sensation for him, this longing for another person's company, and it made him feel both vulnerable and exhilarated.

Lost in thought, he contemplated the events of the day. The revelations about the circus and the fragments of Perihan's life they had unearthed had ignited a spark within him. He was determined to unravel the mystery woven into the handwritten manuscript, still uncertain how much of the fiction drew from Perihan's real life.

Breaking from his reverie, he got up and crossed the room to peer out the window, his eyes scanning the garden below. Satisfied that the surroundings remained undisturbed, he returned to his spot on the corner of the bed. There was no time for relaxation or coziness: he was too anxious, too consumed by the desire to read further in the manuscript. The mysteries it held were like an irresistible magnet, pulling him deeper into the story as he plunged back into the pages, his quest for answers unwavering.

PERIHAN'S MANUSCRIPT

I was captivated by the incredible journey of the monarch butterflies. They migrated an astounding distance of 3,000 miles. I couldn't help but compare their migration to my own. When I calculated the miles between Istanbul and Hatay, it was only around 530 miles. Adding the distance between Istanbul and Milan, approximately 1,600 miles, my entire migration paled in comparison to that of the monarchs. Three thousand miles seemed like an unreachable feat for me, akin to traveling to the moon alone.

The strength and resilience of butterflies fascinated me. However, I soon appreciated that their journey was not undertaken by a solitary insect. They migrated together, as a collective. The butterflies that initiated the journey were not the same ones that reached the destination. The migration was a shared goal, and they moved as a group, constantly striving for something better. Generation after generation, they continued the cycle.

Every fall, the monarch butterflies left the United States and Canada and traveled to southwestern Mexico, where the climate was more favorable. They gathered in immense numbers, huddling together on the branches of sacred firs, patiently awaiting the end of winter. Many of these butterflies eventually returned to warmer regions like Texas to mate and lay their eggs on milkweed plants. Once the eggs hatched, the larvae voraciously consumed the milkweed, transforming first into chrysalises and then emerging as adult butterflies.

The life cycle and migration of the monarch butterflies were a testament to the resilience of nature. Their collective efforts and shared goals echoed the power of unity and collaboration. I couldn't help but be inspired by their journey and reflect on my own path, understanding that progress and growth often require collective effort and shared aspirations.

How butterflies know where to go on their migration is truly fascinating, my dear Riccardo. It's a concept that amazed me when I first learned about it. The most remarkable thing is that their memory is somehow transferred to the following generations, ensuring that even newborn butterflies are aware of the direction they should take. It's an incredible, instinctual knowledge that is passed down from one generation to the next. Can you imagine the depth of that connection and understanding?

The transfer of memories from one generation to another, like the butterflies, fascinated me for a particular reason. It led me to contemplate how inheriting memories could enrich the human experience. Although we may possess videos, sounds, and writings from those who lived before us, these media, while valuable, can never replicate the raw authenticity of firsthand, unfiltered experiences.

Recordings provide us with glimpses into the past, offering valuable insights and knowledge. We can hear the voices, witness the events, and read the thoughts of those who came before us. However, they are still filtered through various lenses, interpretations, and biases. They lack the immediacy and unadulterated perspective that can only be attained through direct personal encounters.

Imagine being able to step into the shoes of our ancestors, to see past historical events unfold through our own eyes, to feel the emotions that coursed through their veins. The richness of their experiences, unfiltered by time and interpretation, would be an unparalleled gift. It would provide us with a profound connection to the past, allowing us to grasp the intricacies and nuances that are often lost in translation.

Anyway, I digress... Returning to that night, I took my foundling to the bathroom next to our bedroom to give her a quick shower. As a gentle breeze flowed in through the open window, a handful of colorful butterflies, whose species names I did not know, entered the room. Each one possessed its unique beauty, with swallowtails shimmering in shades of green and pink, others displaying prominent reddish-pink spots only on their lower wings, and some sporting the familiar orange-and-black pattern associated with monarchs. They flew in harmonious circles above our heads as I unzipped her simple pink dress. Her face remained concealed behind her ginger hair. When she was completely naked, a smile stretched across my face uncontrollably. Her entire body sparkled with different colors beneath her bronze skin.

I was afraid that her enchantment would fade if she entered the water, but she seemed accustomed to showers. She stepped into the tub and lay down, her head resting on the edge. As soon as her body was immersed in the water, other butterflies followed suit through the open window, gently covering the surface of the water, one by one. I couldn't help but wonder: How many miles had she traveled? Where had she come from, accompanied by this gathering of butterflies?

The mysteries and the butterflies surrounding her seemed connected, and I was left in awe of the magical and inexplicable connections that exist in our world.

After she finished washing herself and rose from the tub, a swarm enveloped her entire body. I was at a loss, unsure of what to do. Did she need a towel? A hair dryer, perhaps? As the insects began to depart through the open window, she stepped out of the tub. Once the final butterfly had departed, I closed the window hastily. Time was of the essence: we needed to get ready quickly, leaving behind the captivating swarm. My angel from above, bestowed upon me by the Lucky Virgin of Miracles, was truly breathtaking.

I led her to the room where I stored most of my wardrobe, specifically the section dedicated to the long gowns gifted to me by my mother-in-law. These gowns, with lavish embroidery and other embellishments, rarely saw the light of day. However, this night was different. Tonight, I could indulge in extravagance. But first, I wanted to prepare her. Among the opulent choices, I pulled out an exquisite vintage dress crafted from pleated taffeta. Its vibrant purple hue, almost neon in intensity, featured a plunging neckline and a voluminous skirt. But ultimately, I decided against it. I perused the collection of ornate gowns, recognizing their potential to exude a statuesque elegance reminiscent of Greek sculptures. Yet, I desired a look that was more organic, reflecting her origins closer to nature.

"Flora!" I exclaimed with delight. "None of these will suffice. You should wear one of my dresses," I informed her, closing the wardrobe doors. Turning to my own side, I searched for one of my recent purchases— a silk Gucci dress imprinted with one of Vittorio Accornero's iconic Flora illustrations. The design boasted a simple, conservative cut, featuring a closed neckline and long sleeves. I had glimpsed Jackie Kennedy wearing a similar dress in a magazine. Assisting her in donning the garment, we both knew it was the perfect choice the moment I zipped it up. Standing together before the full-length mirror adjacent to the wardrobe, her beautiful face, radiating a magical sheen, emerged from amid the print depicting nature's most splendid flowers and vibrant insects. She embodied a complete and wondrous offering from the wonders of the natural world. Whispering into her ear, I declared, "You're a miracle." She silently took a seat on the edge of a chair in the corner, looking directly at the floor.

It was my turn to find the perfect attire, striking a balance between glamour and subtlety. I wanted something elegant yet not too attention-grabbing. No plunging necklines, no clingy fabrics. My eyes fell upon a water-green Valentino dress, reminiscent of a sari with its hems embellished with white crystals. I recalled with delight that this very dress had also been worn by Kennedy. Slipping into it, I opted for a light pink lipstick to bring life to my lips. For this night, I had decided to let go of my usual Farrah Fawcett hairdo. I gathered my

hair into a tight chignon. With the chignon, I felt different—stronger. I chose not to wear any jewelry, as my
girl alone would captivate all the attention. Without the
ability to speak, she would be relying on my presence
in her interactions.

We were ready. Opening the door, I let her step out
before closing it behind us. Descending the staircase, I
spotted Marco awaiting us at the entrance. He appeared
enchanted by our presence.

"Sorry for the delay. We're all set," I said.

As I reached the final step, he leaned in closer, his
hand wrapping around my waist as he planted a kiss on
my neck. She stood behind us, observing our interaction with curiosity.

"Off we go, then," he declared.

"Could you at least tell me where we're going?"

He retrieved the car keys from his pocket, dangling
them in the air before revealing, "Casa Mollino."

During the hour and a half ride to Turin, our conversation remained sparse as the melodies of Mina Mazzini's
greatest hits played softly in the background. However,
at one point, your grandfather lowered the volume as
Mina sang "Ancora, ancora, ancora…" and leaned in to
share what seemed like a treasured secret. "Occultists
believe that Turin is the only city where the realms of
white magic and dark magic converge and intertwine."

I couldn't help but wonder where he had acquired such
knowledge, considering his usual disinterest in occultism.

As we finally arrived in the city center, a dense fog
enveloped us, obscuring our view of the road. Both of
us had to remain vigilant at every intersection, double-
checking for any approaching cars to avoid potential ac-

cidents. Throughout the journey, I kept a watchful eye on the girl, periodically glancing back at her slumbering form in the floral-print dress. Despite the occasional gentle bumping of her head against the soft leather seat, her sleep remained undisturbed.

"What is Casa Mollino?" I asked.

"It's the residence of a polymath named Carlo Mollino. He was a photographer, architect, rally-race champion, and an amateur occultist. He spent thirteen years constructing this house but never spent a single night there," Marco explained.

"Sounds like a fascinating character," I murmured, my interest growing.

"Indeed, he was incredibly eclectic. The house is filled with peculiar curiosities. Mollino used to hire prostitutes from the streets, invite them to Casa Mollino, and photograph them with his Polaroid camera. It's said that he captured over two thousand photographs. Can you believe it?" Marco's voice was tinged with intrigue.

Curiosity getting the better of me, I asked, "But how does this connect to the Japanese man?" I struggled to see the link.

"They don't have a direct connection. Carlo Mollino is dead. We're gathering at his house for Fumito's birthday because one of the guests possesses the keys for a television documentary he's producing. They'll sneak us in," Marco explained with a mischievous smile. As we took a sharp turn, heading toward the River Po, my apprehension grew.

"So we're breaking into someone's house? Is that a wise decision?" I said, concerned. Not only were we trespassing, but we were also dragging a stranger who may or may not be fully aware of the situation along for the sake of amusement.

"Don't worry. Nothing can go wrong. We're with a select group of influential individuals. Even if someone were aware, they wouldn't dare interfere…" Marco reassured me with unwavering confidence. As we arrived at the riverside palace, standing solitary in a dark garden adorned with withered flowers, the fog seemed to thicken around its entrance, as if concealing it from prying eyes. I glanced back at our guest, hoping to find her awake, but her eyes remained closed, a purplish sheen accentuating her eyelids against her bronzed skin.

"Via Napione… Here we are. I'll park right here."

Stepping out of the car, I adjusted my water-green silk skirt while Marco gently woke the girl with whispered words in her ear. She seemed surprised to find herself in our presence, taking a few moments to gather herself. With Marco's assistance, she emerged from the car.

As we beheld her standing before the metallic palace gate, enveloped in the grim fog, and surrounded by wilted flowers, excitement surged through us both. Clad in her floral-print dress, her wavy ginger hair cascading, and her skin shimmering with an ethereal glow, she breathed life into the scene. Suddenly, a few orange-black monarch butterflies materialized out of thin air, hovering above her head like a mystical crown. As she emitted her delicate rainbow hues, pushing the fog farther away, it felt as if magic itself had come alive.

I gently nudged Marco toward the gate, captivated by the natural phenomenon surrounding the girl. We had never encountered anything quite like it before. He proceeded into the garden, ascending the three steps toward the entrance, and pressed the buzzer.

"Yes?" a voice responded from inside.

"Fumito Misake," Marco whispered, sharing the secret code.

The gate swung open, and I led her into the entryway while holding her hand. When Marco's attention was diverted, I discreetly checked my hand to see if her iridescent skin had left any marks.

Choosing to forgo the elevator, we ascended the stairs, accompanied by a graceful flight of orange-and-black butterflies. Marco found great amusement in their presence, frequently glancing over his shoulder with a wide grin to ensure they still trailed behind us.

As we approached the entrance to Casa Mollino itself, I noticed an oval mirror hanging on the outer side of the door. Intrigued, the three of us gazed at our reflections. A voice came from behind the door. "Did you look at your reflection?"

"Yes," I replied.

"Both of you?"

"All three of us."

"Welcome," the woman said, swinging the door open wide. She was a vivacious and sensual girl, exuding an aura of playfulness. Her luscious features and captivating charm drew us in, instantly captivating our attention.

She closed the door behind us and showed us the very same oval mirror on the inner side of the door. "Look at yourselves again, but this time in this mirror," she instructed, her voice dripping with mischievousness. Curiously, your grandfather and I examined our reflections, searching for any discernible differences, but found none. Meanwhile, my angel stood behind us, her iridescent skin shimmering under the soft glow of the mirror.

"Internal versus external. Your external self remains

outside. You have left it there. Once you step inside, you enter the realm of the internal world—the world of dreams and thoughts. It is the private world you do not reveal elsewhere," the girl explained, her words carrying a seductive undertone.

With a charming smile, Marco interjected, "Well, I see the reflection of my beautiful wife in both mirrors. You must be Patrizia. I have heard about you."

"Yes, that's me. Patrizia, the girl of many secrets," she replied with a playful giggle, her eyes twinkling mischievously. "The person you see outside is always different from the person you see inside. We all have hidden depths, don't we? It's the beauty of being human."

Marco couldn't help but be enchanted by her charismatic presence.

She led us farther. "Let me take you to the living room. Fumito Misake may be running late, but the other guests have already gathered," she said with a delightful smile.

The monarchs had followed us into the house. Surprised by their presence, she exclaimed, "Where did these enchanting monarch butterflies come from? Look at their colors, so beautiful!" She clapped her hands, her excitement infectious.

As we entered the living room through the sliding doors, the other guests turned their heads toward us, momentarily captivated. I won't delve into describing them, for they were simply a crowd of Milanese individuals with their fashionable attire and sophisticated mannerisms. They yearned for the unexpected, as long as it fit within their predetermined notions of what the evening should entail. They eagerly anticipated the birthday celebration of a very, very old man, hoping Fumito would offer them some sage advice on staying sane and fit until the age of one hundred. Little did they know they were about to embark on a journey beyond their wildest imaginations—a journey into the depths of my angel's origins. However, before such revelations could unfold, they would need a few drinks and indulgence in their favorite vices. As their gazes shifted from me, they fixated on the monarchs gracefully fluttering above our heads.

One of the older gentlemen rose from his seat, radiating excitement as he approached your grandfather. "We're thrilled you could join us! This will be an unforgettable experience. Hopefully, Fumito will share his secrets with us," he exclaimed with fervor. It would later be revealed to me that he was the one who had procured the keys to Casa Mollino, organizing this intimate birthday dinner in honor of the enigmatic Japanese man.

Two women sat closely on the couch, their curious gazes fixated on us, eagerly awaiting an introduction to our mysterious plus-one and her accompanying monarch butterflies. I chose to disregard their scrutiny and instead searched for Elena, whom I had met earlier that day at the hairdresser. She had mentioned attending Costanza's party, but she was conspicuously absent. It seemed she had canceled her plans when Costanza declined the invitation to Casa Mollino. Turning to Patrizia, I asked, "Do you mind if we let my friend rest in one of the rooms until Fumito arrives? I'd like to surprise him."

Patrizia gently held the girl's face between her strong fingers, turning it sideways with a knowing smile. "Glitter mixed with almond oil... I know this trick, darling."

"She's very shy and rarely speaks," I tried to explain, but Patrizia's attention shifted to another aspect. "She radiates such light. Whatever diet she's on, I want to try it too," she remarked with intrigue.

"Patrizia, could you introduce this young girl to us?" one of the women interjected, rising from her seat to approach us. The ethereal rainbow beams surrounding us seemed to emanate from the chandelier in the living area, but I knew their true source.

"She's a bit tired. She just arrived after a long journey for Fumito's birthday. We'll let her rest for now, and later she can join us to enjoy each other's company," I replied, gently guiding her along the narrow, elongated corridor. If Patrizia was unwilling to assist me, I would take matters into my own hands. Your grandfather must have sensed my concern, as he charmingly commented on the woman's outfit, diverting her attention while I led my angel deeper into the house.

The first door on the right revealed a compact, rectangular kitchen decorated with vibrant, colorful tiles on the floor and walls. The intricate floral pattern segued from one square to the next, engulfing the entire space, which felt suffocating. Various plates were arranged on the table, ready to be served. I stepped outside, leaving the door slightly ajar behind us.

The second door on the right led to the bathroom, where a similar pattern repeated itself meticulously on each tile, heightening the feeling of claustrophobia. Even to this day, I struggle to fully articulate the feeling, but within the walls of Casa Mollino, I felt trapped.

"Come with me," I whispered, attempting to coax the butterfly that had landed on the bathroom sink. Despite my efforts with a small guest towel, it refused to depart. We continued down the corridor, accompanied by the other two monarchs fluttering gracefully beside us.

"Maybe there," I suggested, gesturing toward the last door on the left side of the corridor. I attempted to push it open, but it was locked. Knocking on the door in hopes of a response, I received no answer. Determined to find a hiding place for my angel away from prying eyes, I turned the key that was hanging in the lock. What awaited us behind that door, my dear Riccardo, felt like a divine sign.

The room seemed to embody the hidden heart of the entire house. It featured a blue carpet covering the floor, walls covered in leopard-print wallpaper, and vintage butterfly prints neatly arranged in symmetrical frames behind glass. The room was sparsely furnished, with only a vanity and a small bed curved on both ends, re-sembling a boat. "There." I pointed to the bed. "There you can rest." My fallen angel sat down on the corner of the bed, with two monarch butterflies perched on her left shoulder.

"Oh, you've found the room..." I heard Patrizia's voice behind me. "Yes, she can rest here until Fumito arrives, but you must promise me she won't damage anything. This is a very precious bedroom, untouched by anyone before... Do you see this carpet?" Patrizia asked, motion-ing to the blue floor covering. We gazed at it together. "It is the color of a river, a river that can carry away this boatlike bed. The entire house has elements reminiscent of a pharaoh's tomb, you know? Turin boasts a highly esteemed Egyptian museum, and Mollino drew inspi-ration from that culture."

I nodded in agreement, leaving my angel in that room as I rejoined the others in the living area alongside Pa-trizia. Your grandfather thrived in such social settings, effortlessly engaging in conversation with these people. On the other hand, I struggled to blend in. The women showed little interest in getting to know me, their curiosity instead focused on our guest who had been whisked away to another room without a proper introduction. After half an hour of small talk and two glasses of chilled champagne, we heard the doorbell ring. Fumito had arrived.

That night, my dear Riccardo, was when the course of my Kader shifted. If we hadn't been invited to that dinner, perhaps we would never have discovered the secret hidden behind the glittering facade of my enigmatic angel.

"Oh, look at her, with a dazzling three-karat diamond heart on her chest… Kawaii-ne!" we heard a voice exclaim from the living room as Patrizia went to answer the door for the centenarian Fumito Misake. The man's eyes were filled with desire, captivated by Patrizia's sensual curves. "Another mirror? Is this some Italian experiment to entice me? There are weeks when I don't even catch a glimpse of my own face, and here you are asking me to focus on it first to open the door and then to welcome me inside… Well, well, I'll oblige… Here it is, inside and out. Same old Fumito, same unremarkable face. But those magnificent assets of yours, Patrizia… You've truly bewitched me. Let me come in. I'm hungry. Is there cake?"

We were taken aback by his boisterous comments, as we had anticipated meeting a calm and soft-spoken elderly gentleman. Weren't the Japanese known for their reservedness? One of the women stifled her laughter behind a bejeweled hand. I expected Patrizia to respond with a witty comeback, but instead, she gracefully entered the room.

"Ladies and gentlemen, it is my great pleasure to introduce you to the oldest man on earth," Patrizia announced, rolling her eyes and adding under her breath, "and quite possibly the grumpiest as well." With a subtle gesture of her hand, she welcomed Fumito into the living room.

No, my dear Riccardo, Fumito did not look like he held the secret key to unlock the mysteries of immortality for any of us. He did not look healthy. He did not look peaceful. He did not look mysterious.

He waved at us, smiled, and then glanced at the dining table on our right. "Should we dine? I hope you have good wine. I'll spill all the secrets you want, but at this age, I function better when you pour some liquor down this throat…" He chuckled. We curiously watched this short man, trying to capture his persona so that we could analyze it later. He walked toward the table, reached for the appetizer plates with giant green olives, and picked one with his chubby fingers. He was so overweight that he resembled a rolling ball as he moved around the room. He had long lost all his hair, and there were spots on the skin of both hands that revealed signs of a poor liver. Perhaps he was just a fortunate soul. Maybe he hadn't truly earned the privilege of living past a hundred; he had simply stumbled upon it in a stroke of luck.

"Shy girl, can you put on some music? It's my birthday, not my funeral. We should celebrate," he directed, looking directly at me. I think I blushed; I don't remember. I promptly got up and began searching for a musical device. There was a gramophone behind the dining table, and I turned it on without changing the disc that was already playing.

"I'll open the wine," Marco said, rising from the

couch. Two of the women left the room, likely heading to the kitchen to bring more trays of food to the table. Domenico, the guy your grandfather knew, opened one of the windows to let in a breath of fresh air from the River Po. I remember checking to see if any new butterflies had fluttered in through the window, but sadly, there were none.

"Do you mind if I smoke?" Fumito asked us rhetorically as he opened his jacket to pull out a poorly rolled joint. The music playing was familiar, although not very popular among all the guests. It was "Chica Chica Boom Chic" by Carmen Miranda, from that 1940s film *That Night in Rio*. It's important for you to listen to this song if you haven't heard it before, because it recreates the right tone for this part of my evening as you read along. Everything seemed a bit tongue-in-cheek, a bit playful. Thanks to Fumito's attitude and requests, the mysterious room had transformed into a fun party parlor where each one of us came alive, actively engaging in something with loud music in the background, the strong smell of weed seeping into our clothes, and the sounds of chewing coming from various mouths. Fumito might not have been in the best of health, but he had brought life with him. In that moment, we all felt truly alive.

"Chica chica boom chic!" Patrizia danced in a sensual manner, her hands gliding across the smooth silk surface of her dress. "This was actually the song I performed the last time we threw a party in this house," she said, her fingers tracing lightly over the shirt of one of the men. Meanwhile, Marco poured deep red wine into our delicate crystal glasses. Each of us had our names written in thick ink on place cards on our hand-painted ceramic plates. I recall Fumito's curiosity about mine. "Are you Turkish?"

"Yes, I am, but I've been in Italy for as long as I can remember," I replied, using my lengthy residency in Italy as a shield against being perceived as a tourist, a newcomer, or someone who didn't belong to the group. This was my home, and I had no intention of going back.

"Yeter! Is that your real name?" Fumito exclaimed. "I used to shout that word often when my Turkish friends would try to overfeed me. Not that I don't enjoy eating, you know," Fumito continued, stuffing a forkful of spaghetti into his already full mouth.

I quickly glanced at other names: they were all common Italian names comprising at least three surnames. They were represented not just by their basic names but by generations and generations of tightly knit family ties. If it weren't for the surnames Marco had bestowed upon me through our marriage, my card would have appeared like a nickname compared to the others. I took a deep breath and looked toward the open windows, hoping to catch a glimpse of a butterfly or two that would infuse me with strength. A smile formed on my lips as I replied, "Yes, for better or worse, that is my name. I have many sisters, and I'm the youngest, the last one. The one before me is Songül, which means *the last rose*. My parents were exhausted from their efforts to have a son, and then I came along, causing not only disappointment for my father but also a medical condition for my mother, rendering her infertile after my birth. So they named me Yeter." Each word I uttered felt like a fragile butterfly emerging from the depths of my being. I sounded melancholic, as if I sought their compassion and pity. But I didn't. I had my angel waiting for me in the bedroom at the end of the corridor. I didn't need all these unfamiliar faces surrounding me, but it was part of the social game—I had to assimilate if I wanted to belong.

"Songül! That's a beautiful name," Fumito exclaimed. "And yours doesn't sound bad either, if one doesn't know the meaning. Nobody would imagine this story hiding behind that beautiful dress you're wearing, anyways. But if I were to give you the secret to eternal life, would you continue forever with this name? You can live so many lives within this one. You know that, don't you? All of you know that," Fumito remarked, looking both at me and the other guests around the table.

"Well, I had a friend in school named Imdat, which means *Help!*" I shared with a playful wink. "Yeter is a subtle complaint to destiny from my parents, but so far, my own destiny has been quite gentle with me." Your grandfather, thinking my words were directed at him or our paths crossing in life, squeezed my hand under the table. I didn't bother explaining that I was referring to my angel.

"You're funny!" Fumito chuckled. "I've visited Turkey a couple of times, and your people are obsessed with immortality. They've invited me to many TV programs, those that air in the morning for the housewives. Housewives! As if I had a secret recipe for a dish that they could learn in the morning and serve for dinner to the whole family. The TV presenters kept asking me what I had for breakfast, and I always gave the same answer…"

Two Italian ladies dropped their cutlery onto their plates, propping their elbows on the linen tablecloth, eager to hear Fumito reveal the secret.

"Whatever the fuck I wanted!" Fumito said and burst into laughter, his belly jiggling like jelly. Uncomfortable glances were exchanged among us as it became apparent that he was quite drunk at that moment.

"The only way you can be immortal is to love. Only love keeps you alive," he shouted, raising his hands. "Only love can transform you, heal you, help you in life. The more you love, the longer you live. The longer you live, the more chances you get at love." Fumito's words hung in the air. His next revelation surprised us all.

"Take my mother, for example. She was in love with a tree in my hometown, Kyoto. She would caress it, talk to it, and feed it every single day, just to see its cherry blossoms come alive every April. She lived to a hundred and fifteen! A hundred and fifteen! I learned how to love from her," Fumito said, his voice full of reverence as well as nostalgia. He dropped the fork and knife from his hands onto the table, emphasizing his point.

"A hundred and fifteen? That wine must be strong, I think," Marco joked, trying to make light of the astonishing number.

"Ninety-eight, really. Then she stopped. I resumed her life. You can do it as many times as you wish but it's very hard to find a creature and even harder to extract tears really. So, most of us get only one more chance, if any... Anyway, she managed to stay around for another seventeen years for the love of the cherry blossoms," Fumito sighed, taking a heavy breath. He proceeded to roll some more weed into an almost transparent piece of paper. "You don't mind if I smoke, right?"

We were left pondering Fumito's words, contemplating the power of love and the lengths to which it could extend one's life. I felt like I had made the right choice bringing the girl with me here, with all the monarch butterflies that followed her.

"Darling, you are getting lost in translation. What do we have to do?" Patrizia rose from her seat and approached Fumito, firmly gripping his flushed face between her fingers. "How can we live as long as you've done so far?" There was a hint of challenge in her voice, and Fumito seemed momentarily taken aback by her unexpected move, causing him to drop the weed onto the table. He appeared lost in thought for a moment before a mischievous smile curved on his lips.

"Well…" Fumito reached his chubby hand into the depths of his jacket and shirt, searching for something. He retrieved his tightly clenched palm, extending it over the table and opening it. Pastel-colored pills lay nestled in his hand, one for each of us.

"No questions. Take one. Put it under your tongue. Let it melt. Each one has a different effect," he said with a wink. It was then that I noticed the intricately designed wallpapers behind Fumito, depicting a lush forest with various animals weaving between towering trees. As the wallpapers seamlessly merged with the balcony, revealing a breathtaking view of the forest on the other side of the river, it felt symbolic, as if we were immersed in a vast forest that extended from Mollino's living room into the real world outside. I caught sight of a few monarchs gracefully landing on the corner of the balcony. Was my angel awake? Was that why they were drawn to this place?

Patrizia, fueled by the effects of the pill she had taken, became the center of attention as the intimate dinner transformed into a wild house party. Dancing on top of the dinner table in her high heels, she tapped to the rhythmic repetitions of Carmen Miranda's lollipop song, seductively leaning down to touch our faces every few

168 • YIĞIT TURHAN

seconds. One of the women burst into uncontrollable laughter, while the other used the heavy velvet curtains as props for her spontaneous one-woman show. The man who had greeted Marco earlier in the evening became fixated on the arrival of the monarch butterflies through the balcony. Drunk and enthralled, he chased them around the living room, engaging in slurred conversations with them, as if they could understand him.

Meanwhile, Marco had excused himself and left the room, heading toward the bathroom. A surge of worry coursed through me, fearing that he might be succumbing to the very vice he had promised to leave behind: drugs. Despite his reassurances, sometimes our weaknesses overpower our intentions. Your grandfather was one great man; however, during these eclectic parties he liked to entertain his darker side and lose himself to various drugs. He felt like he could be a different Marco if he kept experimenting on himself. I felt compelled to check on him, to intervene if necessary.

I rose from my chair, intending to leave the room and find Marco.

Riccardo's return to his grandmother's world had been a whirlwind of confusion and unsettling revelations. He had come back to a life he had long forgotten, a life in which he had never been an active participant. His relationship with Perihan had been one of minimal interaction, dating back to his elementary school days when she had sent him to Paris for boarding school.

As he sat alone in the dimly lit room, the manuscript clutched tightly in his hands, Riccardo found it all too overwhelming. His mother had long departed from his life, never to return, and his memories of her were a distant blur. The tale spun within those handwritten pages was a bizarre blend of memoir and fiction, blurring the lines between truth and fantasy.

Riccardo reminded himself that his sole purpose for being there was to secure the money that would rescue him from his dire circumstances. He wasn't driven by family, grief, or even love. He was motivated by financial desperation and the opportunity to craft a successful story from this inexplicable manuscript.

The motives of the older individuals surrounding him remained enigmatic. Each seemed to harbor a hidden agenda, their secrets casting shadows over the house. He speculated that their desires ultimately converged on a common goal: Perihan's inheritance. The fortune she left behind was undoubtedly the coveted prize they all sought.

One detail perplexed him, though. If no one had truly cared about him in the past, and these people were desperate to claim Perihan's wealth, why had Maurizio gone to the trouble of bringing him back to the family fold? Why had he encouraged Riccardo to stay in a place he had no intention of relinquishing?

Riccardo decided that he needed some fresh air and a change of scenery. He couldn't bear the feeling of confinement that the room threatened any longer. With the manuscript concealed under his clothes, he left the room quietly, tiptoeing down the stairs to the ground floor. He noticed that everyone had congregated in the kitchen, absorbed in their conversations. Riccardo preferred to avoid drawing attention to himself, so he continued toward the main door and slipped outside.

The cool air greeted him as he strolled down the quiet streets, his AirPods nestled in his ears, the haunting melodies of Portishead enveloping him. With each step, the oppressive feeling of claustrophobia began to ease, replaced by a feeling of liberation.

The warm, golden lights of a nearby Moonbox beckoned to him. It promised the familiar comfort of an international chain coffee shop and the solace to read in peace. He entered the café, where there was no queue, and was greeted by the friendly barista.

"How are you today?" she inquired with a warm smile.

Riccardo considered her question. "Fine, just a bit tired. Maybe craving something sugary, something extra sweet," he replied, his eyes scanning the menu.

The barista continued the conversation, guiding him through the menu options. Eventually, Riccardo settled on a hot white chocolate mocha, his voice softening as he gave the barista a name: *Lorenzo*. He really wanted a piece of Lorenzo with him, even if it was just a Moonbox cup with his name on it.

Beverage in hand, he moved to a comfortable chair situated right in front of the café's expansive window, which framed a view of the bustling street outside. Riccardo was grateful for the brief respite from the bewildering complexities that seemed to have surrounded his return to Milan. As he savored the rich aroma of the hot white chocolate mocha, he took out the manuscript. The shop, with its warm lighting and the low hum of background chatter, offered a tranquil environment in which to immerse himself in the enigmatic pages of his grandmother's work.

The music playing softly in the background provided a soothing backdrop to Riccardo's thoughts. But as he was about to resume reading, his attention was interrupted by the entrance of an unexpected guest. A man, haggard and worn from the harshness of life on the streets, perhaps without a home of his own, shuffled into the café, a hint of desperation in his weary eyes.

The barista, who had served Riccardo earlier, regarded the newcomer with a compassionate expression, a touch of sympathy in her voice as she asked, "How can I help you?"

The homeless man hesitated for a moment, his gaze shifting between the menu board and the other patrons. It was clear that this café visit was a rare indulgence for him.

Feeling a pang of empathy, Riccardo put aside his manuscript and regarded the man. This individual had faced hardships that were beyond Riccardo's own imagination. In the midst of his own tumultuous world, he understood the value of a simple act of kindness.

Gesturing for the man to approach, he asked, "What would you like to drink? My treat."

The weary man's eyes widened in surprise and gratitude. With a voice that carried the weight of his experiences, he replied, "Thank you, young man. A coffee, if you please."

Riccardo signaled to the barista, indicating the man's choice, and a steaming cup of coffee was promptly prepared.

With a heartfelt nod of appreciation, the disheveled man accepted the coffee and joined Riccardo at his table. He leaned his makeshift walking stick against the wall, his worn backpack bearing the signs of countless journeys.

"You know," he began, his voice a raspy whisper, "I don't often come to places like this. But today...today's a bit different."

Riccardo listened to the man's words with curiosity. "Different? How so?"

The man gazed out the window: "I don't know... I saw you from the window. I heard a voice within my head that asked me to tell you."

"Tell me what?"

"That you should take care of yourself, son. You have a big heart, and you need to protect it at all costs."

The weight of those words hung in the air. The man took another sip from his cup, got up, and walked slowly toward the exit. Right before he left the Moonbox, he turned to Riccardo and said, "Also don't forget... Nobody ever suspects the butterfly. Be very careful."

The man's last words sent a shiver down Riccardo's spine. He looked at the barista but realized she was busy preparing another drink and had not heard the conversation. Riccardo leaned back in the chair in front of the window, took the manuscript back in his hands, and got back to reading the rest of Perihan's story.

PERIHAN'S MANUSCRIPT

The man who had been chasing the butterflies, Domenico, took me by the arm and pulled me outside onto the balcony, urging me to witness the incredible sight. The night sky was illuminated by the glow of the streetlamps, casting a purple hue. Hundreds of monarch butterflies moved in synchronized patterns, creating a mesmerizing display against the backdrop of the lush trees. It was a natural phenomenon, perhaps a migration.

As we stood there, Domenico spoke in awe, marveling at the purple sky and confessing that he had never seen such a sight before. He attempted to draw me closer, but I gently pushed him away, feeling an urgent need to find Marco, who had yet to return from the bathroom.

Just as I was about to head back inside, I heard someone call my name twice. Confused, I looked around and realized that everyone else had become deeply immersed in their own experiences induced by the colorful pills. They danced, touched one another intimately, and laughed hysterically, completely unaware of my presence. The atmosphere became increasingly strange and surreal.

During this chaos, the crystals embroidered on the hem of my gown glittered in the weak light that seeped in from the outside, likely from the streetlights. Despite the undetermined swirling, the beauty of the dress remained, contrasting with the bizarre scenario unfolding around me. A part of me was frightened by the strange occurrences, while another part was captivated.

The citrusy taste of the pill still lingered in my mouth, further fueling my disorientation. The transformed view through the windows and balcony, now replaced by three tall screens displaying peculiar scenes, intensified the surreal nature of the moment. It was as if I had been transported into a realm of hallucinations, premonitions, and nightmares, and the allure of the unknown beckoned me, both terrifying and enticing.

"Yeter! Allah'in adi icin yardim et, yavrum…"

As I approached the window, the haunting image of my mother appeared before me. She was suspended from a tree branch, her entire body engulfed by the black cotton of her burka. Her eyes, wet with tears, reflected sheer terror. It was as if she had transformed into a matryoshka doll, but instead of the customary colorful patterns, her outer layer was entirely painted black, with only her eyes visible.

Even in my desperate attempt to convince myself that this was not real, I heard my mother's voice, trembling and fragile. She pleaded for help, expressing her fear of the dark entity that lurked within her. Her words echoed a verse from Sylvia Plath's poem, "Elm." *All day I feel its soft, feathery turnings, its malignity… Are those the faces of love, those pale irretrievables?* These were lines I cherished, but I knew that my mother would never have been able to recite it. This manifestation was a creation of my own imagination, a product of the bewildering circumstances unfolding around me.

Witnessing my mother's profound pain, her tear-streaked face filled with agony, I felt a surge of anguish within me. Tears cascaded from her frightened eyes like an unending waterfall. I watched helplessly as something inexplicable tugged at her, drawing her deeper into the clutches of the tree's branches. The black cloth of her burka constricted her formless body, intensifying the foreboding and despair.

As the unsettling scene played out before me, I over-heard one of the Italian women direct a probing question to Fumito, her voice laced with curiosity and perhaps a hint of seduction. "Is your wife still alive?" she wanted to know.

Fumito was sad all of a sudden. "No, she's been gone for a long time," he murmured softly.

Undeterred, the woman pressed further, her tone suggestive. "Did you cry at her funeral? Was it difficult for you to bid farewell to your lover?"

Fumito vehemently denied attending the funeral, his words infused with defiance and pain. "Why would I go? She didn't come to my funeral!" he exclaimed, attempting to pull the woman closer to him, his repulsive nature on full display.

Meanwhile, the vision of my mother's agony continued to torment me. I hoped to dispel the haunting image, but instead, it persisted against the dark canvas of the night sky, resembling a haunting projection in a summer cinema.

Fumito's laughter, distorted by the effects of the drugs we had ingested, echoed through the room. We had all become detached from reality, lost in our own altered states of consciousness. During it all, my mother's face contorted, her features melting and shifting before my eyes. Her left eye merged into her skin, while her right eye vanished behind the black cloth of her burka. Her body warped, elongated, and sprouted irregular, tumor-like growths.

Suddenly, the black burka became transparent, revealing my mother's naked form to the world. And then, the unimaginable happened: she began to grow wings, iridescent butterfly wings. In a breathtaking metamorphosis, she ceased to be human and was transformed into a magnificent butterfly, breaking free from her dark pupa. Flitting briefly in the air, she vanished into the night sky, embarking on a migratory journey to another existence.

In that moment, overcome with terror and disbelief, I screamed. Yet my cries went unanswered. The others remained lost in their own altered experiences, oblivious to my distress. Once again, I was Yeter, the one nobody truly cared for, even during this gathering of Italians. I screamed once more, my voice piercing the air, as my mother disappeared into the ethereal expanse, leaving behind a profound feeling of loss and longing.

Overwhelmed by the intensity of the moment and still shaken by the sight of my transformed mother, I turned to Patrizia, who stood closely behind me. Desperate for someone to share my experience with, I voiced my bewildered thoughts. "Did you see that?" I gasped.

In response, Patrizia extended her hand, inviting me to join her in a dance. Her offer seemed to carry a subtle invitation to momentarily escape the unsettling reality that surrounded us. But my mind was consumed by my mother's apparition. "My mother..." I struggled to articulate my thoughts, my voice trembling "...that was my mother."

As I grappled with the overwhelming emotions, a flicker of movement in the second window got my attention. Whatever effect the drug had on me, it was far from pleasant. I felt confined within the boundaries of my own body, suffocated by an unexplained weight pressing on my chest. I had not willingly signed up for these haunting visions. Why was I being subjected to this torment?

I looked at the second window, where a distorted fragment of a childhood memory played out before my eyes. I found myself transported back in time, reliving a pivotal moment from my past.

"Run! You must run... Run!" My older sister's urgent voice echoed through my mind. She stumbled and fell, hindered by a stone on our path as we hurried toward the Hatay Archaeological Museum, where our father worked.

Concerned, I slowed my pace and turned back to check on my sister. The once-empty streets were now teeming with an ever-increasing crowd. Hundreds, thousands, tens of thousands of people materialized seemingly out of thin air, running alongside me, ahead of me, behind me. The frenzy of the scene left me bewildered. What were we running from? Was there something pursuing us? And were we all converging on the museum? Would our father grant us entry amid the chaos?

The answers eluded me as I navigated the surreal landscape, torn between the urgency to flee and the uncertainty of our destination. My heart raced with a mix of fear, confusion, and an inexplicable notion of impending doom.

As the memory unfolded before me in rapid succession, Songül's voice rang out once again, urging me to keep running. Her words spurred me on, igniting a fierce courage within me. The competition became intense as we all vied to reach our destination. It felt like a collective migration, a shared purpose propelling us forward.

But then, abruptly, everyone began to fall. One by one, people crashed to the ground, their bodies collapsing under an unseen force. Despite the noise, my father's voice pierced the air. He recited verses from his favorite surah of the Qur'an, foretelling the end of the world. *"What is the striking hour?"* he bellowed, his voice blending with the disarray unfolding around me. *"And what will make you know what the hour is? It is a day whereon mankind will be like butterflies scattered about… And the mountains will be carded wool!"*

I turned toward the distant mountains, but they seemed impossibly far, out of reach. The scene played out like a disjointed dream, as if I was watching myself from a detached perspective, running endlessly on the glass surface of the second window in Casa Mollino's living room.

Finally, I arrived at the entrance of the museum, passing through the gate without encountering any resistance. With an instinctive move, I ascended the steps and made my way into one of the rooms, guided by an unexplained knowledge of what awaited me.

Before me stood a mosaic artwork, composed of three panels. In the center, Eros, the son of Aphrodite and Ares, slumbered peacefully beneath a tree, while Psyche, armed with a bow, and with her butterfly wings spread wide, reached out for a quiver resting on the same tree. To the left and right, geometric mosaics adorned the panels, forming a visual symphony.

As I stood there, a realization washed over me, sending a chill down my spine. I recalled the ancient Greek myth of Psyche, the embodiment of the soul, and how Aristotle had bestowed the name Psyche upon butterflies. In that moment, it struck me with profound significance.

Driven by a desperate need to escape the torment of the night, I pressed two fingers into my mouth, trying to induce vomiting to expel the drug from my system. I yearned for the night to end, for release from the surreal experiences that had engulfed me. All I desired was to find my angel, retrieve the car, and flee from this house and its guests. My focus narrowed solely on saving myself and escaping with the angel.

With my act of purging, the vision softened, leaving me standing in the living room of Casa Mollino, my body heaving with the remnants of the drug-induced nausea. The night had taken its toll on me, but a renewed determination burned within me to find my beloved and make our escape.

During the chaos, a third vision materialized before me, unfolding between the open doors of the balcony. A grotesque and repulsive creature emerged, its slimy body towering over us all. It possessed a dark, moist surface that exuded an aura of malevolence. Its eyes, small and wicked, scanned the room, searching for its target. Despite the diminutive size of its head in proportion to its massive body, it fixated on me, locking eyes with my trembling soul.

Fear gripped me, dear Riccardo, and I found myself paralyzed, feeling impending doom. With closed eyes, I braced myself for the worst, expecting death to claim me at any moment. But to my surprise, nothing happened. Instead, I felt a presence drawing near, inching closer to my face. With my eyes tightly shut, I felt its proximity, the sensation of another living being approaching.

Too terrified to confront the unknown, I waited in anticipation, feeling the pressure against my face, against my lips. Suddenly, a wet, fleshy organ intruded into my mouth. In a moment of instinctual response, I opened my eyes, only to be confronted by one of the men attempting to forcefully kiss me, his tongue already invading my mouth. Overwhelmed by revulsion and fear, I bit down, causing him to recoil and blood to stain my silk dress. In a surge of strength, I pushed him through the open doors of the balcony, desperate to escape his unwanted advances.

Amid the commotion, voices erupted in protest. "Have you lost your mind?" echoed through the room, as the scene descended into further debauchery. Two women indulged in passionate embraces with one of the men near the fireplace, while Patrizia began to unbutton Fumito's shirt, their actions fueled by the effects of the drugs, no doubt. Butterflies, now omnipresent, filled every corner of the living room, their delicate forms invading every inch of space.

Suddenly, Fumito seemed to notice the surreal influx of butterflies, interrupting his lascivious encounter with Patrizia. With an aggressive gesture, he halted her advances, his attention drawn to the insects as they alighted, one by one, upon the furniture. A flicker of alarm crossed his features, and I wondered if the sweat on his forehead was a result of his exertions, the drugs, or the terror of impending discovery. I couldn't discern the true cause amid the chaos that engulfed us all.

"Someone tell me where these insects came from!" The fear in Fumito's voice pierced through the chaotic atmosphere once more, as he demanded an answer about the origin of the insects. Gripping a nearby individual by the hair, he forcefully glanced up at the ceiling, where the monarch butterflies gracefully danced around the lamp. Sensing the escalating tension, I made the decision to leave the room, compelled by my desperate quest to find my young angel.

I hesitated for a moment, contemplating the possibility of her presence, still waiting for me surrounded by the archival prints of butterflies in her boat-bed. Uncertainty gnawed at me, and fear enveloped my thoughts as I grappled with the impending revelation that awaited me. The unknown outcome held a daunting power over me, but the need to uncover the truth propelled me forward, overriding my apprehension. With firm conviction, I embarked on my search, hoping to discover the fate of my angel.

As I made my way down the familiar corridor, memories of the party echoed in my mind. The walls seemed to expand with the pulsating music that still permeated the air, drowning out any other sound. I reached out and placed my hand on the wall, feeling its vibrations as if it were breathing beneath my touch. Polaroids dotted the wall, capturing frozen moments of the lively event.

My steps grew more sure as I approached the bedroom, where I hoped to find the girl resting. However, before I could reach my destination, the bathroom door suddenly swung open with a forceful burst. Startled, I uttered the name Annabelle without thinking. It couldn't possibly be her, could it? The party was over, and there was no need for her performance tonight. I tried to convince myself that she was just another dancer, perhaps masquerading as Peerless Annabelle.

The figure before me had an ethereal beauty, with pale skin and a dress crafted from vibrant pieces of chiffon. A smile played upon her lips, and she remained silent, her movements fluid and hypnotic. With each graceful motion, the red chiffon tied to her hands moved in sync, creating the illusion of a flying butterfly. The contrast of the transparent red fabric against the darkness gave the impression of a bleeding woman suspended in time. It was none other than Peerless Annabelle, who was believed to have been dead for over a decade, performing her renowned act exclusively for my eyes.

I stood transfixed, my heart torn between disbelief and a sense of wonder. The lines between reality and fantasy blurred again in that moment as I witnessed this surreal resurrection. Questions raced through my mind, but before I could gather my thoughts, the performance came to an end, and the enigmatic Annabelle vanished into the night, leaving me with a profound feeling of both awe and unease.

Upset that she was not another dancer but still confident that it was just a hallucination due to the yellow pill I had taken from Fumito, I walked right into her. She jerked her body sharply and moved back deeper into the corridor. I closed my eyes, hoping for her to disappear into the darkness behind my eyelids. When I opened them again, she was near the bedroom door, moving her body in an almost aggressive manner to create the butterfly effect. She pushed the door open and entered

182 • YIĞIT TURHAN

before I could object. My instincts took over, and I ran after her to save my angel.

As I entered the bedroom, my heart pounded in my chest. The room was dimly lit, with many shadows on the walls. The air felt heavy with anticipation. There on the boat-bed lay my angel, her delicate features peaceful in slumber. But the distorted figure that had entered the room was now standing still in the corner.

"Who are you?" I asked, my voice trembling with concern.

The girl on the bed looked up at me, her eyes wide with terror.

I followed her gaze to Marco, who was now hunched over in the corner of the room. His body convulsed with violent retching, and the acrid stench of vomit filled the air. The girl's fear intensified, her eyes welling up with tears.

"Marco, what happened?" I asked, my voice laced with worry.

Marco, struggling to regain his composure, looked up at me with bloodshot eyes. "I—I don't know," he muttered, his voice weak and strained. "I must have taken something...something I shouldn't have." Marco collapsed onto the floor in a state of unconsciousness.

Marco's presence, in his disoriented state, had only amplified the girl's fear, and it was evident that she needed comfort and reassurance. I prioritized her over your grandfather. I held her face gently between my trembling hands, brushing her hair aside to get a clear view. But what I saw before me shattered any sense of reality or hope that remained. My scream echoed through the room, a desperate cry of disbelief and horror.

Her once-delicate features were now distorted and dis-

located, stripped of all beauty and replaced with a grotesque visage. There was no sheen or glitter left, only a
moist and almost slimy texture that sent shivers down my
spine. Her eyes, one on her chin and another on her forehead, stared back at me with an otherworldly gaze. It was
a nightmare, worse than anything I had ever imagined.

Her mouth stretched diagonally across her face, far
too long, filled with teeth resembling small triangles,
their sharp edges glinting in the dim light. Her nose had
shrunk to two little holes, barely discernible between her
eyebrows. The ginger hair that once cascaded like silk
now writhed like tentacles, with a life of its own, moving across the slimy surface as if ready to defend against
any physical contact.

She was something from the depths of hell, a terrifying aberration. Wet and moist, grumpy and crying,
she exuded an aura of fear and despair. Tears streamed
down her face, each droplet falling like the River Po in
front of the house, a haunting reflection of the pain and
torment that had consumed her. My angel, my beloved,
had been cruelly replaced by a monster from the dark-
est corners of existence.

Riccardo was deeply immersed in his grandmother's manuscript, the delicate pages crackling softly beneath his fingers
as he turned them. The café was calm, and the narrative was
a puzzle he was keen to piece together. He found himself so
engrossed in the handwritten words that he failed to notice
the world outside—the people passing by, the Milanese streets
growing darker as evening approached.

As he delved further into the story, the manuscript seemed
to pulsate with life, blurring the line between reality and
fantasy.

Unbeknownst to Riccardo, outside the coffee shop, a figure came to a halt. This individual looked intently through the window, their eyes locked onto him. Gradually, the stare intensified, an unwavering focus on the young man seated by the window.

Feeling someone's eyes on him, Riccardo's focus began to waver. He pulled his eyes away from the pages, slowly realizing that there was more than his reflection in the glass. Another face appeared, and he recognized it instantly. It was Barbara, Lorenzo's mother, in her vibrant red attire, from her wild hair to her coat and shoes. She waved at him.

"Riccardo! What a nice surprise! What are you doing here? You could've come to our bar," she greeted him once inside, drawing an annoyed glance from the barista behind the counter.

Riccardo blinked and contemplated a white lie, the manuscript still clutched in his lap. "Hi, Barbara! I wanted to get something sweet to drink and was reading some documents for research," he offered, hoping to divert her attention from the manuscript.

She glanced at the journal briefly but didn't ask any further questions. Barbara herself was animated, explaining that she had been at the supermarket. The bags she carried appeared heavy, making her shoulders slouch.

Riccardo felt torn between his reading and this unexpected encounter yet had no option but to listen. "I was out buying some milk for tomorrow morning and a few bottles of Aperol. It is not convenient to buy from the supermarket, but we have a birthday party at the bar tonight, so of course Italians will ask for their Aperol spritz! I had to go get some as we finished—never mind, I'm babbling…"

While scanning their surroundings, Barbara said, "Do you

want to stay, or will you come walk with me? I think they're closing…"

He agreed to join her, and with the manuscript rolled up, they walked together back to the bar. "Is Lorenzo there?" Riccardo asked.

Barbara's response came with a smile. "No, he's not. If you want to see him, you can always text him… I know he's glued to his phone waiting for you to call." She laughed with an almost witchlike cackle and hastily added, "I shouldn't have said that! Will you please not tell him I did? He will kill me if he knows. He wants to play it cool, my dear little Lorenzo…"

As redness flushed Riccardo's face, he nodded in agreement, thoroughly amused yet slightly embarrassed. They reached the bar, and he assisted Barbara in placing her shopping on the counter. She gave Riccardo a warm hug, and he departed for the mansion, wondering if he should text Lorenzo, only to find that his phone's battery was almost dead.

Upon reentering the garden and returning to the house, a peculiar scene greeted Riccardo. Inside, a maid was on her knees while Licia supervised. They were fervently cleaning a strange, gooey substance from the floor. The sight was grotesque, and Riccardo felt a chill down his spine.

"Licia, what's happening here?"

"Oh, Riccardo, it's quite a situation, really. We were busy bottling up the cherry jam today, you know, the one we made from Cristina's cherries. The maid wanted to be helpful, but those glass jars can be so slippery. So she…she dropped them. It's all a bloody mess now!"

Riccardo didn't want to push the conversation further. He sensed what he was looking at was not some jam but probably the same substance he had witnessed in the bathroom when he had gotten up to pee the other night. Licia's frustration echoed through the room. As they cleaned the dark, blood-red substance from the floor, the ominous presence of a green bucket lingered, triggering unease. Riccardo recognized these buckets as the ones the maids kept bringing in and out between the house and the greenhouse.

Resolving to distance himself from this perplexing scene, he excused himself. "Listen, I'm going to go upstairs and change, okay?"

Licia mentioned dinner would be served in an hour, and with that, Riccardo climbed the stairs, excited to continue reading. But before that, he wanted to confirm the manuscript's authenticity. He needed to make sure that the handwriting belonged to Perihan. He entered her bedroom once again.

Riccardo checked the wardrobes, the contents of her tuberose-infused coats, but his search yielded nothing. He looked around a few more times for anything with handwriting on it. His hopes were diminishing until his eyes fell upon a cluster of Post-it notes on the vanity. One of them was inscribed with Perihan's elegant handwriting: *Perihan's butterflies never disappoint.*

The discovery sent a shiver down his spine. Trembling, he compared the note's handwriting to that in the manuscript hidden securely between his body and his jeans. The match was undeniable. Perihan had penned the story, a single handwritten copy.

Filled with a renewed excitement, he returned to his room, ready to read the rest.

PERIHAN'S MANUSCRIPT

I recoiled in shock and horror, my mind struggling to process the unfathomable transformation before me. The girl's cries mingled with my own, creating a cacophony of anguish and disbelief. It was a nightmare, a surreal descent into madness that I could no longer deny.

Fear consumed me, but it was not the fear of the unknown or the supernatural. It was the fear of witnessing the destruction of innocence, the violation of beauty, and the loss of everything I held dear. My heart shattered into a million pieces, and I realized that there existed horrors more extreme than anything I could have ever imagined.

The room seemed to close in on me as fear and confusion rose within my mind. The girl, once my angel, now resembled a grotesque reflection of my father. It was a surreal and terrifying transformation that shattered the illusion of safety and love I had associated with her. The dissonance between my feelings of affection and the rising terror made my heart race and my thoughts scatter.

I stumbled backward, my steps faltering as I tried to distance myself from the bed and its nightmarish occupant. The weight of my emotions bore down on me, and in my haste, I lost my footing. Tripping over Marco's unconscious body, I crashed to the floor with a thud, the pain shooting through my back like a searing flame.

Lying there, vulnerable and wounded, I felt the weight of my fear press upon me, threatening to suffocate. The room spun around me, the blue carpet a disorienting blur beneath my gaze. Tears welled up.

As I lay on the carpet, my back throbbing with each heartbeat, I knew that I could not stay there. I had to gather my strength, both physical and emotional, and find a way to confront the nightmarish reality that had engulfed Casa Mollino. I had to save Marco and my angel. I had to save myself!

The journey ahead would be treacherous, my dear

Riccardo, but I would not let fear consume me entirely. I would rise from that blue carpet, with the pain deep in my bones and the weight of uncertainty on my shoulders, ready to face whatever horrors awaited me, accompanied by the reek of vomit. For in the face of fear, the true test of our character lies not in succumbing to it but in finding the strength to overcome and emerge transformed on the other side.

Fumito's heavy footsteps echoed through the corridor, reverberating with urgency. His knocks on the door punctuated the air, jarring my senses as I struggled to regain my composure. Despite the excruciating pain that coursed through my body, I tried to find the strength to raise myself on my elbows, seeking a glimpse of the girl amid the disarray.

The door swung open, revealing Fumito's entrance into the room. A whirlwind of monarch butterflies accompanied him, their delicate wings creating a tempestuous dance in the confined space. Fumito, in his desperation, slapped at his own body, trying to rid himself of their persistent presence. The sight was both mesmerizing and disconcerting, the fluttering insects and their shadows decorating the walls.

His voice trembled with a mixture of fear and disbelief as he looked at the bed. The distorted figure of the girl, her features twisted and contorted, elicited a visceral reaction from Fumito. His voice erupted with a blend of terror and indignation, shaking the very foundation of the room.

"Who brought her here?" Fumito's words hung heavy in the air, a question that demanded answers. His words conveyed a sense of responsibility, as if the intrusion of this aberration within Casa Mollino was a transgression that could not be overlooked.

I met Fumito's gaze, my eyes filled with tears at the scene before us. The weight of the situation bore down upon me, and I found myself at a loss to explain. The girl's presence had disrupted the fragile equilibrium of our reality, leaving us grappling with the incomprehensible.

"Sh—she is my fallen angel," I stammered, my voice laden with vulnerability and confusion. The words slipped through my lips, a feeble attempt to reconcile the enigma that stood before us.

Fumito's expression hardened, his disagreement palpable as he walked toward the bed to assess the girl's condition. He shook his head, rejecting the notion of her angelic nature.

"She is anything but an angel!" Fumito's voice carried a tone of great conviction. His words hung in the air, challenging the illusion of benevolence that had shrouded her. He turned his attention back to me. "She is transforming into what she really is. I won't take responsibility again for this. I've paid my dues. I've obtained what I wished for. She should leave."

With an outstretched hand, Fumito offered his support, pulling me back to my feet. Despite the lingering pain that throbbed through my body, I managed to rise, aided by his steadfast presence. Your grandfather, now half-awake and disoriented, listened intently to our conversation, straining to comprehend the tumultuous events unfolding within the room.

In this hazy realm of reality and nightmare, I sought relief in the companionship of Fumito. Together, we faced the enigma of the girl and the consequences of her presence, determined to navigate the treacherous path that lay ahead.

"What do you know about her?" I asked, my voice trembling with great curiosity. My heart pounded in my chest; fear intermingled with awe. Could it be possible that the queen of all fairies, the one bestowed upon me by The Lucky Virgin of Miracles, held a dangerous secret? The thought sent shivers down my spine, challenging the very foundation of my beliefs.

Fumito's expression remained inscrutable as he listened to my inquiry. His silence was heavy with the weight of knowledge and understanding, as if he held the key to unraveling the enigma before us. With a slow nod, he indicated his willingness to share what he knew.

"You first," he responded, his voice calm and measured. "Where did you find her?"

I proceeded to recount the circumstances that led to the girl's arrival, my words pouring forth in a hurried yet meticulous manner. Fumito absorbed the details, his nodding offering a silent acknowledgment of my account. It was as if he were piecing together a puzzle, connecting the dots that would reveal the truth hidden beneath the surface.

"I see… I see." Fumito's voice carried deep gravity as he motioned for me to check the corridor, instructing me to close the door and take a seat. The presence of the monarchs, their silent observation, created a sinister atmosphere, as if they were privy to the unfolding secrets of our discussion.

Once I had followed his instructions, settling down in anticipation, Fumito began his tale. His voice took on a cadence, weaving a narrative that seemed to transcend time and space.

"Once upon a time—but really, even before the time itself was invented—" Fumito's words resonated with an air of mysticism and ancient wisdom "—there existed a land where trees grew out of water and the sun shone only once a year..."

As I listened intently to his story, the room became enveloped in an ethereal ambience. The fluttering butterflies seemed to dance to the rhythm of his words, their delicate wings casting enchanting shadows on the walls. It was in that moment, suspended between reality and the realm of dreams, that I awaited the revelation that would shed light on the true nature of the girl who had entered my life so unexpectedly.

Fumito's voice carried a captivating allure as he began his tale. The room seemed to fade away, and I found myself drawn into the depths of his words.

The description painted a vivid picture in my mind—a land of perpetual darkness and mystical beauty. Fumito's words held an air of secrecy, emphasizing the importance of listening attentively, for this story would not be repeated.

"This land still exists today, near Mexico," he continued, his voice a whisper that seemed to echo through the room. "It is called the Forest of Immortals. For three hundred and sixty-four days a year, it remains shrouded in darkness, untouched by the rays of the sun. But on the three hundred and sixty-fifth day, something magical occurs."

I leaned forward, captivated by the tale unfolding before me. The Forest of Immortals—it was a place I had never heard of, hidden away from the prying eyes of the world.

"The sun cannot usually penetrate into this forest,"

Fumito explained, his voice filled with wonder. "Yet, on that special day, the forest is bathed in light, as if touched by some other celestial force. The trees extend their branches high into the sky, reaching toward an unseen source of illumination. And then something incredible happens."

Awe washed over me as Fumito revealed the phenomenon that brought light to the darkness: branches joining together, emitting a gentle glow from their tips. The forest, once cloaked in night, transformed into a realm of shimmering radiance.

"They call these trees the praying trees," he continued, his voice tinged with reverence. "For they seem to commune with the heavens, offering their branches as conduits for the ethereal light. It is a sight that fills the hearts of those who witness it with wonder and reverence."

As Fumito spoke, it became clear that the Forest of Immortals held a profound significance. It was a place of natural magic, untouched by the bustling tourism of the modern world. A place where secrets whispered among the trees, waiting to be discovered by those who sought them.

Riccardo was deep in his reading when the sound from downstairs pierced his concentration. At first, it was merely a distant rumble, like thunder in the far-off horizon, but then it grew louder and more distinct.

Intrigued, he set the manuscript aside and leaned over the edge of the bed, his ear pressed to the old parquet. The voices below became clearer, though the words were fragmented.

Maurizio's voice was unmistakable. He spoke in agitated, urgent tones, his words marked by an ominous thud against the wall. It was as if he had punched one of the walls in frustration. However, Riccardo could only catch snippets of his speech. *Monarchs* and *psychosis* were fragments that found their way to Riccardo's ears.

Maurizio spoke again, his voice rising with intensity. "We have to postpone the ritual until we have it! That's it!" He bellowed these words, leaving them hanging in the air.

Riccardo felt his unease intensify as he strained to hear more, but the dialogue below grew indistinct and muffled, as though hidden behind a heavy curtain.

Frustration and fear welled up within him, and he reached for his phone, which was still plugged into the charger. Desperation drove him to check the price of a ticket back to Paris, his lifeline to escape this increasingly enigmatic and disconcerting situation. The website loaded slowly, teasing him with hopes of freedom.

But as the prices flickered on the screen, Riccardo's heart sank. Even the longest train journey back to Milan was more expensive than he could currently afford. The weight of his predicament bore down on him, and with a heavy sigh, he closed the browser. His only relief lay in continuing to read his grandmother's strange manuscript, despite the unnerving events taking place in the house around him. If he wanted to free himself, he had to know what happened next in Perihan's story, which had way too many resemblances to real life after all.

PERIHAN'S MANUSCRIPT

"Information about this place is scarce," Fumito concluded, his voice a soft murmur in the stillness. "It remains a hidden gem, known only to a select few. The Forest of Immortals—the mysterious land where trees grow out of water and light emerges from the branches, transforming darkness into a fleeting day."

The room seemed to hold its breath, the weight of

the story lingering in the air. The monarch butterflies darted about delicately, their presence a testament to the enchantment that dwelled within the narrative. And as I absorbed the tale of the Forest of Immortals, I couldn't help but wonder what connection it held to the girl, my angel, who now resided in my midst.

"Anyway, the story goes that a long, long time ago the first humans stumbled upon the Forest of Immortals on that extraordinary day when the sky illuminated. The sight of the trees with roots immersed in water fascinated them, and they couldn't resist taking cuttings to take with them. To their astonishment, the places where they made the cuts sprouted new branches immediately. It was as if these trees possessed an immortal nature, capable of regenerating and growing at an incredible speed.

"One courageous human from the group decided to stay in the forest overnight, commanding the rest of the tribe to leave. His purpose was to uncover the secret of immortality and bring it back to his village. However, he vanished without a trace, and no one ever saw him again.

"This event sparked a fierce competition among tribes. Each day, they would send individuals from their community to the forest, armed with hidden blades and hopes of returning as carriers of the secret to eternal life. At the forest's entrance they would gather, ready to confront whatever awaited them in the darkness. Swimming through the ever-growing trees, they braved the unknown.

"Outside the forest, those awaiting their return would sometimes hear agonizing, high-pitched screams, followed by an unsettling silence. No one who ventured into the darkness ever made it back. They became lost to the depths of the forest, and the cause of their demise remained a mystery.

"The fear of the unknown gripped the hearts of those who watched their loved ones disappear among the trees. The Forest of Immortals held secrets that defied comprehension, and the cost of seeking its treasures was immeasurable. The question of what lay hidden within haunted the minds of the living, as they grappled with the unyielding darkness and the fates of those who ventured into it."

As Fumito's voice faded, foreboding settled over the room. The legend of the forest had introduced a mix of danger and allure, its enigmatic power beckoning to be discovered. I couldn't help but wonder again how this ancient tale intertwined with the presence of my angel and what truths awaited us as we delved further into the mysteries that surrounded her.

"On the three hundred and sixty-fifth day, when the praying trees illuminated the sky over the forest, one of the kings of the tribes decided to venture in accompanied by his blind servant, Idak. The servant was a frail figure unbothered by his lack of sight, moving as effortlessly as any other member of the tribe. The king envisioned Idak, this unfortunate chattel, as potential bait for the lurking and terrifying monsters if they chose to stay overnight. They spent the entire day swimming around the trees but found nothing of significance. Eventually, they ascended a tree, with the king taking the lead to settle upon one of the higher branches, followed closely by Idak. As night descended, they discerned the swift movement of water beneath them, the rhythm of the waves altered by the intrusion of an unknown entity. Straining their ears, they listened intently, attempting to decipher the identity of this wild creature. Idak perceived additional movements behind him and to his right. Gradually, the noise intensified, now emanating from all directions. Realizing they were surrounded by these monsters, the king instructed Idak to go down into the water, diverting their attention away from himself. Idak shrugged nonchalantly and lowered his body into the warm water. In the darkness, his hand brushed against something slimy, and he heard an aggressive hiss.

"However, Idak refused to succumb to fear. Instead, he tenderly caressed the creature's slick surface, inquiring whether it was injured, his inability to see rendering him impervious to its menacing nature. The king vehemently rebuked him for engaging with the dark forces of the forest but was swiftly silenced by a violent scream that echoed into the depths. Meanwhile, Idak listened as one of the monsters voraciously devoured the king's flesh and bones, consumed by insatiable greed.

"Days passed in complete darkness, but Idak couldn't care less as he couldn't distinguish between day and night anyway. In his tribe, he had never experienced affection since the servants were kept in individual cages during their off-duty hours, and nobody dared touch them. However, in the forest, it was different. Idak could freely caress these animals and listen to their stories. They whispered in their peculiar little voices, sharing their secret powers. According to Idak, these creatures were long tubular reptiles with large bodies and tiny feet and faces. Some had fur, others had spikes, and most had small bumps on their bodies. If you saw them today, Yeter, you would think they were giant caterpillars—slimy and ugly with aggressive attitudes.

"After spending a month in the forest, Idak learned several facts about the creatures. Even monsters endured their own suffering in their monstrous hearts. The more affection they received, the less aggressive they became. As Idak listened to their stories and asked questions, the slime on their bodies decreased. They fed on small fish-like creatures in the water and only resorted to eating humans for self-defense. Each monster had a unique venom, and with it came a specific superpower. One could ignite anything on fire, another could make blood cells explode in veins, one could crush bones to dust, and another could strangle like a boa snake. Idak discovered that immortality was just one of the many secrets held by the forest. Through conversations with the creatures, he learned that they could grant powers of invisibility, flight, time travel, precognition, night vision, and even mimicry, among other extraordinary abilities.

"Idak fell in love. He had formed a special connection with one monster, the one that claimed to possess the secret of immortality. He spent all his time with it, doing everything possible to make it happy. Day by day, he felt a physical transformation in the monster under his touch. The slime vanished, the bumps diminished, and its shape became more humanlike and huggable. Idak realized that through the love he showered upon the monster, it was gradually taking on a real human form.

"When the transformation was complete, the newly formed human began to cry. In its monstrous voice, it said to Idak, 'The tears that fall from my eyes hold the elixir of immortality. The tear that rolled down my face today is a result of the joy from the transformation you granted me. Open your mouth...'

"Unaware of the significance, Idak tasted the tear of happiness on his tongue, unknowingly receiving the gift of immortality. The tear swiftly dissolved, leaving a tingling sensation in his stomach. Idak, being blind, couldn't see it, but with a single drop of this elixir, a butterfly was born inside him, stealing a heartbeat from his heart.

"'When you consume my tears, a butterfly will be born within you. It will capture one heartbeat from your heart, preserving it until the day you pass away. After your death, the butterfly will locate your lifeless body and return your heartbeat, allowing you to resume your life from where you left off. This is the essence of immortality: the opportunity to continue one's existence.'

"Idak had attained immortality. Despite the objections of the other monsters, Idak and his newfound companion decided to leave the forest together and return to the servant's village. Surely, the new king would welcome him with open arms once he shared the secret of immortality. So they departed from the forest, swimming through the praying trees and returning to the city.

"Did they live happily ever after? Well, I have never personally met Idak, but the monster remains right here in front of us, shedding tears containing the elixir of immortality once again..."

When Fumito finished recounting his story, an uncomfortable silence engulfed the small room. Marco lay on the floor, exhausted and semiconscious, trying his best to follow Fumito's words. His head was uncomfortably close to a drying pool of vomit on the carpet. He clearly struggled to focus on the story. The butterflies, motionless and serene, adorned the surroundings, but Marco's attention was divided between Fumito's words and the unpleasant scene before him.

"Now you know," Fumito finally broke the silence, looking directly at her.

"My angel is not a monster."

"Your monster has never been an angel. Perhaps it resembled a fairy on the day it emerged from the Forest of Immortals, but nothing more. I have only told you the beginning of this story... It has caused chaos wherever it has gone for a long time." Fumito's tone was grave. I struggled to comprehend it all. The distorted face of the angel was the only reason I was inclined to believe him. What I had seen beyond the living, writhing tentacles of hair was far from human.

"Who told you this story?"

"We can't linger here all night. You need to get rid of her quickly."

"Who told you this story?" I repeated, looking at my dress, torn on one side. One of the monarchs took flight, landing curiously on my shoulder. I gently pushed it away, but it returned to its original position.

"Old books...ones that are kept locked away in important libraries around the world, not accessible to the public. It's a long, long story. What you need to know is that this creature once saved my life," Fumito replied. "I had heard about the Forest of Immortals from professors at the university in Kyoto, which led me on a trip to Mexico. However, upon arriving there, I discovered that nobody had any knowledge of this story or the whereabouts of the forest. But I didn't give up easily. When you're in search of the secret to eternal life, giving up is not an option. I spent three months in a small village mentioned in a couple of research papers, making peculiar connections with healers, fortune-tellers, shamans, magicians, and psychics. However, I never encountered any monsters or fairies, and nobody had heard of Idak."

Fumito paused as we heard a knock on the door.

200 • YIĞIT TURHAN

"We're coming, give us ten minutes," Fumito said, making his way toward the door to block it with his own weight.

On the other side, it was Patrizia's voice. "I'll bring out the birthday cake soon. Let me know if you want me to join your little gathering in there."

"Fumito," I interjected, "we should hurry."

He remained focused and responded firmly, "Ten minutes." We waited for Patrizia's reply, but her footsteps gradually faded away from the door.

Without wasting a moment, he resumed his story. "I was exhausted. I wanted to return home. I packed my bags, bought my ticket, and went to bed. However, that night, a young boy knocked on my door, panting heavily with enthusiasm. He was so eager that he could barely contain himself. Despite my attempts to calm him down, he wouldn't listen. He spoke in a rapid, strong Spanish dialect and urged me to follow him. Curiosity got the better of me, and I found myself following the boy barefoot out of town and into the forest. It may have seemed insane, but after spending three months in search of a miracle, I didn't mind sharing in the boy's excitement. I had no expectations, never imagining that he would lead me to this very monster—"

I interrupted, intrigued. "You found the forest?"

"No, it wasn't the Forest of Immortals. It was just a small plot of land with numerous trees. I wouldn't even consider it a proper forest. The creature was there, in its most horrifying form, hissing aggressively in the darkness. I felt sheer terror coursing through every cell of my body. It's the kind of sight that can cause a heart attack. That's how terrifying it was," Fumito explained.

At that moment, your grandfather opened his eyes

and placed his hand on my shoes. "I don't feel well," he said, followed by a hiccup. He didn't look good either. His eyes were bloodshot, and the wound on his face was still moist and weeping. "I took too much of it," he mumbled, likely referring to the cocaine he had taken earlier. Unfortunately, he had this terrible addiction that he could never overcome.

Although Marco's condition concerned me, I remained focused on Fumito's story. "I don't believe you," I protested.

Fumito calmly responded, "You don't have to believe me. I'm simply sharing the information I have, and it's up to you to decide what you do with it. I continued to show the monster love and affection for another month, visiting the forest late at night. At first, I stayed far away from it, singing at the top of my lungs. Then gradually, I got closer to its perimeter as it grew more beautiful each day. When it finally transformed into a fairy, I asked for its teardrop. I was lucky that she let me have a tear. It's easier, though much more dangerous, to keep her as a monster and let her shed as many tears as possible. As a monster, it has a vicious and dangerous nature... I didn't want to risk my life. I only desired to extend it for eternity."

"So you drank it?"

"So I drank it, just one drop. It was a moment of magic... A peculiar sensation in my stomach. You know, like butterflies in your stomach, as the saying goes when you're in love. I felt a sharp pain in my heart, followed by something like a little lump moving inside my mouth. I parted my lips to release it. A beautiful purple emperor butterfly, with its shimmering wings, fluttered under the first rays of morning light in the forest. It gradually ceased its movement, gracefully descending onto my palm. I took it, expressed my gratitude to the fairy, and departed. Well, not entirely… I asked for another teardrop, just in case. As a matter of fact, that extra tear was the one I used for my mother years later. And all of this happened before the circus people discovered the creature and abducted her to Italy."

"You died and came back?" I felt as though I had fully crossed the threshold between reality and the surreal. This realm of fantasy held such vast possibilities that I didn't want this experience to end quickly.

"Yes. I died years later in an accident, but the butterfly came to life with my heartbeat, found me, and brought me back. It helped me resume my life from where it had halted." Fumito's words didn't sound crazy; rather, they seemed quite believable.

"Who are the circus people?" I was like a hungry caterpillar, eager to devour the knowledge from Fumito, but I knew time was running short as Patrizia wanted him back in the living room.

"I'll make sure you find out," Fumito responded, casting one final glance at the monster on the boat-bed. By then, the monarchs fluttering around the room had grown restless. I couldn't explain how, but I felt that something extraordinary was about to happen. The room seemed charged with an imminent burst of magic. Your grandfather grasped my ankle tightly, struggling to utter, "Yeter… I don't…"

That was the breaking point. He started coughing heavily, struggling to prop himself up on one elbow. I knelt to assist him, but it was already too late. He began vomiting uncontrollably all over again.

"Oh God… Marco!" I exclaimed in despair. Fumito

gazed at us with pity in his eyes, too old and overweight to be of any assistance. The vomit was everywhere, and Marco had fainted. His body convulsed and twitched in strange movements. My dear Riccardo, your grandfather was dying before our eyes.

"Do something! Call an ambulance, please! Patrizia!" I pleaded, but my voice came out weak and feeble, unable to penetrate the closed door and the noise of the music resonating from the living room.

"He will die," Fumito confirmed with a heavy tone.

I felt desperate. Slapping Marco's cheeks, I tried desperately to bring him back to consciousness, but my efforts proved fruitless. Tears streamed down my face as I reluctantly let him go and turned to face the monster on the bed. Overcoming my fear of its distorted visage and hairlike tentacles, I sat beside it, sobbing uncontrollably. "Please, please help me. Please, do something. He's dying…"

"The monster is not crying. You must make it cry. You must hurt it. Time is running out, and you don't have enough time to turn it into a fairy. Instead, you must do the opposite. All you need is one teardrop," Fumito said. I looked at him, a mix of anger and pain in my eyes, before redirecting my attention to the monster.

"You are so ugly," I uttered, but it remained motionless. "You are so ugly, so damn ugly!" I screamed at it. It let out a pained moan, its ginger hair-tentacles attempting to shield its face. I focused on one of its dislocated eyes, searching for a tear, but there was none. I struck its body forcefully, repeating, "You are so hideous and unwanted. Not in the heavens above, not in your stupid forest, and not here with us. You disgust me, you are repulsive!" A surge of rage welled up inside me, and

I became afraid of the intensity of my own emotions. The monster began to howl, emitting a sound filled with profound sadness. I questioned whether I was crying out of desperation for Marco's condition or out of sympathy for the sorrow this creature evoked.

"Once more," Fumito commanded.

"I wish you were dead, you worthless piece of trash," I spat at its face. It started to cry. Two streams of tears flowed down its moist skin, unconnected. I had to act swiftly. "How do I collect the tears?" I asked, but Fumito remained silent. I thought quickly, scanning the room for something to use. However, I found nothing suitable. With so many tears now present, I attempted to gather some on the tip of my finger, but it proved ineffective. Then I noticed a loose piece of fabric hanging from the torn hem of my dress, a casualty of my earlier encounter with Marco. I tore it off and placed it gently on the corner of the monster's right eye. The water-green silk became damp with its tears. Hurriedly, I returned to Marco, who was still alive but barely breathing, teetering on the edge of death. Using both hands, I pried open his mouth, sliding the piece of fabric beneath his tongue.

The monster's anguished howls continued to echo behind me, but I didn't divert my gaze from Marco. At first, nothing appeared to be happening. Then, a series of small hiccups followed one after another. One more. His eyes closed, Marco entered a hiccup-induced stupor, which, given the circumstances, was far from amusing. Yet it somehow provoked laughter within me. He resembled one of those comically intoxicated cartoon characters with flushed cheeks, bloodshot eyes, and vomit splattered everywhere, emitting peculiar little hiccups. He opened his eyes first, then his mouth, and there it was.

A rather large morpho butterfly, its wings shimmering with iridescent blue, emerged from Marco's mouth.

"Bismillahirrahmanirahim," I uttered in Arabic, in awe of this miraculous sight. I glanced at Fumito, who wore a smile of contentment.

However, the butterfly swiftly tumbled lifelessly through the air, descending slowly onto Marco's shirt. "A but—" Marco began, his expression one of astonishment, but he turned over on the floor, regurgitating once more. This time, only white foam was expelled from his mouth. Both Fumito and I rushed to his side, attempting to support him, but he was lifeless in our arms. Fumito appeared unaffected, but I lost control. I lashed out, striking Fumito as if it were his fault that your grandfather had succumbed to a drug overdose. How could he be dead? Was it because of the butterfly, perhaps? Had Fumito deceived me into doing something I shouldn't have?

"He's dead!" I screamed.

Fumito gently squeezed my hand and spoke softly. "Yeter, everyone's butterfly is as unique as their soul. But they all use the same way of restoring life. Watch closely." I turned my attention to Fumito, eager to understand what was about to unfold.

As if in response to Fumito's words, the morpho on Marco's chest started to flutter its wings with renewed vigor. In a mesmerizing display, it soared through the air, making its way back to his lifeless body and landing on his chin with horrifying precision. It was a sinister insect, its presence unsettling rather than beautiful. With a flicker of its wings, it unveiled a mesmerizing display of iridescent blue. As it fluttered them once, then twice, the many hues of blue hidden within them were revealed in a breathtaking dance of color.

Its thin, spindly legs made minute, delicate steps along the contours of Marco's chin, crawling closer and closer to his slightly parted lips. The creature's body was an eerie spectacle that seemed more like an artist's grotesque creation than a natural phenomenon. An insect shaman acting upon a dark ritual to bring a man back from dead…

The butterfly's two compound eyes, each bearing countless minuscule lenses, roamed in every direction. They observed the world around them with an alien curiosity, devoid of any semblance of grace. Advancing farther, the butterfly extended its repulsive antennae, feeling its way through the alien landscape of Marco's skin. Its exploration was both uncanny and sickening to behold. I could not watch the scene. It was all too much for me. My husband was dead, and we were placing all our hopes in one insect on his mouth.

With an almost malevolent drive, it thrust its proboscis into Marco's mouth, wedging itself between the parted lips. A twisted sight unfolded as the creature sipped greedily, drawing forth Marco's bubbling saliva like a perverse meal. I felt it was almost feeding on the dead body of my love.

I imagined that, as it traversed the wet terrain of his lips, it was leaving a trail of moist footprints. Of course I had no way of telling: my eyes could not adjust to that fine a detail. Marco's saliva clung to the butterfly, coating its legs with a glistening layer of mucus. This monster seemed to have a desire to infiltrate Marco's insides, its actions an unsettling dance that straddled the line between the surreal and the nightmarish.

It finally took another step and passed through the bubbling sea of saliva into the dark abyss of Marco's mouth. It left a delicate and shimmering blue dust that sparkled like stardust on his lips.

I held my breath, my heart pounding with anticipation. A moment passed, and then I saw it: a faint movement, a subtle rise and fall of Marco's chest. Color slowly returned to his face, and his eyes batted open. He was alive.

I couldn't contain my joy and relief. Tears streamed down my cheeks as Marco sat up, looking around with a mixture of confusion and wonder. Fumito's claim had come to life before our eyes. The butterfly had brought Marco's heart back, reviving him from the brink of death.

Overwhelmed with gratitude, I embraced Fumito, thanking him for his wisdom and guidance. The room was filled with a renewed hope. The butterfly, having completed its extraordinary task, flew away, disappearing into the depths of the shrine.

Marco, still in disbelief, reached out and held my hand, his grip firm and full of life. We knew that this experience had changed us forever. We had witnessed a miracle, a testament to the power of the unseen and the resilience of the human spirit. And as we stood there, surrounded by the echoes of life and the enchantment of the butterfly's visit, we understood that our journey was far from over.

In that moment of joy and newfound purpose, I shared my revelation with Fumito. "Perihan," I said, with confidence. "If our paths ever cross again, you can call me Perihan."

Fumito nodded, his eyes filled with understanding

and acceptance. "Perihan," he repeated, as if savoring the taste of my new name. "A name fit for the Queen of All Fairies."

As we stepped out of the room, I felt a surge of energy coursing through me. The monarchs continued to dance around us, their delicate wings creating a dizzying display of colors. I knew that my journey had just begun, that I had been given a gift—the ability to bring life back from the brink of death.

With Marco by my side, his hand tightly clasped in mine, we walked out of that shrine, ready to embrace the unknown. I had shed the weight of my past, of the name that had held me back, and embraced a new identity, a new purpose.

Perihan, the Queen of All Fairies—for that was what my new name meant in Turkish—ready to explore the mysteries of the world and use my newfound power to bring hope and healing to those in need. With the monarchs as my loyal companions, I embarked on a path that would forever shape my destiny.

And as I looked back one last time, taking in the shrine and the magic it held, I whispered a silent prayer of gratitude—for the second chance at life, for the love that had brought Marco back, and for the profound transformation that had taken place within me.

15

As Riccardo delved deeper into the pages, confusion swirled in his mind. The revelations about Maurizio's circus past and the connections to Perihan's draft left him perplexed. Each chapter he read added to the intricate web of connected stories. He admired Perihan's skill in turning mundane information into a captivating plotline but couldn't help but be surprised at the level of detail she had poured into the narrative. It almost felt as if she had set out to write her autobiography but had instead transformed it into a work of fantastic literature—or at least attempted to do so, he thought.

With the book still in his hands, Riccardo reached for his phone, intending to call Lorenzo and suggest going out for drinks. However, just as he was about to dial, a knock on his door startled him. It was as if someone had caught him in the middle of an intimate act. He leaped off the bed, hastily shoving the book into the narrow crevice next to the library. He winced as he watched the first few pages of the book fold and tear in the process, disappearing into the dark recess.

Wanting to buy himself some time, Riccardo called out,

"Give me a second!" and swung the door open slightly. In the dimly lit corridor, he saw Licia standing there. "Is it dinner time already?" he asked, hoping for a brief reprieve.

Licia stiffened, absent-mindedly brushing invisible crumbs off her skirt. "No, there's still an hour until dinner, but we have an unexpected guest who insists on seeing you," she explained, her voice filled with annoyance. "I tried to send him away, but he claims you invited him over."

A fleeting moment of confusion passed through Riccardo's mind as he tried to recall inviting anyone. Then, a spark of recognition flickered in his thoughts. *It must be Lorenzo*, he surmised, and a rush of happiness washed over him. "Perhaps it's Lorenzo? Send him upstairs," he instructed Licia, reluctant to open the door wider.

Licia hesitated, clearly uncomfortable with the idea of unannounced guests. "Upstairs? We're not accustomed to guests who arrive without prior notice. Maybe you could come down to see what he wants?" she suggested, her stance growing even stiffer.

Riccardo pushed back, trying to assert his authority. "I'm sure you'll get used to it. In my house, guests are always welcome. Send him upstairs, please. I'll see you later at dinner," he replied, the tone of his voice indicating his resolve. Just before closing the door in Licia's face, he couldn't resist a final jab, "Oh, and don't forget to set an extra place. Our guest might like to join us for dinner."

As he shut the door, a surge of anger welled up within him, seemingly out of nowhere. He felt threatened by this old friend of his grandmother, how she still wanted to micromanage everything. He couldn't wait to see Perihan's will—and Licia's face when she found out who the sole owner of the house was.

Riccardo checked his armpits and tested his breath by

breathing into his palm, a nervous habit he had picked up, before Lorenzo's arrival. A flutter of excitement danced in his stomach, but he tried to ignore it. He wanted to smoke but decided against it. He initially sat on his bed but quickly stood up, then moved to the edge of the window before changing his mind and opening the door to his room. As the door creaked open, the sound of solitary footsteps echoed up the stairs.

Riccardo leaned over the threshold to catch a glimpse of Lorenzo, and his warm smile instantly brightened Riccardo's face. Lorenzo carried a small box in his hand and said, "I should've called, but I thought I would just come by and try my luck."

"I'm glad you came," Riccardo replied, leaving his room to accompany Lorenzo to the Art Deco window door in the corridor. The door led to a spacious balcony, and together they stepped out into the crisp afternoon. The view of the garden was disappointing, with the dilapidated greenhouse and a lack of flowers anywhere.

Taking a seat on the comfortable chairs, Lorenzo handed Riccardo the box, but Riccardo's attention remained fixed on the terrace. "I swear this is not how I imagined the garden from outside," Lorenzo remarked. "It's such a stark contrast to the lush street it resides in, don't you think?"

"Apparently, it wasn't always like this," Riccardo replied, recalling the encounter with the strange woman who had trespassed earlier that day and expressed shock at the state of the garden. "Everyone talks about it as if it was a piece of heaven, with tuberose flowers cascading like waterfalls, but all I see is emptiness."

Lorenzo looked down at his hands and said, "I've always had a green thumb. I love taking care of plants, but I never had a garden like this, of course," he added with a smile. As he smiled, a small dimple appeared on his cheek, making him even more attractive. Riccardo loved Lorenzo's deep blue eyes, now resembling a wavy ocean under a potential thunderstorm, filled with darkness and curiosity.

Riccardo tried to avert his gaze, knowing that when their eyes met, unfamiliar emotions surged within him. "I'd love it if you could help me fix the garden," he said, finally tearing his eyes away from Lorenzo. Opening the box, he discovered the two cannoli desserts. "For later!" he exclaimed. "Would you like to stay for dinner?"

"Oh, no, no, don't worry." Lorenzo initially declined, but Riccardo insisted, mentioning how spending time reminiscing about the past with his grandmother's friends was tiresome. "I'd love to have a guest for dinner if you don't have other plans," Riccardo added.

Lorenzo smiled again, somewhat shyly, and pulled out his phone from his pocket. His posture changed, his voice lightened as he said, "I also wanted to come by because there's something I thought you should see, but I didn't want to show it to you in front of my mom." He scrolled through his phone, adjusted the volume, and handed it to Riccardo.

Uncertain of what to expect, Riccardo took the cell and pressed Play to watch the video on Lorenzo's phone. The fifteen-second video was from the perspective of someone standing on the street where Perihan resided. "It's our street," Riccardo mumbled, captivated by the unfolding scene. Tall trees lined the road, creating a gloomy yet picturesque setting, seemingly accompanied by rain. People were engrossed in recording something with their mobiles, their attention focused on the grand villa.

Suddenly, Perihan emerged onto the street, carrying shopping bags. Riccardo brought the phone closer to catch more details. Perihan glanced at the crowd, puzzled by their intense fascination. The bags slipped from her hands as she discovered what had caught their attention. Desperation and terror washed over her, and she started running back toward her house, her shoes splattered with mud. As the camera panned upward, a breathtaking sight unfolded: a massive swarm of butterflies flitted through the sky above her house. Their vibrant colors and patterns created a surreal spectacle. Perihan, now inside, slammed the door shut and let out a startled scream. The video ended, leaving the viewer yearning for more insight into this intriguing moment.

Riccardo watched the video repeatedly, then turned to Lorenzo with a puzzled expression. Lorenzo remained silent, his eyes locked with Riccardo's. "When is this from?" Riccardo asked.

"I believe it was a day or two before her death, maybe less than a week ago. The video went viral on social media because of the abundance of butterflies," Lorenzo explained. "I read the comments, and many mention that these butterflies, like some birds, migrate between countries at certain times of the year. Perhaps it was just a natural phenomenon that happened here."

"But she screams," Riccardo added.

"True, but we don't see what happens inside the garden once she enters. Considering the state of the garden and how people remember it," Lorenzo remarked as he stood up to get a better view from the balcony, "maybe she screamed at the sight of butterflies devouring all the flowers or something. I thought I should show you because you mentioned her unexpected heart attack. Perhaps witnessing something so wild in her own home had an impact. Maybe I should have kept it to myself," he trailed off.

"No, no, I appreciate it," Riccardo replied slowly, his thoughts racing. He regretted lying to Lorenzo earlier about the cause of Perihan's death. Now that he knew she had taken her own life by swallowing pills, he wondered if there were a connection to the butterflies in her book. Did anyone else witness the butterflies when Perihan was present, or was she alone? It seemed unlikely, since there was usually someone around the house. Why hadn't anyone mentioned it to him? Lost in a whirlwind of thought, Riccardo struggled to undersatand what was really happening.

"I should ask Licia or Maurizio," Riccardo muttered to himself, considering his options.

Lorenzo overheard and suggested, "They might be able to tell you what really happened." His attention then turned to the greenhouse, where two maids emerged, locking the door behind them. "What's in there?" Lorenzo asked, pointing toward the greenhouse. Riccardo joined him at the balcony's edge, peering down at the structure.

"As far as I know, there's nothing inside," Riccardo responded, though his mind wandered elsewhere. He pondered Barbara's mention of the circus, Perihan's draft referencing it, the viral butterfly swirl on TikTok, and the abundance of butterflies around the house, particularly in Perihan's room. Strangely, he felt a newfound trust in Lorenzo, possibly due to his own isolation and lack of people he could confide in. Riccardo took Lorenzo's hand and pulled him back into the house, leaving Lorenzo puzzled about their destination.

"Where are we—" Lorenzo began to ask, but they found themselves back in the corridor.

"Come with me," Riccardo whispered, surveying both ends of the corridor before guiding Lorenzo forward. "We can't stay for long, but you have to see the collection of butterflies. Maybe there's a link between these and the video you showed me?" They moved cautiously, careful to avoid making noise. Riccardo led Lorenzo to Perihan's room, opened the door, gestured for his friend to enter, and closed the door behind them.

"Quickly," Riccardo urged in a hushed tone, leading Lorenzo behind the silk screen. Lorenzo's eyes darted around the room, captivated by the beauty and intricate details. From numerous crystal bottles atop a vanity to the original Picasso painting on the wall, the room exuded a magical aura. However, Riccardo pushed Lorenzo back out despite his desire to analyze every detail. Once they were outside, they returned to the balcony in Riccardo's room.

Lorenzo was about to speak, but Riccardo placed a finger on his lips, silencing him. "Take a moment to absorb it all," he said, contemplating whether to show Lorenzo the draft of Perihan's novel and seek his opinion. Lorenzo's deep blue eyes remained fixed on Riccardo's. Their connection was interrupted by a tap on the glass door from one of the maids, who announced, "Dinner's ready!"

Leaving the balcony, they descended the stairs, Riccardo taking the box with the cannoli with him.

The dinner passed without any company joining them at the table, leaving emptiness in the air. Lorenzo didn't seem to mind the solitude, but Riccardo grew increasingly irritated, feeling as though they were leeches clinging to a shelter that no longer belonged to them. Finishing their meal in silence, Riccardo couldn't shake off the fear that someone might have been eavesdropping on their conversation.

After they went back upstairs, Riccardo led Lorenzo into his room and motioned for him to sit on the bed. Riccardo paced nervously, his hands fidgeting with a desire to smoke a cigarette. He knew he needed to confide in someone about his recent actions and seek advice.

"I have a secret I need to share with someone," Riccardo

finally spoke, staring at the carpet. "It's been weighing on me since I arrived. My grandmother...she was working on a novel before she passed away. I stumbled upon the draft by accident on the day I arrived."

Lorenzo's smile was warm and curious. "It must be in the genes," he chuckled lightly, placing an arm around Riccardo's shoulder as he joined Lorenzo on the bed. "Tell me more."

Taking a deep breath, Riccardo continued. "I took the draft without telling anyone. Soon enough, I realized that everyone was searching for it, whispering among themselves at the funeral and even speculating on who might have stolen it."

Intrigued, Lorenzo asked, "Is it really that good? Have you read it?"

Riccardo's eyes lit up, a blend of enthusiasm and guilt crossing his face. "It's incredible. Written from her perspective, it starts as a sort of memoir but quickly transforms into a wild fantasy. It draws inspiration from the mundane things that happen here—the greenhouse, the butterflies. And the writing itself is engaging. It's a shame she never submitted it anywhere—someone might have published it."

Lorenzo nodded, captivated by the tale. "Interesting! It's wonderful that you get to discover this hidden talent of your grandmother. But what do you plan to do with it?"

Uncertainty clouded Riccardo's expression. "I'm not sure yet. I haven't finished reading it, and I'm not even sure if it's complete. There are some plot holes and parts that are a bit too extreme to be believable. I checked if she had written anything else, but I couldn't find anything online. Perhaps it was just a pastime for her."

Suddenly, Lorenzo's hand rested on Riccardo's shoulder. "Why don't you turn it into something of your own? You've been struggling with writer's block, and this material could be the breakthrough you need."

Riccardo's eyes widened, a spark of an idea igniting within him. He hadn't considered this possibility before. The hand-written manuscript with scattered handwritten notes was the only copy, and its contents remained a secret known only to those currently searching for it. It could be an opportunity to collaborate with his agent, a chance to submit something before the looming deadline.

A thrill surged through Riccardo's veins, overwhelming him with a surge of emotions. Without a second thought, he turned to Lorenzo and, propelled by his newfound inspiration, pressed his lips against Lorenzo's in a passionate kiss.

16

After Lorenzo left, Riccardo went out to the balcony to smoke and decided to text his agent, Louis. He took out his phone and, without much thought, wrote I have it. It was around one in the morning, and Riccardo thought his agent must be asleep. However, as soon as he hit Send, he saw his agent's name pop up on his screen. The agent was calling.

"Tell me you were not drunk, nor high, nor trying to prank me," Louis demanded.

"No, I wasn't. I didn't tell you much, and I'm sorry about it, but I have been working on a new idea," Riccardo confessed as he lit a cigarette. He needed to share his secret with someone and seek advice.

"Another story?" The agent's voice lacked enthusiasm, aware of the challenges that came with Riccardo's initial attempts at plotting. "Give me a hint."

"I can't tell you much. You'll need to read it, but think *magic*, think *butterflies*, and think *fantasy*," Riccardo explained, his eyes drawn to the faint light emanating from the greenhouse and the shadows dancing on the dirty windows. He squinted, trying to see, but the night was too dark, revealing nothing.

The agent's tone grew stiff. "Riccardo, I am fed up with your indecisiveness and your half-assed projects. I need a full synopsis by this weekend, or…you won't have an agent anymore," the agent warned before hanging up.

A drop of sweat trickled from Riccardo's hairline down to his forehead and gently ran along his cheek. He still had more pages to read, and the agent's request for a full synopsis added to his stress. He didn't think he could submit the whole thing as it was; he needed to make a few modifications to protect the work, in case there were another copy somewhere. He thought about Lorenzo's phone and the viral TikTok video: perhaps it could serve as an intriguing first chapter. Extinguishing his cigarette on the balcony with his foot, he went down to the garden to see what was happening inside the greenhouse.

Once there, he approached the greenhouse door and saw one of the maids coming out with two heavy buckets covered in muslin cloth. Riccardo remembered offering help before, but the girl had declined. He felt bothered by their secrecy, so he pushed the door open and entered the greenhouse. At the end of the long corridor, he spotted Maurizio, bathed in light. The interior was divided into rows of long, metallic tables with giant vases holding what appeared to be dead branches or remnants of past flowers. Riccardo's attention was drawn to a small, chimneylike structure that provided the light.

"The light…" Riccardo started.

Maurizio completed his thought. "That never goes out. I knew you would come here, sooner or later. You were fixated on some metaphorical meaning, but it was just a small chimney, used to maintain the right temperature for the tuberose flowers we used to have here. So yes, everything died, and nothing is special anymore, but it wasn't always like this." Maurizio sighed, turning around, and went back to where Riccardo had come from.

Realizing Riccardo wasn't following him, Maurizio called out, "I want to show you Perihan's butterfly collection, if you don't mind."

Riccardo was about to thank him and mention that he had already seen it, having secretly entered Perihan's room twice before—once alone to investigate and eventually steal the book, and earlier that night with Lorenzo to show him the butterflies. But, to make it appear natural, he simply nodded and added, "I thought you would never give me a full tour of…my house." Maurizio visibly flinched at that, but they didn't exchange any further words as they went back inside together.

17

As Lorenzo arrived at the bar, he noticed a few teenagers standing outside, chatting, and holding plastic glasses, probably filled with gin and soda. Apart from those patrons, the bar seemed to be closing, with only a few customers tonight. He entered and saw his mother behind the cash register talking to someone on the phone, her makeup smudged as she tried to wipe away her tears with a white napkin she found in the kitchen.

"Thank you, Licia. Of course… Of course, I'll never forget…" she said before hanging up.

"Mom, is everything all right?" Lorenzo asked, walking behind the counter to console her.

Barbara looked at him with teary eyes and burst into sobs, embracing her son tightly. "Mom, come on. What's going on?" he pressed, scanning the surroundings for any signs of trouble, but everything seemed fine. One of the teenagers glanced through the window, witnessing their embrace, and smiled before turning back to his friends.

"It's nothing. Don't worry… I was talking to Licia, and I

just had a flood of memories come back to me from when you were a kid," she managed to say between her sobs.

"But why? I'm not a kid anymore. I'm taller than you, Mom. Stop crying," Lorenzo insisted, feeling helpless as he had no idea what had upset his mother. "Please, tell me what happened."

"Licia…" Barbara snorted. "Well, Licia called to tell me that you went to Riccardo's house, and that you might help them find some book or something."

"Licia, the woman at Riccardo's?" Lorenzo's eyebrows furrowed in confusion.

"Yes, Perihan's best friend… She called to tell me that they're searching for a book that is very important, and they believe Riccardo might have it. I didn't want to believe he would steal something that wasn't his to begin with but…you never know. I ran into him earlier at Moonbox. Well, I had to get a few things from the supermarket and saw him sitting by himself reading what seemed to be a manuscript. I went in to say hi. I could tell he seemed surprised. I have no idea what the book was about, but apparently it was very important to Perihan. Licia said since you are his only friend, they thought you could help," Barbara explained, her voice trembling with emotion.

"Mom, slow down. I just met the guy. I have no idea what you're talking about," Lorenzo lied, his mind first going to the book Riccardo had mentioned, then to the passionate kiss they'd shared on the bed before he left.

"Does Riccardo know that you knew his grandmother?" Barbara asked.

"No, I didn't tell him. I didn't know how to bring it up without having to go through all the past drama… She cured me or something, right? You said so. I don't remember much.

I was just a kid," Lorenzo responded, memories from his childhood resurfacing.

"She cured you of cancer, and I'll forever be grateful to her, even after her death. Is there no way you can get this book for them? We owe this to them. They gave you your life back… My love, my son, you wouldn't be here today without Perihan," Barbara pleaded.

"He didn't mention any book to me, but I promise I'll talk to him. Now, please stop crying," Lorenzo said, trying to comfort his mother. "Let's go. There are no more customers left for tonight." He assisted Barbara in settling the bills, locking the door, and they walked back home together. On their way, all Lorenzo could think about were Riccardo's soft lips.

18

It wasn't Riccardo's first time entering Perihan's room, yet his fascination with the decor was stronger than ever. His eyes wandered from the Picasso to the vanity with its crystal bottles and the luxurious silk screen that separated the room from the enchanting area behind where butterflies rested under the glass domes.

"As you can see, she had impeccable taste," Maurizio remarked, gesturing toward the room in general. Riccardo nodded, trying to discover new things he hadn't noticed during his previous, hurried visits to this room.

"This room has such a distinct scent," Riccardo commented, inhaling the tuberose that permeated everything.

"Fracas. It was her signature scent," Maurizio replied as he walked behind the screen. "Come, take a look at this."

Riccardo followed Maurizio, and they stood before the domes containing the butterflies.

"I'm quite knowledgeable about these," Maurizio declared confidently, then proceeded to name each butterfly species one by one. "Papilio palinurus in the next dome... Genus caligo, my favorite, as well as Cristina's. Cymothoe sangaris, twin butterflies in what Perihan used to call Valentino Red, two iridescent morphos, a light blue large blue, and finally, the most magnificent of them all, Queen Alexandra…"

Riccardo found the sight mesmerizing, each dome holding its own mystery, but there was one little detail he could not share with Maurizio without revealing he had already been in the room: one dome, the one with the blue butterfly, phengaris arion, was missing from the shelves.

"Why did she have such a fascination with taxidermy and butterflies?" Riccardo asked, his mind still busy with potential answers for the missing dome.

"Oh, it's like when Alejandro Jodorowsky talked about how awakening was not a thing… That if the caterpillar kept thinking only about turning into a butterfly and designing its wings and antennae, it wouldn't have really changed. It's important for the butterfly to come out and that the caterpillar accepts its disappearance during the metamorphosis. I couldn't have said it better. Reflect upon this," Maurizio replied with a wink, before leading Riccardo out of the area and back to the main part of the room.

"Take one if you like," Maurizio offered, gesturing to the crystal bottles.

Riccardo shrugged and, without much thought, responded, "No need, they're all empty." However, he immediately realized his mistake as Maurizio noticed.

"How do you know they're empty?" Maurizio asked curiously.

Riccardo stammered for a moment, searching for an excuse to evade trouble, but he took a bit too long to respond and finally shrugged. "I don't know. They just look empty," he said, picking up one of the bottles, removed its cap, and turned it over. Nothing came out. "See?" he said, placing it back.

Maurizio nodded, bidding Riccardo goodnight and mentioning that it was quite late. All Riccardo desired was to return to his room and finish reading Perihan's novel, so that he could send the synopsis to Louis before the deadline. He made his way to his room.

"He has the book..." Maurizio whispered to himself in a dark tone, as he descended the stairs into the darkness below to go inform all the others.

Time had run out, and so had his patience.

PERIHAN'S MANUSCRIPT

We left Casa Mollino right after the incident. Your grandfather had returned to life, albeit in a weakened state, and I was in disarray, my gown shredded and stained with blood, my makeup smudged. Additionally, we had the presence of the deformed monster in its human body to contend with. As Fumito headed to the living room to celebrate his birthday with the others, I seized the opportunity to discreetly escort Marco and the monster out of the house.

Thankfully, everyone was still immersed in the euphoria of Fumito's birthday celebration, their attention diverted from the door. I guided Marco and the monster into the elevator and descended to the ground floor. Stepping out into the silent garden beneath the starlit sky, I knew that leaving the monster behind would have been the easy choice, but I couldn't bring myself to do it. I had just witnessed a miracle, and it had awakened something within me.

For the first time in my life, I felt the possibility of meaning something to people, of being seen and valued, even as an immigrant in a foreign land against all odds.

So, purposefully, I urged them both toward the waiting car parked outside, retrieved the keys from Marco's coat, and settled into the driver's seat.

During the two-hour journey back home, we remained mostly silent. One of us was a resurrected man, still grappling with the shock of returning from the clutches of death. The other was a transformed monster, now in human form but undoubtedly carrying the weight of its past. And then there was me, brimming with anticipation for what fate, or Kader as we call it, had in store for me.

As I turned on the radio, a John Denver song filled the car, its lyrics resonating with my newfound sense of self. Today was, indeed, the first day of the rest of my life.

Overwhelmed with emotions, I couldn't help but shout in exhilaration at the monster's reflection in the rearview mirror.

"Perihan! Perihan! Perihan!" I exclaimed, embracing the name that now defined me. "All hail Perihan, the Queen of All Fairies!"

And so, as we journeyed on, the car carrying us toward an uncertain future, I held on to the transformative power of my new name and the possibilities that lay ahead. This was the first day of the rest of my life, and I was ready to seize it with all the strength and magic within me.

That night, as we arrived home, I asked Marco to retrieve the keys to the greenhouse in the garden. He moved with a slowness reminiscent of one of the zombies from George A. Romero's films. It would take some time for him to fully come back to life in his own body, I presumed. Meanwhile, I guided the monster out of the car and led it into the garden. It remained silent, its face concealed by a cascade of wavy ginger hair, its floral-print Gucci dress appearing out of place in the moonlight.

Ah, the moonlight… It cast an enchanting glow over the glass facade of the greenhouse. I struggled to recall the last time I had ventured inside. Neither Marco nor I had a particular passion for gardening, but when we moved in, the greenhouse was already there, so we left it untouched. Now it seemed like a suitable place to keep the monster. After the exposure to its dark side earlier that night, I was hesitant to have it sleep under the same roof as us. Come morning, I would figure out a solution. Besides, I had to be cautious with Marco as well. Did those who visit the other side ever return unchanged? The thought of sharing a bed with a zombie sent shivers down my spine.

"Here… I feel much better now," Marco said in his usual affectionate tone. He glanced at my tattered dress in horror, starting to express concern about his mother's reaction. However, his attention then shifted to the monster standing beside us. "Oh, are you okay?" he asked.

"Marco, I promise I'll explain everything tomorrow. Just help me with one more thing, and then we can take a shower, go to bed, and rest," I replied, hoping to allay his worries. He seemed uncertain but ultimately nodded in agreement.

I gently took the keys from his cold hands. "Come," I beckoned to the monster. It followed me silently, resembling a shadow, as we entered the greenhouse. I inserted the key into the rusty lock, struggling for a moment before finally opening it. The air inside carried the scent of earth, and loneliness. It was evident that nobody had set foot in this place for a long time. There were no flowers, no vases, no traces of life from earlier days. Under the moonlight, the thick waves of the monster's ginger hair seemed like flames from the depths of hell. The angel I had believed it to be was now burning with an inner fire. I sighed, overwhelmed by sadness.

"You will stay here tonight. Tomorrow, I will come to take you inside. I'm sorry about earlier…and thank you for bringing him back," I murmured, feeling a pang of sorrow at the sight of this peculiar creature. It emitted some indiscernible sounds, and as I turned my back and headed for the door, a few colorful butterflies fluttered in, as if expressing gratitude. With a simple thank-you, I had infused a touch of magic into the space. I stole one final glance at the monster before locking the door of the greenhouse.

Returning home to your grandfather, I tried to sleep but found it impossible. Perihan had just been born, and her energy surged within me, making it impossible to close my eyes. I took a long shower, steam enveloping my body. With my damp, heated flesh, I entered the bedroom to awaken Marco. Desire consumed me. He had just returned from the clutches of death, reborn anew. How could he possibly sleep? As soon as he opened his eyes and his strong hands caressed my warm, wet skin, I lowered my face to his and sensuously licked his lips. He sat up, his gaze intense, grasping my breasts with both hands and showering them with kisses. Our room was bathed only in the moonlight that filtered through the window. Under its luminous glow, we experienced the wildest, most passionate encounter of our relationship.

Upon awakening, I hastily threw on a robe and dashed outside to the greenhouse. My curiosity was insatiable.

I needed to see if it was still there, behind the locked door, waiting for me to come and rescue it. The morning greeted me with its usual coldness, accompanied by the dull, gray light that enveloped Milan. The distant chirping of birds reminded me that I wasn't alone; life existed beyond these walls.

Unlocking the rusty door, I stepped inside, my pink slippers sinking into the dark brown earth. Overnight, something had transformed within this space. An intoxicating scent, thick and sweet, assailed my senses. Its familiarity eluded me momentarily. As I scanned the area, I discovered the source: flowers had bloomed overnight, scattered haphazardly across the soil inside the glasshouse.

Yet perhaps it is not accurate to call them simply *flowers*. In my eyes at that time, it was as if life had blossomed within this long-neglected space, dear Riccardo. Life— tuberoses, that was the name of the flowers. Tuberoses had sprouted from the earth in various corners of the greenhouse—some solitary, others in small clusters. The once-lifeless soil I had walked upon the night before now teemed with green stems reaching skyward, crowned by the unmistakable white blooms of tuberoses. Had death itself been transformed into a garden of flowers? I couldn't discern. The fragrance was so potent that it became difficult to breathe.

"Hello?" I called out amid the sea of tuberoses. "Hello? Where are you hiding? Where did these tuberoses come from?" I yearned for explanations, for a miracle a day proved too much for the simple life I had grown accustomed to. Circling the group of flowers, I searched for my monster. Finally, I found it, lying at the far end of the structure. Kneeling beside it, I gently pushed back its hair, revealing a face where the mouth and nose had returned to their rightful places, while the eyes remained widely spaced…and moist. It must have wept throughout the night. I watched as the final teardrop clung to the corner of its eye before slowly falling to the ground.

"Please don't cry. It's a new day today," I said, attempting to console it. I couldn't fathom why I felt a surge of affection toward this peculiar creature. As the tear landed, something stirred beneath the earth. The dark soil shifted, and if not for my fear, I would have thought it to be an insect. With trepidation, I stood up, not taking my eyes off that spot for a second.

A saturated green shoot emerged, pushing itself upward, reminiscent of the magic bean in the fairy tale where it had been discarded, only to watch it grow into a magical ladder toward the heavens. The shoot grew several inches, sprouting leaves and finally revealing beautiful white flowers: tuberoses. Their unmistakable fragrance filled the air. It took me a moment to piece it together, but the connection became apparent: the tears that granted a second chance at life could also revive the barren earth, giving birth to tuberose flowers. Well, we would later discover that the tears weren't directly linked to the tuberoses—they simply revived whatever had once existed in those patches of earth. In the case of our greenhouse, it was a room filled with those flowers.

I plucked one of them and brought it close to my nose, savoring its heady aroma before crushing it between my fingers. With the oily residue, I massaged my neck, leaving behind a trace of the scent.

"I must return to the house now. It's rather chilly here," I informed the creature, my mind preoccupied with thoughts of Fumito's mention of circus people from the previous night. What had he meant by that? He had promised I would find out, but when? As I left the greenhouse, I made a mental note that I would have to create a small stove to maintain a consistent temperature and keep the tuberoses alive with warmth.

No, Fumito didn't send anything that day, or the next, or the one after that. The waiting was driving me mad. Without a complete understanding of the situation, I was hesitant to take any action. I needed information, knowledge to delve deeper before I could put my plans into motion. That's how it had always been for me, even back in school: a diligent student, the teacher's favorite, striving for excellence.

On the fourth morning, Marco looked out from our bedroom window. "Did you see the greenhouse?" he asked.

"What about it?" I replied.

"I can only see white through the glass walls. The monster seems to keep crying. Yesterday, when I took out the garbage, I could hear its weeping. I thought maybe we should set it free."

"Set it free for what?" I countered. "You are the living testament to what it can do for us, for others... I'm not letting it go. After all, I was the one who found it in the first place."

Just then, the door of our bedroom opened, and Licia, our nineteen-year-old maid, entered, carrying a tray with two plates of omelets. Her green eyes sparkled with concern as she carefully placed the tray on the bed, ensuring not to spill any orange juice on the pristine linen. Licia had been working for me for almost a year, and I had come to rely on her loyalty and trustworthiness. Despite her small figure, she possessed a surprising strength and resilience. She seemed concerned. "I brought you both breakfast," she said.

"The gardener was supposed to come this morning, but I postponed it until you figure out what to do with it..." Licia's eyes revealed her worry. She didn't know much about the monster, only that she had seen "a strange girl" sleeping amid the tuberose garden. I had told Licia that she was a homeless girl we had taken in to care for. When questioned about the tuberoses, I struggled to come up with a plausible explanation. "Marco's mother...she came by on your day off with her own gardener to plant everything. She thought we should have a fragrant flower bed at the entrance..." I hoped my fabricated story would satisfy her curiosity.

"Fragrant? It stinks. People are complaining about the smell three streets over," Licia had grumbled, expressing her disdain for the overwhelming scent of the tuberoses. She had a valid point. Despite the closed doors of the greenhouse, the heavy fragrance still managed to permeate the air, finding its way into our home through the open windows. Over time, I would grow accustomed to the tuberose's heavy sweetness, my mind associating it with the miraculous presence of Perihan.

Interrupting our conversation, Marco asked about any incoming mail. Licia informed him of a parcel from a foreigner, suggesting it was meant for me. Marco seemed puzzled by the mention of a foreigner, questioning who it could be. Licia's mention of the name Fumito got my attention. Finally, a sign of communication from him! Without uttering a word, I swiftly left the room, leaving Marco and Licia behind.

Making my way downstairs, I located the unassuming yellow package resting atop the dark cherry table.

Fumito's name was elegantly handwritten in one corner in thick, purple ink. The weight of the parcel hinted at something substantial, perhaps a book or a significant document. Carefully, I began to unravel the mystery, savoring the anticipation.

As I opened the package, my eyes fell upon a note, confirming my earlier suspicions. Fumito had indeed chosen me as the recipient of his knowledge, as he had alluded to before. The realization sent a surge of thrill through my veins. Fumito, in his enigmatic manner, had found me worthy of receiving the wisdom he possessed about immortality.

Perihan, remember my mention of the circus? Terrible things happened there... Maurizio and Elettra abducted the monster after I set her free in that Mexican forest. I know for a fact that Maurizio is still alive and lives in Milan. The only person who has seen him since the incident is Cristina; she owns a small bookshop on Corso Magenta. I'll leave her address for you in case you'd like to meet her... Good luck. F.

Within the parcel, aside from the note, I discovered a small, weathered poster from an old circus. It was a captivating piece of advertisement, though time had not been kind to its vibrant neon colors, leaving them faded and muted. The poster depicted an appealing scene, capturing the essence of the circus with its whimsical illustrations. The focal point was the face of Elettra, rendered like a mask with an enigmatic expression. Her eyes seemed to hold a secret, a hint of the mysterious events that unfolded in that fateful place.

As I examined the address of the bookstore provided by Fumito, a surge of recognition washed over me. Cristina—the name struck a chord in my memory. She was the good soul who had shown me unexpected kindness during my days of struggling to survive on a scholarship in Milan. Back then, I would visit her bookstore, and she would occasionally gift me a book or two, understanding my passion for knowledge despite my limited means. Our paths had never crossed again after those encounters, until now.

Riccardo stopped reading. He took his phone and his fingers danced across his its screen, composing a message to Lorenzo. The weight of the words pressed upon him as he shared his thoughts.

Just read about Cristina in Perihan's book. It's like she's a mirror of the real Cristina. This isn't fiction, Lorenzo. It's more like a memoir. The lines between reality and fantasy are blurred. I can't help but wonder if my grandmother's imagination went wild in her final days…or if something darker was at play…

With the text sent, Riccardo placed his phone on his chest awaiting Lorenzo's response as he went back to reading.

PERIHAN'S MANUSCRIPT

It struck me as serendipitous. The universe had orchestrated this meeting, guiding me back to Cristina, the person who had unknowingly played a part in shaping my journey. The connection between us, dormant for so long, was now rekindled through the enigmatic circumstances surrounding the mysterious girl and the circus.

With a renewed sense of purpose, I understood that meeting Cristina was not only a path to deciphering the secrets of Maurizio and Elettra but also an opportunity to express my gratitude for her past acts of kindness. This convergence of fate, the intertwining of our lives once more, held a deeper significance that I couldn't ignore.

On the day of my meeting with Cristina, I made a detour to the greenhouse, carefully selecting a handful of fragrant tuberoses to take with me. Their delicate petals and dizzying scent would serve as a token of appreciation and a connection to the miracle that had unfolded within those glass walls.

Cristina's bookstore, nestled behind a popular bar on Corso Magenta, exuded an enchanting charm. The small space was full of remnants of theatrical history—posters of past plays, aged book covers, and eclectic artifacts. The weathered parquet floor creaked with every step, bearing witness to the countless visitors who had wandered through its literary sanctuary.

Having moved to Milan two decades ago for love, Cristina's journey as a talented actress had taken an unexpected turn. Hindered by her thick Italian accent, she found herself relegated to minor roles on stage, perpetually cast as an immigrant—an all-too-real reflection of her own life. When questioned about her decision to stay in Milan, she would simply shrug and confess, "Life has its own plans. I find comfort within the pages of these plays… I earn more selling books here than I ever did pursuing my acting career back home. Besides, I still have to support my mother."

During my arduous days as a student, Cristina had extended kindness and support. Her warmth and hospitality left a lasting impression on me, fostering a mix of gratitude and connection.

Now, as I ventured into her bookstore once more, clutching the tuberoses in my hand, I couldn't help but feel a mingling of excitement and nostalgia. The meeting with Cristina held the promise of decoding the enigma surrounding the circus disaster Fumito had alluded to. But beyond that, it was an opportunity to rekindle a bond forged in literature, and to uncover the untold stories hidden within the pages of our lives.

I gazed through the bookstore's window, peering inside before stepping through the door. Cristina was busy talking to someone on the phone. She didn't notice me, while an older woman diligently organized the shelves. Holding the bouquet of tuberoses, I entered, capturing the attention of the girl who turned and greeted me warmly.

"Welcome," she said, setting aside a stack of books on a nearby table. I returned her smile, appreciating her friendly tone. Cristina, still unaware of my arrival, continued her conversation. Seizing the opportunity, I feigned interest in the book selection, leisurely browsing their titles.

"My name is Allegra. Let me know if you need any assistance," the young woman offered kindly.

"Thank you, just browsing," I replied, enjoying the ambience.

Cristina abruptly ended her phone call, audibly frustrated. Taking a deep breath to regain her composure, she raised her head and caught sight of me. Recognition flickered across her face, and her joyous exclamation filled the air.

"Yeter!" Cristina called out, her voice brimming with delight. Unable to perform onstage, she brought her theatrical flair to the bookstore, transforming herself into various characters each day. Her attire, a sequined skirt paired with a simple white T-shirt, hardly registered as I corrected her.

"Perihan... Call me Perihan from now on," I insisted.

"Perihan? What does that signify? When did you change your name?" Cristina asked.

"It means *the queen of all fairies*... It's a long story, but I'll share it with you later. Let me catch my breath first. I practically ran here from the other side of the city," I explained, settling comfortably into the leather chair across from Cristina's cash desk. The room was filled with the strong scent of the flowers I had brought with me. I handed them to Allegra.

"Let me find a vase. These're quite hard to come by in Milan, especially this time of year," Allegra murmured, almost to herself, in a hushed tone. She discovered an unattractive blue vase beneath Cristina's desk and filled it with water from a plastic bottle. She carefully placed the flowers inside, seemingly attempting to inhale their entire fragrance into her lungs with a couple of deep sniffs.

"It's been such a long time since we last saw each other! How have you been?" Cristina inquired of me. We briefly updated each other on our lives before I gathered the courage to ask what I had come for.

"Have you ever heard of a circus accident? A tragedy where children lost their lives? It was apparently a national story," I said. I noticed Cristina flinch in her chair, clearly struck by my words. She glanced around the room, as if searching for an invisible audience. Leaning closer to me, she whispered in the lowest tone.

"Nobody ever talks about that in Milan. Why are you asking me about it now?"

"Fumito instructed me to speak with you," I revealed.

"You met Fumito? How?" Cristina appeared surprised.

"It was at a friend's gathering, a random event... Will you please tell me what happened? I truly need to know," I pleaded. Allegra, positioned close to us, seemed disconnected from the conversation, our faces near each other and our voices hushed.

Cristina straightened up in her chair, briefly glancing at her fingers and then at Allegra before speaking.

"Well," she began, "it was a few years ago. The circus was owned by the most famous showgirl, who reportedly committed suicide shortly after. Many children lost their lives, many—"

"I've heard about it," Allegra interjected. "But I thought it was an urban legend."

Both Cristina and I turned our attention to Allegra, who seemed to possess more knowledge on the matter. She played with her long, black hair as she spoke, her thin figure and deep eyes adding to her mysterious aura.

"Well, you know... Silly things people make up... Like the rumor that there was a monster, discovered by Elettra during her travels, and that it was this monster who consumed some of the children," Allegra shared.

"Was there also an influx of butterflies?" I whispered.

"Oh, yes... I remember that very well," Cristina responded. "For days, we would walk through various streets and witness these groups of orange butterflies circling in the air above us. There were hundreds, maybe thousands, of them in Milan following the tragedy. We became fearful of these beautiful creatures due to their sheer numbers. Beauty can captivate us individually, but in overwhelming swarms, it becomes scary...because it holds such power, you know? Beauty, I mean."

"I'm not here to listen to old tales. Listen to me, Cristina. I'm onto something. I need to meet Maurizio, the sole survivor from that circus," I insisted.

"Maurizio? I've never heard of him. I wish I had kept the newspaper articles about the accident, but I didn't. It was such a heart-wrenching event that I didn't want to keep that energy within these walls. I don't want that kind of darkness here," Cristina explained.

"Do you think anyone else survived the incident?" Allegra asked.

"Apparently, according to Fumito, Maurizio did," I replied.

"Why are you searching for him?" Allegra's curiosity was evident, and I felt that she was intelligent and open-minded. While I didn't want to divulge the entire story, I decided to give her a hint.

"Well...the urban legend may not be just a legend. I believe I saw the monster myself," I hinted cautiously.

Both Allegra and Cristina gasped in disbelief.

"You saw it? What does that mean?" Allegra asked, her eyes wide with intrigue.

"No, it's nothing... Forget I mentioned it. I'll discuss it with Maurizio if our paths ever cross. I should go now. Please let me know if you find anything about Maurizio. It's important to me," I said, leaving my contact number on a piece of paper that I found on the table between us. I handed it to Allegra. "Both of you," I added.

"How could we ever forget, especially now that you've brought all these tuberoses? The scent is overwhelming... Peri-an," Cristina remarked, emphasizing my new name. "You know, you should change your fragrance. This powdery scent doesn't match who you want to be... I mean, the queen of all fairies."

"What do you mean?" I replied, puzzled. I can't recall now the fragrance I used to wear. Although it had a powdery quality, it had also provided me with a sense of comfort and tranquility. My fragrance was not a weapon; it invited others to approach rather than pushed them away.

"Try Fracas, you'll love it. That way, you won't have to carry freshly cut tuberoses everywhere," Cristina suggested, rolling her eyes.

Riccardo's heart raced as he read about Fracas in the text. Things were beginning to add up, and the line between fiction and real life blurred further. He couldn't forget Maurizio's recent mention of Fracas, the same word now staring at him from Perihan's handwritten manuscript. It was undeniable: this story had to be connected to the real world. The word *butterfly* stayed in his thoughts, like an enchanting mystery. He wanted to watch the viral video of Perihan again, that creepy scene with the sky filled with butterflies, a sight that still gave him chills.

He tried searching for the video using his phone, but his efforts were in vain. Frustration mounted. As a last-ditch effort, he downloaded TikTok, registered quickly, and searched with the keywords *butterfly infestation Milan*. The search results appeared, like a message from another time. He found the video—Perihan caught in a digital memory of the strange event. The video showed her initial anger as she scolded people for filming her. But then the camera turned upwards to capture the astonishing sight in the sky—a colorful sea of monarch butterflies.

Perihan, initially defiant, hesitantly ventured into the garden, her movements unsure. The video ended with her letting out a piercing scream, marking the conclusion of this bizarre spectacle. A shiver ran down Riccardo's spine, and his skin tingled. He couldn't bring himself to watch the video again; it was as unsettling as the words he'd been reading. There was something they were not telling him. His grandmother had not simply committed suicide but died in excruciating agony... But if that were so, how come she looked okay in the open-casket ceremony? Or had she? The more Riccardo thought about it, the less of a precise answer he could come up with: in the end, he hadn't seen her up close.

His brow became damp with sweat, and his heart raced in his ears as he placed his phone on the bed. Lorenzo hadn't responded, and his phone calls went unanswered. Unresolved questions swirled in his mind, but the manuscript compelled him to read further. Before he concentrated on the words in front of him, he remembered once again the words of the home-less man at Moonbox. "Nobody ever suspects the butterfly..."

PERIHAN'S MANUSCRIPT

I dismissed her comment with a wave of my hand, embraced both, and left the store. Cristina had handed me a book of letters from Nabokov to his wife before I departed. Outside, the sun had disappeared completely behind the clouds, casting a gloomy atmosphere over Milan. I glanced at the book, which featured a black-and-white photograph of Vladimir Nabokov carrying a net, ready to catch butterflies. The circular plastic frame was affixed to a white net and came with a long stick to extend it toward the fluttering creatures. Lost in the book, I failed to notice the uneven cobblestone in front of me, stumbling and nearly falling face-first into its pages, causing my legs to scrape against the pavement and my socks to tear.

"Damn it," I swore, brushing off the dirt from my

socks and picking up the books I had bought from Cristina. I surveyed the area, searching for a store where I could purchase new socks. Across the street, I spotted a small lingerie store. I crossed the deserted road and entered.

"How can I assist you?" the girl behind the counter asked, her smile appearing rather cold.

"Oh, you see…" I pointed at my torn socks. "I want a new pair of these," I stated matter-of-factly. However, my attention was drawn to a pair of black fishnets hanging loosely on a thread between two shelves. I had never worn fishnets before, but a particular memory flashed in my mind, associated with those stockings.

I was transported back to my time in Hatay, when I was a middle-grade student in a classroom filled with struggling students trying to learn English. Our teacher, Didem, had come from Istanbul to teach us. Despite her unconventional appearance, with features that were not conventionally beautiful, Didem possessed an alluring body. She wore black fishnet socks to school every day, displaying a courageous defiance that seemed to emanate from within.

Unbeknownst to my classmates, I had overheard a conversation between Didem and our dean during a break. She was battling breast cancer. I admired her audacity, knowing that wearing those fishnets could lead to punishment or scorn. It was the type of courage that arises when one realizes their time is limited and the finish line is approaching.

As months passed, Didem's health deteriorated, and one day, she was no longer there. We were never informed of her fate. Whether she had passed away or simply left, I couldn't say for sure. But her memory lingered, and I thought of her as a butterfly trapped in the black net of her own creation.

Returning to the present, I declined the sales assistant's offer and pointed to the black fishnet stockings on display. If I was no longer Yeter, I had to dress the part of Perihan. I asked about procuring some Fracas, the fragrance Cristina had recommended earlier, and was given the address of a nearby niche perfumery.

That day marked a turning point for me. I began to transform my appearance, shedding my old self like a pupa, emerging as the butterfly I had always aspired to be. However, the authenticity of this transformative power demanded verification. I questioned whether it was a genuine force or merely a transient illusion, particularly as it had originated in the midst of a party at Casa Mollino entangled with drugs, alcohol, and a diverse group of people, allowing our imaginations to run wild.

Before claiming to have access to otherworldly magic, especially in the presence of individuals of a certain status, I felt the need for tangible proof. I had to know! I had to see it happen again outside Casa Mollino. Perhaps the lingering immigrant within me, fueled by impostor syndrome, insisted on avoiding potential ridicule in front of society's powerful figures—Marco's friend circles, people who I had to interact with on a daily basis, the women at the hairdresser who I kept bumping into at every event. I recognized that true power demanded sacrifice. I had to test these tears whose miraculous attribute seemed to bring the dead back to life. Marco was back, you see?

In a risky and morally very challenging decision, I decided to experiment first on those society cared least for: the poor and the outcast. This required a dark leap into the realm of murder, of course, a calculated gamble to play God and bring them back from the brink of death... If they came back to life, as Marco did, I would be prepared for the next chapter of my life... If they did not, I would have to live the rest of my life knowing I was nothing but a murderer...

My dear Riccardo, I understand if this revelation unsettles you, but I feel compelled to share the narrative of my first kill, a very important moment that set the stage for my transformation.

The moon illuminated the night sky, casting its ethereal glow over the greenhouse where the monster lay dormant. As I prepared to venture out, Marco, with his garish bathrobe and casual indifference, questioned my late-night excursion.

Ignoring his presence, I rummaged through my belongings in search of a suitable scarf to conceal my hair. Opting for a burgundy silk scarf, I tightly tied it around my head, securing it beneath my chin. Marco's attempts to tease me with his jokes fell flat, as he failed to grasp the gravity of my quest for immortality. To him, it was merely a night of drug-induced illusions, an opportunity to revel in altered perceptions and discard the strange girl we had brought home as a mere transient.

When I confronted Marco about the sudden appearance of tuberoses in our long-forgotten greenhouse, he offered no explanation or theory, his interest waning. I was fortunate in that regard, for he would not interfere with my plans or insist on involving the authorities.

"I am going to the Duomo," I declared, clutching the bottle of Fracas I had acquired earlier that day. Unveiling the jet-black box, I revealed the black crystal bottle with its name written in a playful shade of pink.

Curiosity tinged Marco's voice as he asked about my intentions and offered to accompany me. I declined his company, knowing that this was a journey I had to undertake alone. Spraying the perfume on my wrists, the initial burst of orange blossom filled the room, gradually giving way to the mysterious allure of tuberose. There was a darkness underlying Fracas, beneath its initially cheerful and citrusy facade. It reminded me of decaying fruit concealed with freshly cut tuberoses, and the slumbering monster at the heart of our greenhouse. The perfumer at the shop had cautioned me about the synthetic civet note that I might detest, but instead, I found myself enamored by its heavy blend. The scent embraced me with its enigmatic aura, drawing me deeper into its mysterious depths.

As the fragrance enveloped me, I became acutely aware of the power it held—the power to unlock the secrets of the monster and potentially grant me immortality. It was time to put my plan into action, to drink the tears of the beast, and to seize the forbidden knowledge that lay dormant within. The moonlight guided my path as I ventured into the night, driven by a stubbornness that surpassed all rationality.

As I caught Marco's eyes in the mirror, I reconsidered my decision to go alone and invited him to accompany me. It was true that a woman walking alone at this late hour could attract unwanted attention, and having Marco by my side would provide a suitable cover story. I sprayed more perfume on various parts of my body, ensuring the fragrance enveloped me completely. Marco coughed in response, seemingly affected by the intensity of the scent.

His insistence on our existing romantic relationship annoyed me. In my mind, I had distanced myself from Yeter, from the reality of our relationship. I felt the need to detach myself from that identity and fully embrace the powerful transformation into Perihan. The knowledge that I was about to take a life sent shivers down my spine, making my hands tremble and my heart beat with an unfamiliar rhythm.

I had no interest in playing the role of a romantic couple with him. He was a reminder of the reality I was trying to escape. I proceeded to dress, again disregarding his presence. In a lace bra and high-waisted black pants, I bypassed his Armani suits and opted for a simple double-breasted black jacket. Its oversize shoulders, large lapels, and a diamond pin adorning the neckline added a touch of elegance. I draped the jacket over my shoulders, the silk lining caressing my skin.

Looking at my reflection in the mirror, I saw a transformed woman: a burgundy headscarf, a men's jacket, and black pants. The fishnets peeking out from the hem added a hint of allure. In this somewhat masculine ensemble, I felt powerful and authentic as Perihan. Gone were the soft and feminine Kennedy dresses favored by Yeter. Perihan embraced the scratch of tough wool against her skin and the crispness of cotton on her body. My fragrance choice further solidified this transformation. It was no longer the comforting, powdery scent Yeter preferred but a fragrance that smelled of sweaty skin after an orgasm. It provoked rather than comforted, embodying Perihan's essence.

Asserting my newfound power, I claimed the black

jacket as my own and slipped into a pair of black patent leather high heels with pointed toes. I grabbed a Lalique crystal bottle within which I kept the monster's tears, embellished with a butterfly stopper, and placed it in my clutch. Another small pack, prepared earlier in the kitchen where the rat poison was kept, found its place among my belongings.

Without hesitation, I ordered Marco to join me, leaving behind the trappings of seduction as I strode toward the door. Yeter evaporated within those walls, but Perihan emerged with determination, leaving a trail of intrigue in her wake.

"What are we looking for, exactly?" Marco's lack of enthusiasm was palpable as he stood with his hands buried in his pockets. We stood in front of the deserted Duomo, its grandeur dimmed under the glow of the full moon. The hand-painted windows depicting biblical scenes remained unlit, devoid of their usual vibrant colors.

"An outcast…someone homeless, perhaps," I whispered, scanning the surroundings. Typically, the city center was their gathering place. These unfortunate souls would travel the streets during the day, scavenging for food scraps or collecting spare change from tourists. At night, they would return to the center, constructing makeshift shelters out of cardboard boxes.

"They are usually behind the Duomo in Piazza Diaz," Marco pointed out, gesturing toward a dark pathway. I followed his lead, the hypnotic fragrance of my new perfume trailing in my wake.

Your grandfather's information proved accurate. Two women were standing some distance apart. I wondered why they didn't form a bond under their shared circumstances. Perhaps, together, they could have found a way out of their current predicament and forged a new future. I approached a woman with dirty blond hair, who had a dog nestled on her lap as a companion.

"Good evening," I spoke softly, crouched on my pointy black heels. The overpowering stench emanating from her made it difficult for me to breathe, even with Fracas's darker notes. I awaited her acknowledgment, hoping she would engage in conversation. She appeared dazed, and I noticed the presence of cheap wine boxes from the supermarket nearby.

"Are you hungry?" I asked, my impatience evident. All I desired was to offer her a drop of the elixir and witness its effect.

"Yeter, I will wait for you over there," Marco interjected gently, distancing himself from the unbearable odor. The woman's clothes bore stains of various colors, riddled with holes exposing her flesh. Her bare feet, plagued with painful sores, had turned an ashen gray. I wondered why her dog chose to remain by her side, unfazed by the inhospitable conditions.

"Hungry." She smiled, revealing a single yellow tooth. There was a gentle warmth in her gaze as she looked at me. "Hungry? Hungry!" she repeated the word, as if the mere pronunciation could satiate her hunger. Growing increasingly anxious, I retrieved the crystal bottle from my bag. The cold touch of the butterfly stopper pressed into my palm, providing a slight reassurance.

"Ablam, paran var mı?" she repeated in Turkish.

"What did you say?" I asked, confused.

"Ablam… Ben senin dilden anlamaz…" She laughed; her deep green eyes filled with softness. I couldn't help but wonder how this Turkish woman had ended up homeless on the streets of Milan. It was difficult to discern her exact origins, as her accent carried variations in pronunciation. Perhaps she was from a neighboring country.

"What is your name?" I asked in Turkish, seeking to establish a connection. This time, it was her turn to be surprised. She let out an exclamation of wonder, opening her mouth wide and searching the empty surroundings for a witness. We were alone, with Marco now a distant dot in the background.

"Ismin ne?" I repeated, feeling the strain on my legs. I adjusted my bag on my shoulder and began twirling the butterfly stopper, preparing to test the elixir of immortality on this woman.

"Songül," she proudly replied. I looked at her intently, struck by the choice of name. Songül, of all the names? It was the same name as my sister's. "Ismim Songül, ablam," she added.

I stood there, gazing down at the woman covered in dirt. My dear Riccardo, in that moment, I felt a surge of emotions—pity, sadness, and a dark nostalgia—flowing through my veins. How could I do this to her? I knew nothing about her past, why she had come to Italy in the first place. Was she a political refugee? A victim of love? An unfortunate soul whose plans had gone awry?

"İçki mi o, ablam?" she asked, pointing at the crystal bottle in my hand.

Once again, I knelt, inhaling the combination of her repugnant odor and my intoxicating fragrance. Speaking in Turkish, I responded, "What I have here is not good for you. I could give you the gift of immortality, but then it wouldn't truly be a gift. It would be a punishment, binding you to this life once more, as if your first experience in it wasn't enough. I cannot do this to you, Songül…"

I stood up, opened my bag, and took out all the cash I had in my wallet. I offered it to her, saying, "Enjoy the rest of your time. I hope life treats you better in the future." She expressed her gratitude multiple times, her eyes shining with a fairylike glow. My heart sank, dear Riccardo, because I saw my sisters in her place. I imagined them immigrating to another country, seeking refuge from their suffering in Hatay, only to end up in a similar condition, in a foreign land where they didn't even speak the language. Imagine being among the most vulnerable in a city yet lacking the means to communicate your needs. A tear fell from the corner of my eye and traced its path to the contour of my mouth. I extended my tongue and tasted it. No butterfly materialized. My tears were in vain.

I walked toward the second woman, a few steps ahead of me.

"You…" I felt sadness morph into rage. "You!" I shouted at the woman, who was so drunk that she could barely comprehend the direction of my voice. I wanted to get this over with quickly. I kneeled and investigated her face.

"Are you hungry? Do you want something to drink?" I asked. Unlike the previous woman, this person was much older, with gray hair sticking out in all directions like a witch. Her face had a malicious look to it. Her clothes were overly baggy, but relatively new. Her hands, though weathered, were covered in dirt. She smelled like a combination of sour milk and cat urine.

"Leave me alone, lady!" she roared in Italian, shooing me away with her filthy hands.

"Do you want some alcohol?" I asked her again.

"Where?" she asked, looking around me. It was true that she was older, but she seemed to be in relatively good health. I began to despise this old witch, as I felt she was not earning her living but surviving off others like a parasite.

I opened the crystal bottle and handed it to her. She stared at it for a few seconds, turning it in her hands. She held it in front of her eye and tried to see through it. "Cheers!" she said without enthusiasm and went to pour the contents of the bottle down her throat. But there was only a single drop of the elixir inside, and I watched as it clung to the rim of the bottle while the woman tapped it in the air a few times. Finally, it surrendered and fell into her dark mouth. The woman aggressively threw the bottle away. "Where the fuck is the drink? There's nothing inside this shitty bottle! Who are you kidding, woman?"

I didn't say a word. My heart raced, waiting for the elixir to take effect. I went to retrieve the rolling bottle from the ground, bringing it back to the dark path we'd been in. I placed the stopper back on it and returned both pieces to my bag. Then, I went back to where the woman was.

"Shitty whore," she mumbled, seething with rage against an invisible adversary. "Get me a drink!" she roared again, this time directing her anger at me. I didn't move, just continued observing. Slowly, I could feel something happening. Marco must have noticed it too, because he had come closer to witness it. The old woman placed her hands on her stomach, pushing against it with determination.

Riccardo's heart raced as he glanced at his phone and saw a message from Lorenzo. He opened it, his back straightening as he read the text.

Hey! I was with Mum. This might all be fiction just the same, maybe your grandmother wanted to take her real life friends and put them in the heart of a fantasy or something... Did you tell anyone else you have the book?

Did you tell anyone else you have the book? echoed in his thoughts. He read it again, his brow furrowing in concern. Had someone else been informed of his possession of the manuscript? Anxious to allay his fears, he swiftly typed out a reply.

No, absolutely not, they're still looking for it. Did you??

Riccardo's heart drummed in his chest as he waited for Lorenzo's response. Each passing second felt like an eternity. Finally, a message appeared on the screen.

NO! But they know you have it...

A surge of panic coursed through Riccardo's veins, and he leaped to his feet. It was all too much, too bewildering. He dialed Lorenzo's number, a mix of dread and frustration in his voice. Lorenzo picked up but then hung up. Riccardo's fingers flew across the screen as he sent another text. How do you know?

Lorenzo's reply was terse but held an underlying promise. Wait for me, okay?

Restless and agitated, Riccardo abandoned the book on his bed. He moved to the window, the night having swallowed the world outside. Disheartened by the darkness, he decided to perch on the windowsill, with the manuscript ready to re-veal its final chapters. His fingers traced the remaining pages, guiding him through the enigmatic narrative.

PERIHAN'S MANUSCRIPT

"Are you okay?" I whispered but received no response.

Once again, she placed both hands on her stomach and hiccupped. Once. Then once more. "I don't feel good," I heard her say to herself. "Oh!" Her whole body jerked back in a painful motion, as if unnatural forces were taking hold of her. Her body twisted; her hands clenched tightly next to her legs. "Oh!" she exclaimed in agony.

"She is dying." Marco panicked. "We should leave!"

I stood up, walking farther away with Marco but keeping my eyes on the scene. "I don't think so... Look!"

The woman opened her mouth so wide, that it seemed like we could put our feet inside and disappear into the depths. A small green butterfly with swallowtail wings emerged from the darkness, fluttering in the air.

"It works!" I jumped with joy on my pointy heels. "It works!" I screamed again, hugging Marco.

The woman attempted to catch the little butterfly, but after a few unsuccessful attempts she forgot about it. The swallowtail fluttered for a few seconds, then suddenly stopped in the air, and started descending in a spiral motion toward the dirty wool blanket on which the woman was sitting.

We both watched the scene in silence, wondering what would happen next. I knew what was coming, but I struggled to muster the courage to do it.

"I have to complete the task. Otherwise, we will never know," I said. Marco took hold of my arm, but I pushed him back.

"Eat some," I instructed the woman, taking out a small plastic container from my bag. Inside was a piece of quiche that I had laced with rat poison. Even if she died, nobody in Italy would go the extra mile to investigate whether it was a suicide, an accident, or an actual murder. They would simply dispose of the body, relieved to be rid of the burden. One less thing to worry about—who would say no?

The woman took the container, opened it, and greedily bit into the quiche. She stuffed the entire piece into her mouth and then struggled to chew it slowly. I don't remember if we heard her cry out or saw the white foam bubbling from her mouth first, but both occurred. The poison, which I had added in such an exaggerated amount that it could potentially kill an entire country with just one bite, took effect, destroying the woman from within. She looked at us, pleading for mercy, but I personally had none. She was the rat I was testing my drug on, and if the rat had to die, it had to die. Nothing personal.

"She is dead," Marco commented, looking at the woman, whose head had fallen to one side, her palms open, and her legs twisted strangely from the pain she had endured in her final moments.

"Well, let's watch that little miracle now," I said, confident that the butterfly would come to her rescue. We both gazed at the green butterfly on the blanket, still motionless. Suddenly, in an instant, the butterfly came to life, flapping its wings urgently like an ambulance trying to navigate through traffic to reach a patient. It ascended in the same spiral motion it had descended, fluttering around to land on the woman's lifeless body. Once it did, it settled on her chest and made its way up to her neck, where it came to rest.

I couldn't utter a word. The elixir of immortality was

working. I felt that I deserved to be Perihan more than anyone else in the world.

The most intriguing aspect was that the elixir was so potent, the woman appeared ten years younger than before her resurrection. It not only brought her back to life but also reversed her aging. I would later discover that not all tears possessed the same power. The cycle was simple: if you were nice to the monster, it would turn into its humanlike form, and if you mistreated it, it would transform into a monster, shed tears which would then either give you another chance at life...or tuberose gardens, of course. But the more we mistreated it and neglected to transform it back to its humanlike form, the more energy we extracted from it. How far can you go when you are unhappy all the time, dear Riccardo? This had an impact on the quality of the tears as time passed by, of course...

The first people I brought back from the dead did not only come back to life, but all came back younger, healthier, happier. As the years passed and we overused the monster's power, we destroyed its potency. Sometimes the last ones would come back from the dead, only to die of a heart attack an hour or so later... I turned to Marco, who still seemed astonished, his gaze fixed on the woman.

"Marco, snap out of it. You've already experienced this at Casa Mollino. We can't afford to lose any more time to your bewilderment. Now, follow me. We need to go back home," I instructed him before turning to head home.

And there you have it, my dear Riccardo. This is the tale of my first murder, where I had to take another person's life to test the tears of the monster. But let me pose a question to you. Am I still guilty of a crime if I can return the life I took? Is it still considered murder if I can resurrect the victim immediately afterward? These thoughts consumed me as we made our way back home. I must admit, Riccardo, the night didn't end there. I walked back home with your grandfather, unaware that there was a body buried in the greenhouse. I don't believe anyone will ever discover it, but as you will be inheriting this house, it is only fair that you know this information.

Upon our arrival at the door, we heard a voice shouting at us from behind. "Hey! Hey! I want more of what you have…" The potency of my fragrance, Fracas, probably masked the foul odor of the homeless woman who had followed us to our house. Nevertheless, we were startled by the late-night shout. We feared that someone might have witnessed our actions.

"Oh, not you," Marco exclaimed, pushing the woman away from the entrance.

"I want more! That bitch has it in her purse," she protested.

"Watch your language, lady, and get lost," I retorted, pushing the door open to let us both inside before closing it firmly.

"I will go to the police!" she shouted in defiance.

"Good, go and waste their time instead," I shouted back. I turned to Marco. "She can't enter here, and by morning, she'll think it was just another bad dream. Let's go back to bed."

And so, we did. We went back to bed.

However, our slumber was abruptly interrupted half an hour later by a piercing scream. The sound came through our window, assaulting our ears mercilessly. I sat up in bed immediately and turned on the bedside lamp.

"Did you hear that?" I asked Marco, who was already alert and off the bed, trying to catch a glimpse of what was happening outside.

"I don't see anything. It's all dark and quiet now. Maybe it was a cat?" he suggested.

"A cat? When was the last time you saw a cat roaming the streets of Milan? This isn't Istanbul, you know."

I witnessed your grandfather donning his velvet bathrobe and leaving the room. I followed him to the garden, wearing my pink slippers and silk nightgown. I couldn't help but feel sorry for him. I had uprooted him from his monotonous Milanese life, with his mundane Milanese friends, all dressed in varying shades of beige khaki pants, blue shirts, and duck-green cashmere V-necks. I hoped he was at least finding some enjoyment in all this mysterious chaos.

The air outside was cold in the early hours of the morning. We made our way to the greenhouse, where we believed the scream had originated.

"Look." Marco pointed to something on the grass outside the greenhouse door. It was the blanket of the homeless woman who had followed us to our house. A shiver ran down my spine. If she had harmed the monster, I was ready to end her life once and for all. Marco opened the door slowly and silently, and we entered the greenhouse.

19

It was the faint whispers that stirred Lorenzo from his sleep in the middle of the night. His hands fumbled in the darkness, searching for his phone, and as the blue glow illuminated his face, he squinted at the screen to see that it was a few minutes past three. He tried to convince himself that it was just a dream and attempted to lull himself back to sleep. But as soon as the screen dimmed and his head sank back into his soft pillow, he heard his mother's voice next door, filtering through the thin wall.

In the darkness, Lorenzo sat up in bed, his ear pressed against the wall, straining to decipher the words. At first, the whispers eluded him, and he wondered if his mother was talking in her sleep. However, when he heard Licia's name, he realized that his mother was on the phone. *Weird…at this hour,* he thought, imagining that something dreadful might have happened to Licia, prompting her to call his mother in an emergency. Holding his breath, Lorenzo focused on his mother's words in the room next door.

"We need it… We all do, of course… But are you sure?

When I asked Lorenzo earlier, he knew nothing of it... Yes... Yes, of course, Licia, it's three in the morning, he's sleeping." Barbara's voice carried a tinge of worry. A prolonged silence followed, during which she made noises indicating agreement and understanding, affirming their shared perspective.

Suddenly, the silence was shattered by Barbara's comment. "I'll talk to him in the morning. If there's anything we can do to bring Perihan back, I'm certain he won't be opposed to helping us. Riccardo trusts him, that's what I observed. I'm sure Lorenzo can sort this out... I just don't want anyone to get hurt in the process. Do you think that's possible?"

Lorenzo's blood ran cold. He wondered if he were imagining the conversation or trapped in some kind of nightmare. He couldn't comprehend what bringing Perihan back entailed, and he wanted no part in anything that could harm him or Riccardo. He retreated under his duvet, stiff and motionless on his bed, his eyes fixed on the ceiling, even though he saw nothing in the pitch blackness.

"I have the keys to the greenhouse. I noticed you left them at the bar by mistake. Don't worry, I'll bring them to you tomorrow. For now, go back to sleep. We will sort this out... Anything for our Perihan," Barbara said, ending the call, and the night once again returned to silence.

Lorenzo waited a while longer, to ensure his mother had returned to sleep. He turned restlessly in his bed, contemplating Riccardo's lovely face and how he had entrusted Lorenzo with the secret of the novel written by his grandmother. He felt a pang of guilt for the people around him, who were trying to take something that didn't belong to them. Driven by his affection for Riccardo, he made up his mind.

"Off we go," he decided, rising from the bed. He grabbed whatever clothes his hands found in the darkness, quietly slipped out of his room, tiptoed past his mother's closed bedroom door, and used the flashlight on his phone to scan both the round table by the entrance and the kitchen counter in search of the greenhouse keys.

Bingo! he thought triumphantly as the light illuminated the rusty old keys on the table. He slipped them into his pocket and silently exited through the door, ready to help Riccardo any way he could. Before he disappeared into the darkness, he texted him.

Stay strong, I'm on my way.

20

As Riccardo neared the final pages of the book, he felt the weight of exhaustion pressing down on his eyelids. His attention wavered under the relentless pull of drowsiness, yet he knew that giving in to sleep was not an option. He fought to stay awake, willing himself to remain vigilant. He opened the window and smoked a cigarette while watching the darkness outside. The manuscript, with its secrets and mysteries, demanded his focus. With Lorenzo en route, Riccardo hoped for a newfound strength to keep his senses sharp and alert, prepared for whatever twist lay ahead.

PERIHAN'S MANUSCRIPT

"When did you get that?" I asked Marco as I saw him turn on a small flashlight.

"I always keep it in my bathrobe…for emergencies," he replied. For him, *emergencies* meant unexpected earthquakes, not battles between good and evil.

He illuminated the area with the light as we ventured

deeper into the tuberose garden. The scent was intoxicatingly sweet, causing your grandfather to cough a few times, struggling to breathe there.

As we approached the end of the greenhouse, we first saw the monster. It was still in its human form, but its hair appeared more alive than ever, long tendrils of waves slowly moving across its concealed face. I would have assumed it had been sleeping for hours if it hadn't been for the red spots splattered across its floral-print dress.

"There's blood," I informed Marco.

"I see that," he replied, his voice betraying a hint of fear. He took a few steps back, shining the light around, searching for clues as to where the blood had come from. "Oh my God," he whispered, fixating the light on a particular spot.

And then, I saw it. Blood defaced a couple of white tuberose flowers, as if someone had exploded inside the greenhouse, staining a significant portion of these delicate blossoms. I took two steps closer to the flowers, and that's when I saw the body of the homeless woman. It lay there, most of it obliterated, a grotesque mass of blood and flesh. I let out a shriek and instinctively covered my eyes with my hands. Marco embraced me from behind and slowly guided me toward the exit.

"There's not much left of the woman…just blood and bones," I kept repeating to him. I was petrified that we might awaken the monster. It had never shown aggression toward me, so it was a shock to witness the results of its violence in such a brutal manner.

Once we were outside, Marco locked the door. I noticed bloodstains on some of the windows, already drying to a darker shade of brown.

"Well, she's gone… Maybe we should get rid of

this," Marco suggested, but his words enraged me, and I slapped him.

"If it leaves, I leave with it. It's our destiny in life. I won't let it go. That woman was deranged, and she would have harmed us. She trespassed on our property. How do you know the monster wasn't protecting us?" I argued fiercely.

"Protecting *you*, perhaps... I don't have this special bond with the creature," Marco replied, sounding bewildered. I knew he would eventually agree to let me keep it, but he always enjoyed being a headache before reaching any agreement.

"Go to bed. I'll go back inside and clean up the mess. I don't want Licia to discover this scene tomorrow morning," I declared firmly.

"Then, cancel Licia. She can come another day. You can clean it tomorrow in daylight," Marco suggested, correcting himself. "I mean...we'll clean it together."

But I had no intention of waiting until morning, my dear Riccardo. So I entered the greenhouse, fetched a bucket of water and a mop, and began the arduous task of washing the glass panels, disposing of the bloodied flowers, and digging a hole to bury the remains. By the time the first rays of morning light touched the greenhouse, everything would be restored to its previous state.

Perihan, on the rise, back on track.

Oh my dear Riccardo, in this new world, I discovered the power that came with my newfound immortality. I became the center of attention for political figures, influential collectors, and socialites, all of whom sought eternal life for their own reasons. They were captivated by the elixir's potential, and I became the embodiment of their desires. My story spread like wildfire in small but influential circles, and soon I found myself surrounded by a web of intrigue and fascination.

At a glamorous fashion show, I encountered a top model whose beauty graced the covers of magazines worldwide. She, too, sought to extend her fleeting existence, and her desperation was palpable. We struck up a conversation, and I shared my secret with her in whispered confidence. She clung to my every word; her eyes filled with hope. It was there, amid the glitz and glamour, that I offered her a vial of the elixir. In return, she promised to keep my secret and ensure my name remained unlinked to the mystery that surrounded my existence.

In another instance, a politician approached me with fear on his face. He had risen through the ranks, and with power came enemies. He believed that by obtaining multiple butterflies, he could deflect any potential threats aimed at his life. Intrigued by his paranoia, I obliged. We met discreetly in a dimly lit room, where I presented him with the elixir. The monster was in great health back then—its tears were very powerful and could give birth to butterflies that would not only resume life but reverse aging as well. As he drank multiple drops of it and let butterflies come out of his mouth, his anxiety began to subside. As I observed him, I knew that my influence and mysterious powers had once again left an indelible mark. These encounters, mixed into the story of my existence, solidified my position as a captivating enigma in the eyes of the world, while my true purpose remained shrouded in secrecy.

I carefully crafted my image as an opaque yet alluring figure. My presence at high-profile events and social gatherings became commonplace, my name whispered in hushed tones among the elite. I maintained an air of intrigue, revealing just enough to keep them curious, but never disclosing the true nature of my powers. The public remained oblivious to my identity and purpose, viewing me merely as one of the faces of high society.

In this realm of desire and ambition, the mystery of my existence was my greatest asset. It allowed me to shape the narrative, ensuring my secret remained hidden while I basked in the adoration and adulation of those who sought immortality by my side. Everything seemed to be in my favor until that one night... Oh, my Riccardo...

One night about a year later, I woke up suddenly, startled by a loud, crashing sound coming from the garden. The room was dark, with heavy curtains blocking out the moonlight. Beside me, Marco snored peacefully, unaware of my growing fear. Clutching my silk nightgown, I whispered his name, hoping for comfort, but he remained fast asleep.

Who could have made that noise? Did someone break into our sanctuary? Or was it the monster itself, trying to escape its confines? Questions flooded my mind as I struggled to figure out the situation. The gut-wrenching scream that followed only intensified my concern.

Unable to ignore the chaos unfolding outside, I mustered the courage to investigate. The moon cast a pale glow, guiding my path as I left the room. I tried to find Licia, who had moved into our house as her responsibilities grew, but her door remained closed. Reluctantly, I decided not to disturb her, knowing she needed her rest.

With a mixture of trepidation and determination, I made my way to the kitchen. In the dim light, I grasped a knife, its reassuring weight offering a semblance of protection. Step-by-step, my heart pounding, I ventured into the garden, the dew-drenched grass cool beneath my feet.

As I stepped out, the air was filled with the intoxicating scent of tuberose flowers. Their fragrance enveloped me, making me dizzy with their heady allure. It was as if the very essence of the night had taken on a floral form, weaving its way through the garden.

Drawing closer to the greenhouse, I noticed dark stains on its windows, a stark contrast against the moonlight. Shadows moved within, and I was entranced by their ethereal dance. A chill ran down my spine, mingling with the warmth of curiosity that pulsed through my veins.

The combination of the heavy aroma and the enigmatic shadows sent a shiver of anticipation through me. I felt a pull, an inexplicable desire to uncover the secrets hidden within those glass walls. The windows seemed to hold stories of their own, stained with remnants of unknown events that had unfolded in the night.

I approached the door cautiously, my hand trembling as I reached out to open it. The hinges creaked in protest, echoing through the night, as if warning me of the mysteries that awaited within. With each step, the scent of tuberose grew stronger, its presence overwhelming yet captivating.

As I peered into the darkness within the greenhouse, the shifting shadows played tricks on my eyes. They seemed to dance and swirl, whispering secrets that only the night could understand. My heart raced, torn between fear and curiosity, as I took a tentative step forward.

The moon's gentle light filtered through the glass, revealing glimpses of the world within. It was a sanctuary of nature's beauty, a place where life and mystery connected. The tuberose flowers stood tall, their delicate white petals bathed in the moon's ethereal glow. They held secrets, I was certain of it.

The stains on the windows seemed to grow darker, like splotches of hidden truths. They beckoned me further, urging me to explore the enigmatic depths of the greenhouse. My hand tightened around the knife, a reassurance in the face of the unknown.

Feeling a mix of curiosity and terror, I entered the greenhouse and closed the door behind me. The powerful scent of the flowers enveloped me, wrapping me in its fragrant embrace. The same thought from a few minutes ago raced through my mind: Was the monster trying to break free?

The silence within the greenhouse was oppressive, as if it were a tangible force engulfing the room. It pressed against my eardrums, muffling any sound that dared to breach its domain. Every footstep I took echoed like thunder, shattering the tranquility that should have prevailed. My heart pounded in my chest, a constant reminder of the fear that gripped me tightly.

I conducted a thorough search, my eyes scanning every corner, every nook and cranny. Yet there was nothing amiss, no trace of the disturbance that had sent me spiraling into this maze of uncertainty. The silence remained unbroken, unforgiving, as if taunting me with its impenetrable mystery.

Anxiety gnawed at my insides as I turned to make

my way toward the exit. But then, a glimmer caught my eye—a pair of legs protruding from behind one of the giant vases containing tuberoses. My heart lurched in my chest, my breath catching in my throat. I cautiously approached, my mind conjuring the image of a fainted figure.

As I drew closer, my trembling hands instinctively moved to cover my mouth, attempting to stifle the scream that threatened to escape. Tears welled up in my eyes, uncontrollable and streaming down my cheeks, as terror surged through every fiber of my being. There, amid the fragrant blooms, lay a gruesome sight—a mangled mess of muscles, fat, and bones. The head was nowhere to be found.

Horror consumed me, choking any coherent thought that struggled to rise. My naked feet had unwittingly stepped into the pool of blood, adding another layer of macabre reality to the nightmare I found myself in. The instinct for self-preservation propelled me backward, my eyes widening with each step.

Just as I reached the door, a disturbing sight stopped me in my tracks: a severed head, discarded on the floor. For a fleeting moment, I struggled to recognize the face, a name lingering at the edge of my consciousness. And then, it hit me with a force that sent me reeling: the lifeless visage belonged to Allegra, the girl from Cristina's shop. She had met her demise within the confines of my sanctuary, her body crushed to a grotesque pulp.

Terror gripped me, rendering me momentarily paralyzed. Confusion, disbelief, and fear mingled together, clouding my judgment. I knew I had to act, to escape this house of horrors that had invaded my once-tranquil abode. Without hesitation, I fled from the greenhouse, my mind racing to find a solution, a lifeline in this sea of darkness.

I rushed back to the house, my footsteps echoing through the empty corridors. The urgency spurred me forward as I searched desperately for the telephone, my lifeline to the outside world. Panic and indecision fought within me: Should I wake Marco? Should I seek guidance from Licia? Or should I call Cristina, who held the answers to the world we had stumbled into?

Summoning all the strength I had left, I dialed Cristina's number. Fear and a touch of relief flooded my veins as her voice crackled through the receiver. With each passing second, I struggled to form coherent sentences, my words stumbling over the horror that lay within the confines of my garden.

The thought of involving the authorities did not cross my mind. I knew too well the intricacies of the world we inhabited, the shadows that danced beneath the surface. But now, in this moment of darkness, I sought guidance, a lifeline to navigate the treacherous path that had unfolded before me.

I started to explain to Cristina, but as the words began to form on my lips, I hesitated. Cristina was not a confidante, merely someone from my past, someone I held fondly in my heart. Confessing such a nightmarish scene to her seemed unthinkable. With a heavy heart, I swiftly ended the call.

Returning to the greenhouse, I stood before its door, bathed in the soft, weird glow emanating from within. The scent of tuberoses clung to the air, their intoxicating fragrance mingling with the unsettling atmosphere. As I lowered my gaze to my feet, stained crimson with blood, a realization washed over me: the stains extended beyond the confines of the greenhouse. They led toward the garden exit, a gruesome trail that hinted at a horrifying event.

With trembling hands, I swung open the main Art Deco door and ventured outside. The moon's feeble light cast elongated shadows, stretching like grotesque specters along the path. And there, in the dim glow, lay the evidence of a macabre struggle. Bloodied prints meandered in a chaotic dance, as if someone had been dragged across the ground, their entire body leaving a chilling imprint.

Dread weighed heavily upon me as I contemplated the possibility—it could have been the girl, trapped within the monstrous form, attempting to flee our abode. But was she alone? The uncertainty gnawed at my consciousness, each possibility more terrifying than the last. Yet, my thirst for answers eclipsed my fear.

Returning indoors, I slipped into a pair of shoes, their practicality at odds with the sinister events that had transpired. The jingle of keys resonated in the silence as I made my way to the car. With trembling hands clutching the steering wheel, I embarked on a haunting journey through the night, my eyes scanning the darkness, searching for any sign of the elusive monster that had escaped our sanctuary.

The eerie silence engulfed me, broken only by the hum of the engine and the racing thoughts in my mind. Each shadow lurking in the periphery of my vision seemed to hold untold secrets, a disturbing presence that kept me on edge. The streets, usually familiar and welcoming, now twisted into sinister passages, hiding the truth from me.

As I drove, the weight of the unknown pressed upon me, amplifying the notion of dread that had settled deep within my bones. I yearned for answers, for an end to the torment that now plagued my existence. The night stretched on, filled with uncertainty, as I traversed the city's labyrinthine streets, chasing a ghostly specter that eluded my grasp.

The night was pregnant with shadows and secrets, and I, Perihan, found myself entangled in a web of darkness. Only time would reveal the truth, but until then, I remained on this desolate path, determined to confront the horrors that lay hidden in the shadows of the night.

I cruised through the desolate streets of Milan, the sinister silence broken only by the soft hum of the engine. As I neared Stazione Centrale, a faint sound pierced the stillness, disrupting the night's tranquility. Intrigued, I drove a little farther and caught a glimpse of the monster's reflection in the car's headlights. They loomed over a figure on the street, terrorizing them as they desperately attempted to escape its clutches. Beside the creature sat a tall, thin man with a desperate facial expression. Although I didn't recognize him, I understood that he was the one who had escaped with the monster.

Without hesitation, I parked the car immediately, leaving it in the middle of the road. Hastily, I approached the man. "Who are you?"

His sad eyes met mine, and in a trembling voice, he uttered words that sent a chill down my spine. "Allegra… It devoured Allegra…"

I pressed him for more information, eager to understand the connection between them, but he appeared shell-shocked by the trauma he had witnessed.

Aware that the grotesque creature's presence could attract unwanted attention, I decided to take matters into my own hands. Approaching the slimy monstrosity, I summoned the courage to touch its repulsive form, all while closing my eyes to shield myself from the disgust it evoked. With an improvised lullaby on my lips, whispered in Turkish, I coaxed the creature into a state of calm. Remarkably, it began to transform again, shedding its monstrous exterior and assuming a more humanlike guise.

Satisfied with the creature's newfound passivity, I escorted it back to the car, settling it in the back seat. Returning to the man, I aimed to extract more information. "What's your name?" I asked firmly, my grip on his arm tightening.

He hesitated before responding. "I'm Maurizio." His appearance reflected the hardships of a destitute existence: tattered clothing, unkempt hair, and an overall malnourished appearance.

My eyes widened in recognition. "I've been looking for you," I uttered, a flicker of hope kindling within me.

Maurizio attempted to distance himself, stepping away from me. However, I held fast to his arm, refusing to let him slip away. "You're not going anywhere, Maurizio. Get in the car," I asserted, my voice leaving no room for argument. With both Maurizio and the transformed creature now seated in the car, I steered us back toward the sanctuary of my home.

As we drove, the weight of curiosity consumed me, and I addressed Maurizio. "So tell me everything," I demanded, my voice filled with urgency and determination. He sighed heavily, his eyes filled with desperation. "Please don't leave me on the streets. I have nowhere to go," he pleaded. Sympathy welled within me, and I nodded, assuring him that his story would be heard. But first, we needed to return home and confront the grim aftermath of the chaos he had wrought.

After a long night of cleaning up the gruesome mess in the greenhouse, I led Maurizio to the comfort of my home. Exhausted and in need of comfort, we settled into the cozy living room. I brewed a pot of fragrant tea, its steam rising and mingling with the heavy atmosphere. As we sat together, the flickering candlelight casting creepy shadows on the walls, Maurizio began to recount the harrowing events that led us to this point.

He shared the tale of Elettra's ill-fated circus performance, how Allegra had once worked alongside him, assisting Elettra in her shows. Together, they had journeyed to Mexico, where they stumbled upon the monstrous creature that now resided in my greenhouse. Driven by ambition and the lure of eternal life, Allegra dreamed of exploiting the creature's elixir of immortality for financial gain.

Their grand plans came crashing down when the monster, freed during Elettra's televised spectacle, unleashed chaos upon the unsuspecting audience. Hundreds perished in its rampage, and Elettra's career plummeted into darkness. The weight of guilt and despair became too much for Elettra, leading her to take her own life. Maurizio and Allegra fled, seeking to forge a new path away from the horrors that had unfolded. I thought they must have had a fallout as Allegra had started working at Cristina's store...

The fateful encounter at Cristina's store brought them back into my life, intertwining our destinies. I imagined Allegra searching for Maurizio in the months that followed only to inform him that the monster was alive and kicking, in my very greenhouse, where they could make an attempt to abduct it once again... Allegra's untimely demise in the greenhouse and Maurizio's desperate attempt to transport the creature had left a trail of bloodshed and confusion. The story was as tragic as it was convoluted.

Turning to Maurizio, I posed a question that carried the weight of uncertainty. "Would you like to stay? Help me take care of this creature?" The proposition hung heavy in the air, a pivotal moment that would shape our future. Together, we lured the monster back into the confines of the greenhouse, its wails reverberating through the night.

In the following years, Maurizio and I built a peculiar empire. We established the Tuberose Club, a haven for immigrants, where diverse life stories converged. Amid the walls of our establishment, we tried to offer support and hope, providing solace to those who sought refuge from their troubled pasts.

While our outward mission carried an air of benevolence, behind closed doors we subjected the captive monster to ruthless exploitation. Utilizing cutting-edge technologies, we extracted its teardrops. It was a dark juxtaposition, our altruism mixed with the exploitation of a tortured being.

Our partnership, born from chaos and tragedy, yielded unforeseen consequences. The tale of Perihan and Maurizio echoed through the corridors of time, a saga that danced on the edges of morality, power, and the alluring prospect of immortality.

Riccardo's eyelids closed as he finished reading the first sentence of the last paragraph. He had no energy left in him to keep him awake.

21

In what seemed like a fever dream, Riccardo found himself standing at the entrance of a grand circus tent. The colors had been saturated, and the sounds were deafening, with a marching band of clowns blending with children's shouts to their parents. The air was filled with the aroma of popcorn and candied apples. He drew back the curtains and entered what appeared to be the backstage area. Elettra stood before him, accompanied by a much younger Maurizio, both unaware of his presence. Elettra was squeezed into a sequined bodysuit, concealed under a matching cape. As she held Maurizio's hand, she said, "I'm ready."

Riccardo found himself among the audience, watching the stage. Although he didn't understand what was happening, he went along with it, driven by curiosity. The lights dimmed, leaving only the spotlights. The audience held their breath, their eyes fixed on the center. With a slight delay, Elettra emerged in the middle of the tent. Her attire captured every ray of spotlight and reflected it back to the audience as a sparkling rainbow. Her transformation into a disco ball was astounding.

"Ladies and gentlemen, welcome to Elettra's Circus, where elephants roar and lions sing," Elettra spoke into the microphone covered with rhinestones, a wide grin on her face. The mention of singing lions amused the children, who burst into giggles. Elettra's voice grew louder with each word as she continued, "You'll encounter dancing tigers and turtles with wings… But now, allow me to introduce her…" Elettra paused, creating suspense. She looked at the children in the front row, one by one, and exclaimed, "Monarch!"

The girl didn't react to Elettra's words. From the opening of the curtains behind Elettra, Riccardo observed Maurizio pushing the butterfly girl onto the stage. With both hands, Monarch shielded her face from the spotlights. The audience now focused on her stunning ginger hair, long silk gloves, and velvet dress. Nobody had any idea what her performance would entail.

Gradually, the buzzing of butterflies outside grew louder. One monarch butterfly entered the tent, followed by another, and then two more. Soon, there was a kaleidoscope of butterflies rushing inside, accompanied by the sound of gasps, giggles, and cries from the children. The entire scene seemed like real life but embellished with special effects. Monarch lowered her hands and gazed up at the tent's ceiling. The monarch butterflies landed in various corners of the tent, but most of them chose to perch on the tightrope hanging above Monarch's head.

Elettra was so captivated by the spectacle before her that she failed to notice how the large group of butterflies frightened most of the children in the audience, causing them to scream. Misunderstanding the screams as directed at her, Monarch trembled with anxiety in the middle of the stage, now in tears. As the audience witnessed her increasing distress, they noticed her appearance growing more and more grotesque. It seemed as if her face was melting into something else, becoming slimy. Riccardo wanted to leave the tent but realized he was trapped in his seat, forced to witness this shocking spectacle unfold. Monarch's face contorted, her features randomly shifting. Her body lost its shape, transforming into an ugly, large, caterpillarlike alien. Witnessing this transformation, all the children started to flee.

Riccardo heard Maurizio trying to warn Elettra, shouting repeatedly, "Elettra! Run away! Run away!"

Riccardo wanted to rush back into the tent to save them both, but it was already too late. Elettra's horrified face appeared in the rear, stage right. She stared in horror at the small screen from which she observed the act on stage, witnessing the fairy turning into a monstrous creature from hell. The animals also detected the presence of the alien and broke free from their cages, charging violently into the crowd. The two large cats ran full speed into the audience, reaching the front row where the children sat. One of them opened its mouth wide enough to engulf the entire head of a blonde little girl. The sound of her delicate bones being crushed and blood spurting from her face froze Maurizio's blood. Paralyzed by fear, he stood motionless, unable to move.

The lion and tiger had entered the tent while attempting to escape and, overwhelmed by the sense of danger, began attacking the audience. They bit into anything that crossed their path. The teacher lost her entire left arm as the tiger shredded it into pieces. The tent was now littered with bloody remains of children.

"Oh my God… Laura… Davide… Run away! Everybody,

run away!" one of the teachers shouted. The lion pounced on the child seated in the front row, its claws tearing into his angelic face, cutting it in two. Blood spurted onto the girl next to him, who now writhed in pain with her face split open. The lion, a few meters away, chewed on the arm of a student, while they all remained alive, crying in agony. Birds flew directly into the heads of the children, pecking at their skulls in a frenzy, trying to crack them open. Elettra attempted to save some of the children, but she saw the elephant tear through the entrance curtains, charging inside at full speed. She threw herself to the side, narrowly escaping being crushed underfoot. Instead, the elephant trampled a child, squashing his legs. The tent became drenched in blood and tears. There were screams and cries. The air was permeated with pain. Monarch watched the disaster unfold around her, greedily devouring bits and pieces of children that came her way from the aftermath of the animal attacks.

Within a few minutes, all the children lay dead, their bodies contorted and bloodstained. Some teachers were missing limbs, while others had fainted from fear. Elettra had succumbed to complete shock, her body trembling within her bloodstained, glittery bodysuit.

"Elettra!" Maurizio shouted as he entered the tent, but the animals had already left. Riccardo finally broke free from whatever spell he was under and ran toward them. However, as soon as he started running, the scene transformed. Everything around him melted away, and hundreds of balloons emerged, rising into the night sky. Baffled by the morbid sight of these colorful balloons appearing out of nowhere against the starless sky, Riccardo continued to run. It was then that he realized he was back in the villa's garden. The house lay buried in darkness, while the greenhouse radiated a magnetic energy. Despite his mind's attempts to resist,

Riccardo's feet compelled him forward. He approached the greenhouse, and the unending light within turned into a blazing inferno. Flames emerged from every crack in the greenhouse's glass. He stepped inside and let out a scream, as he beheld the giant caterpillars hanging in chrysalis form at the center of the structure. Their iridescent, hard shells contained human faces on what should have been their sides. One of them resembled Perihan, while the other two were the blind twins. The last chrysalis at the end shattered, and enormous iridescent wings emerged, stretching into the air. Riccardo heard a voice say, "Hey, come here!" He turned to see Lorenzo and realized that his right arm was trapped inside the slimy jaws of a hellish monster lurking behind the vases.

Riccardo awakened from the nightmare, panting with an urgent instinct to read the final part of the manuscript. Thanks to the nightmare, his senses were alert. He turned the page from where he had left off before dozing.

PERIHAN'S MANUSCRIPT

So how does this story arrive to you, my dear Riccardo? Where is your mother in all this? Do you know how I found out I was pregnant? While I was looking for eternal life… Your grandfather and I had planned a weekend getaway to Portofino, and I had packed one of the Lalique crystal bottles containing the monster's tears in my bag, just in case. It was a beautiful Friday afternoon, and Marco was enjoying the songs of his favorite singer, Mina, on the radio as we made our way to the beachside destination. However, as we approached a sharp turn on the road, Marco made a mistake, and for a moment, it felt like we were about to crash into a tree. Thankfully, we narrowly avoided the collision, but the near miss left me shaken.

As soon as we arrived at the hotel, I excused myself and made my way to the bathroom. The harsh, fluorescent lights revealed in the mirror that despite the stress of the near accident, my skin still glowed with a natural radiance. I decided to freshen up, splashing cold water on my face and drying it gently with a soft pink towel. I opened the crystal bottle. Closing my eyes, I let the glass touch my lips, and the monster's teardrop trickled onto my tongue, dissolving within. At first, nothing seemed to happen, and I wondered if anything would occur at all.

But then it started—a series of small hiccups, one after another. I couldn't help but open my mouth wide and examine my reflection in the mirror. To my astonishment, a magnificent light blue butterfly emerged, its wings outstretched. It fluttered toward the fluorescent bulb, its beauty short-lived as it met an untimely demise, falling gently into the sink. Carefully, I retrieved the fragile creature, placing it between layers of tissue for safekeeping.

Just as I was about to turn off the lights and leave the bathroom, another hiccup interrupted me. I brought my concerned face closer to the mirror, searching for answers. Two more hiccups followed, and a knot formed in my throat. I opened my mouth wider, attempting to catch a glimpse of what was happening inside, but found nothing.

The hiccups persisted, growing more frequent and forceful. I gripped the marble sink, seeking support as immense fear and anticipation filled my being. And then, there it was—a second large blue phengaris arion emerged, smaller than the first, from the darkness into the fluorescent-lit bathroom.

"Bismillahirrahmanirrahim," I uttered, a tremor of fear present in my voice. Two butterflies, two heartbeats within the same body.

The blue insect fluttered its wings with joy before meeting the same fate as its predecessor, joining it in the sink. It was in that moment that everything became clear: I was carrying life within me: my own and that of your mother's.

To be honest, I wasn't thrilled about the prospect of having a child. After fighting so hard for my freedom, the idea of being responsible for another life didn't sit well with me. Children were not part of my plans. Marco, on the other hand, was ecstatic when he learned about my pregnancy. He saw it as a wake-up call, a reason for me to let go of the monster. He wanted us to return it to the canals in Navigli, setting it free for someone else to experience its magical powers. But I refused.

"If you want to see your child, you'll have to let me keep the monster. Otherwise, I'll do everything in my power to have a miscarriage. I promise you," I declared.

He knew I wasn't bluffing, so he reluctantly accepted. There wasn't much he could do anyway.

The rest of my story unfolds in a more straightforward manner. Exactly nine months later, your mother came into the world. She was a sweet little baby, but I was too consumed with bringing magic into the lives of important individuals. Licia and Marco took on the role of raising her, while I traveled with Maurizio. I had become well-known in influential circles, not just in Milan, but also in cities like Paris, New York, London, Moscow, Vienna, and Istanbul. Maurizio and I mingled with the rich and powerful, selling them drops of eternal life. We encountered everyone from famous princesses to dangerous criminals. Sometimes they would meet sudden and mysterious deaths, only to miraculously return to the public eye hours later, boasting about their restored health. There was even an occasion when a prominent English newspaper mistakenly reported the death of a young prince, only to issue a hasty retraction in the afternoon. Wrong news indeed! It was I, Perihan, the queen of miracles, who had brought the prince back to life.

I must confess, my dear Riccardo, that I didn't have much of a relationship with your mother. In fact, to be completely honest, I resented her. Every day, I prayed for her to vanish from my life. However, we should always be cautious about what we wish for.

When she became pregnant, I took her to the doctor to discuss the option of an abortion, which she adamantly refused. But who had the time or desire to become a grandmother? Certainly not me! Little did I know that her pregnancy was not driven by maternal instincts but rather by a deep thirst for revenge. She wanted to have you so that she could abandon you to my care and escape. And that's exactly what she did. When you were just a few months old, she left for Australia—or was it somewhere else? I can't quite recall—with her boyfriend at the time. Since then, I haven't heard a word from her, nor did it ever occur to me to search for her. But Marco, he tried. He even hired a private investigator, sending him all the way to Sydney, using the money I earned through my magical abilities. But it yielded no results. Your mother had simply vanished into thin air. She was here one moment and gone the next. I would be lying if I said I was upset about the whole thing. I wasn't.

I or, rather, Marco and I did everything in our power to keep you away from the monster. We never let it go. We raised you in what I believed was a safe and joyful environment, until your early years of elementary school. After that, I made the decision to send you off to Paris, not only for a better education but also for a safer life. I never felt affection for you. You were constantly needy. Craving love, seeking protection, always requiring my presence. However, I needed you too. I had to play my part and cultivate a strong bond...

Meanwhile, the monster had grown more grotesque and violent with each passing year, leaving a trail of death in its wake. Despite the occasional mishap, my connections with the top figures in public security kept the police from bothering me too much. Maurizio often pointed out how we were overwhelming the monster, how its tears had become of poor quality. People were being brought back from death, yes, but they weren't experiencing true rejuvenation. Their scars remained; their broken bones didn't mend. The tears seemed to act more like a mediocre adhesive. And to make matters worse, the tears became scarce. Not only were they of inferior quality, but their quantity had significantly decreased. It was a disaster for me. The monster had grown accustomed to being mistreated, so it grew a rather thick skin and didn't let go of its tears as easily. Butterflies emerged from people's mouths with damaged wings or in dull hues. The magic was growing weary. We even witnessed someone spitting out a caterpillar in chrysalis form once; it wasn't even a butterfly.

Both Licia and Maurizio suggested that we shield you from all this. I then made every effort to maintain a strong bond with you. I shared with you the concepts of Jungian rebirth, discussing metempsychosis, reincarnation, resurrection, psychological rebirth, and indirect transformation. I truly believed in it. I knew that there would come a point in my life when this body would no longer be healthy enough to sustain me. Maurizio was aware of this as well, and he began working on a wild idea he had heard from Fumito years ago.

Maurizio read. He spent endless hours reading Jodorowsky, Jung, de Sade. He called people from the other side of the world, he left for weeks to go meet shamans, professors at prestigious universities, scientists. He was onto something, and once he was back, I saw him finally bring all his knowledge into play. One rainy afternoon, someone buzzed at our door, and a very old woman, with no hair and a sullen face, entered. She was dripping in amazing jewelry. She was also carrying a fluffy white cat with green eyes in her arms. She talked to Maurizio in a barely audible manner, then they passed to the living room. Licia served tea and biscuits as Maurizio asked me to leave them alone. I would not. I wanted to see who this person was and what they were discussing so secretly. Maurizio saw me watch them and invited me over. I went there and sat down next to him. The very old lady told me her name was Anjelique. I smiled.

Maurizio began recounting the myth of Er from Plato's *Republic*, his voice carrying a lot of excitement. "What you are about to witness is nothing new. Plato wrote about it in *The Republic*. In the story, Er, the son of Armenius, dies, and on the twelfth day, he miraculously returns to share the secrets of the afterlife. Er witnesses how souls gather in the place of judgment and how they embark on new lives, some as wild animals, others as domesticated ones. Some souls return to the world as humans, inhabiting different bodies. But the number of souls remains constant, for it is fixed. Er sees—" Maurizio's voice grew more fervent "—he sees how the soul of Orpheus transforms into a swan! He sees Thamyris's soul become a nightingale! Who wouldn't want to be a nightingale, with all its elegance and beauty? Atalanta turns into an athlete. It's a perpetual cycle of change and transformation between souls. Plato shows us that the soul is not created anew but rather undergoes transmigration—"

"Transmigration?" Anjelique interrupted, curiously. Maurizio retrieved a Lalique bottle, opened it, and prepared a drop, bringing it closer to her mouth. "Transmigration," he nodded, his eyes shining. "The migration of one body to another…"

Anjelique allowed the drop to dissolve on her tongue, closing her eyes in anticipation. When she opened them again, she saw the delicate legs of a butterfly emerging from her mouth. With a gentle touch, she used her long, pink nails to hold her mouth wide-open, allowing the butterfly to take flight.

"Greta oto, my favorite master of camouflage," Maurizio remarked. "The wings have such a unique structure that they appear transparent through various reflections of light." It was evident that Maurizio held a deep fascination with the subject of lepidoptery. He assisted Anjelique in carefully placing the butterfly within a tissue, ensuring its safety.

"Now is the time," Maurizio declared, turning his attention to the cat, administering a tear to the animal. "Just as in the myth of Er, the great philosopher Carl Jung also discusses the concept of metempsychosis. According to the Jungian archetypes of rebirth, metempsychosis refers to the soul's journey through different bodily existences—a life sequence interrupted by various reincarnations. And that is precisely what we are about to attempt, what I have been working on. Thank you, Anjelique, for granting me this opportunity to try..."

As the colossal butterfly, with a wingspan of about thirty centimeters, emerged, Anjelique's cat let out a whimper. The magnificent Queen Alexandra butterfly, with its captivating beauty, landed softly on Anjelique's lap. It was impossible to overlook its precious presence. However, before I could close my eyes as Maurizio instructed, curiosity held my gaze fixed. Even Licia observed silently from the corner, and I wondered if Marco was still present in the house or if he had ventured outside.

Maurizio took hold of the cat and swiftly snapped its neck, causing it to make no sound. He then approached Anjelique, and in a decisive moment, without giving her any chance to protest, he did the same to her. Both lifeless bodies collapsed onto the sofa. I gasped in disbelief, but my astonishment heightened as the two exquisite butterflies on the sofa suddenly stirred to life. Their wings fluttered with renewed vigor, soaring back into the sky, exchanging destinations. Anjelique's butterfly flew toward Anjelique's demised cat and vice versa. Metempsychosis, my dear Riccardo, metempsychosis akin to the ancient Greek myths.

Anjelique's transformation after being revived was truly perplexing. As she settled onto the sofa, her posture underwent an uncanny alteration. Slowly, she shifted her weight, arching her back in a way that mirrored a feline stretch. Her once-human eyes, now reflecting an enigmatic emptiness, fixated on some invisible point as if she had become a part of an alternate reality.

Then, in an unsettling move, Anjelique began to groom herself. Like a cat, she started licking her hands and running them through her hair. The room fell silent, except for the rhythmic sound of her tongue against her skin. It was as if she had effortlessly adopted the behaviors of a feline creature, displaying an uncanny precision in mimicking their movements.

I was shocked, witnessing this transformation that seemed to go beyond mere physical changes. Anjelique's actions spoke of a profound shift in her essence, blurring the lines between her humanity and the mysterious presence that now seemed to inhabit her. The air in the room hung heavy. As for the cat, it displayed an excessive surge of energy, a stark contrast to its mood mere moments before.

"We've done it," Maurizio proclaimed.

"What just happened?" I asked, still trying to understand the extraordinary events unfolding before me.

"Metempsychosis... Anjelique's soul has transferred to her cat and vice versa," Maurizio explained. "You can swap bodies between different species, such as a human and an animal, or even between two humans, though that only seems to work when they share the same bloodline. However, upon awakening, all memories and identities from the previous body are completely erased."

The concept sank in—same bloodline, body swaps, no memory, no previous identity, and the allure of eternal youth, my dear Riccardo. Eternal youth for an eternity...

Every detail has been meticulously orchestrated, a testament to the intricacies of my master plan. A day before my long-awaited birthday, I sought the guidance of my trusted lawyer, ensuring that every possession I owned would be transferred into your name. The inheritance, a testament to my unwavering trust in you, held the key to my ultimate liberation. With all arrangements made, contentment washed over me as I laid my head to rest that fateful night.

The sun rose, casting its warm rays upon the world as I embarked on a day of celebration. Shopping bags in hand, I returned to the haven of my luxurious villa, brimming with energy. But as I approached, a disconcerting sight greeted me: an entire street overrun by a swarm of butterflies. Curious onlookers recorded the enchanting spectacle, their fascination evident in the glow of their screens.

Driven by a great curiosity, I hurriedly made my way to the garden, where a troubling atmosphere hung heavy in the air. There, I encountered a disheveled maid fleeing the greenhouse, her attire marred by sticky crimson stains. Panic-stricken, she attempted to communicate something urgent, her words lost amid a symphony of fear. With trepidation clawing at my heart, I flung open the door, unleashing a maelstrom of decay and the frenzied flight of monarch butterflies.

The pungent scent of decay, mingled with the sickly sweet aroma of rotting tuberoses, assaulted my senses as I ventured into the heart of the greenhouse. The heavy door closed behind me, sealing my fate within its dark confines. An air of menace permeated the stillness, the silence amplifying the weight of the moment. And there, amid the withered flora, lay the monster in its most grotesque and vulnerable state, sprawled upon the ground in a pool of viscous dark-burgundy fluid that bore an unsettling resemblance to blood.

Overwhelmed by a rush of conflicting emotions, tears cascaded down my cheeks, a testament to the years of torment endured at the monster's hands. It was a moment of reckoning, as the magnitude of the creature's demise settled upon me. No longer would it hold sway over my existence, for its power had been vanquished, its influence forever silenced. With this realization, my mind raced, concocting plans on how to seize the opportunity presented—a chance to utilize my escape card, to reclaim my freedom and reshape my destiny.

The monster's defeat served as a catalyst for a grand metamorphosis, a rebirth of both body and spirit. Amid the tears and contemplation, the weight of my inheritance, now securely placed in your hands, magnified the possibilities that lay before me.

As I stood within the hallowed sanctuary of the greenhouse, my mind buzzed with excitement. The door closed behind me, shutting out the world that had long held me captive. With resolve coursing through my veins, I wiped away the tears and steeled myself for the challenges that lay ahead. The monster's reign had come to an end, and it was now time to take advantage of the situation that had been so cunningly crafted. The inheritance, the exit strategy meticulously prepared, would serve as a gateway to a life where I could finally dictate my own fate, unburdened by the shadows of the past.

A plan formed in my mind, ready to be set into motion. The world awaited, and I was prepared to seize my chance and embark on a new chapter of my life, Riccardo...

Riccardo's heart was beating at an unprecedented speed. As he finished reading the last handwritten sentence of the manuscript, he jolted by the sound of a door slamming shut. He leaped out of bed, only to discover that the real nightmare was about to begin. He saw Maurizio standing by the bedroom door, his expression malicious as he uttered, "You have what I need."

22

Downstairs, perched on the grand sofa, Licia waited patiently. Her eyes remained fixed on the ashtray positioned before her. Like a wild nocturnal creature, she was alert, attempting to capture any sound that might signal victory from the upper floors. The room was heavy with anticipation, tension humming in the air.

Licia's thoughts raced, contemplating the crucial moment at hand. *The time has come,* she mused, her mind consumed by the need to set things right. She placed her unwavering trust in Maurizio to fulfill their shared plan. The cat and mouse game they had been playing had dragged on for far too long. *We should have been celebrating our triumph by now,* she thought bitterly, recalling the arduous work that had led them to this point. Her frustration manifested physically as she scratched the back of her thumb aggressively, inadvertently scraping off layers of skin.

Beside her, Cristina rested her head on the plush sofa, her eyes closed. She, too, awaited the unfolding events. "It would be a disaster," Cristina muttered with a heavy heart. "If Riccardo were to acquire the entirety of the inheritance, we would be left with nothing at this age, cast out the door," she lamented. "She can't just come back and say it was all a joke," Cristina continued. "No, she must remain dead at this point, and the rest will be pure hell for us...pure hell."

As the tension mounted, another voice spoke. "Maybe you should go inform her," Greta, one of the blind twins, spoke softly, her words hanging in the air without a specific target. She clung to her sister's hand, as if seeking comfort in their unbreakable bond. Greta's remark carried an undercurrent of urgency. Time was of the essence, and the ritual could no longer be delayed.

Licia avoided offering a direct response to Greta's suggestion. Sensing the gravity of the situation, she rose from the sofa with determination. She made her way down the corridor behind the majestic staircase, passing by numerous closed doors. Each step brought her closer to the room where they had held the funeral, a room shrouded in memories and secrets.

Upon reaching the door, Licia paused, her hand poised to knock. She hesitated for a moment; then, with a deep breath, she knocked twice on the door before pushing it open and stepping inside. The room greeted her with a strange silence, the remnants of the funeral lingering in the air. Her eyes were drawn to the butterfly dome, a delicate and transparent enclosure that housed the phengaris arion. Its ethereal beauty stood in stark contrast to the weight of the situation at hand.

"We're almost ready," Licia announced. Her gaze lingered on the butterfly dome, knowing that their carefully orchestrated plan hinged on the delicate creature within. The room seemed to hold its breath, as if aware of the gravity of the impending events that would unfold within its walls.

23

Riccardo's senses jolted as he quickly regained composure, his mind still reeling from the macabre nightmare he had just experienced and the grand reveal at the end of the manuscript. He knew he had to act swiftly to both protect Perihan's draft lying on his chest and save his own life, as Maurizio stood ominously at the threshold. Riccardo attempted to make a move toward the exit, only to have Maurizio block his path completely.

"That book is mine!" Maurizio demanded.

"Nothing is yours. You're blocking the door. Move away," Riccardo retorted, attempting to buy some time and divert Maurizio's attention. However, the man remained resolute, refusing to budge.

"That book was not intended for you. You may have thought otherwise when you saw your name on it, but it was *not* meant for you," he said.

Riccardo's eyes darted around the room, seeking a potential advantage. His gaze landed on a small green lamp with a marble base on a nearby table. As he continued the conversation with Maurizio, he mentally calculated the distance to the lamp.

"Everything under this roof, and more, is intended for me. I am the sole survivor of this story," Riccardo stated. In one swift motion, he lunged at the lamp, snatched it up, and hurled it forcefully at Maurizio's chest. Caught off guard by the sudden move and the heavy marble base, the older man stumbled and fell into the corridor.

Seizing the opportunity, Riccardo swiftly retrieved the book, leaped over Maurizio's prone form, and dashed toward the stairs. The sound of Maurizio's scream echoed behind him as he struggled to regain his footing and give chase.

Descending the staircase, Riccardo's eyes fell upon the two blind twins and Cristina seated on the sofas in the living room. Their mouths moved, shouting something at him, but he paid them no heed. With a final burst of energy, he leaped from the last step, turned the corner, and headed for the main door of the house. However, as he stood with one hand on the doorknob and the other clutching the book, a figure emerged from the dark corridor behind the grand staircase—Licia.

"Where are you going, dear Riccardo? It's finally over for you," she said softly, her voice dripping with a sinister tone. Slowly, she advanced toward him, cradling a butterfly dome with a phengaris butterfly trapped in its confines. Riccardo stared at her, transfixed, and his eyes widened in astonishment as he got a glimpse of Perihan standing behind Licia.

It was his grandmother, in a blond hairdo, flawless makeup, and a blood-red gown that evoked memories from his childhood. Perihan seemed surprised to see him, or perhaps taken aback by the unfolding climax they had all orchestrated. Time stood still, and all Riccardo could hear was the thunderous beat of his own heart.

Was it all a lie, then? Did she lure me into this trap with the fake suicide? Or am I witnessing a ghost for the first time in my life? Is she here before me? Riccardo's mind raced, bombarded by a flood of questions. *What do these people want from me, and why is this book so important?* Doubt consumed him as he contemplated the true intentions behind their actions. *Could it be their ego, desiring the one thing my grandmother truly meant for me alone after her death?* The whirlwind of thoughts threatened to overwhelm him.

Perihan stepped forward, intertwining her hands in what seemed to be a gesture to inspect the perfection of her manicure. She took a moment of deliberate silence, avoiding eye contact with Riccardo, allowing the already-heavy atmosphere to intensify. Her sudden and unexpected presence obliterated the fragile boundary between fantasy and reality, making Riccardo very aware that his grandmother was indeed alive.

Looking directly at her grandson, she looked deeply into his eyes. Despite his search, Riccardo found no trace of emotion in her expression. With a feigned cough, Perihan signaled the beginning of her speech. She clasped her arms to her chest, atop her striking gown, and began speaking in her captivatingly rich voice.

"Listen closely, my precious Riccardo, for life begins with migration. It is the moment we depart the secure confines of our mother's womb and venture into the chaotic world. We cry, instinctively aware of the mistake in leaving our mother's embrace, yet there is no turning back. Survival demands that we keep moving forward. We migrate to escape the clutches of famine, poverty, violence, ignorance, and hatred. Countless reasons propel us to run…"

Perihan held Riccardo captive with her magnetic presence. Aware that his fate teetered on the brink of life or death, Riccardo believed his best chance for survival might lie just beyond the main door of the house. The imperative to turn the knob and flee surged within him, yet Perihan's allure immobilized him. Her voice possessed a hypnotic quality that rendered him powerless.

For years, Riccardo had yearned for a connection, a familiar bond. Now, with his grandmother standing before him, prepared to offer explanations, he found himself unable to break free from this mesmerizing grip. Perihan continued without changing her pose as Licia moved closer to Riccardo, probably in an attempt to block his potential escape.

"But here's the bitter truth. Mere physical migration cannot guarantee a better life. It slams into our consciousness within the endless queues of unfamiliar police stations, where we yearn for a residence permit in foreign lands. It strikes when the authorities perceive us as potential criminals, our faces deemed alien in their eyes. It hits hard when urgent medical situations arise, and language barriers render our pain inexpressible in anything but our mother tongue. And it crushes us when we find ourselves confined within the rigid boundaries of our assigned gender. As time passes, the blows become more frequent, and we grow desensitized to this ghostly violence. We internalize it, accepting it as our own. We strive to make the best of it because what other choice do we have? We decorate the walls of our new homes with the wallpaper of this violence, yet they remain mere houses, devoid of true belonging."

Despite her frail figure and advanced age, Licia took one of Riccardo's arms, signaling to Maurizio to do the same. Entranced by Perihan's monologue, Riccardo found himself trapped, positioned in front of the door with both Licia and Maurizio holding on to him. In the midst of this enchantment, Maurizio removed the manuscript from Riccardo's hands.

Perihan continued. "But mark my words, my precious one, and look to the caterpillar. Sometimes, moving a mere few meters or endless kilometers is not enough. The caterpillar knows the secret to survival lies in transformation. We must change our very bodies, migrate from one form to another, and embrace the power of metamorphosis. In this memoir, dedicated to you, Riccardo, I reveal the truth of my existence. I will very soon inhabit your body, but I will have lost all memories from my previous life due to metempsychosis. I will need a bit of refreshing, though nothing I can't recover from. Do you see? I will wake up, in your body, and feel like I'm in a room with foggy windows… I will have a very faint idea of who I am in my essence, but reading that manuscript will help me clear out all the fog and resume where I left off."

"You are a monster! You're the real monster. How could you do this to me? How?" Riccardo screamed, now clearly very angry at both how naive he had been and how unaffectionate his whole family had been with him.

Taking his question seriously, Perihan deliberated for a moment before moving a few steps closer to him. The rich scent of tuberose enveloped Riccardo as she began to answer.

"Let me explain how this plan unfolded, with Maurizio's help. Of course, you have a right to know, my little one. My new shelter… We devised a grand scheme. Maurizio went to Paris to find you and bring you back for a fake funeral, a pivotal moment in our transformation. You were supposed to be drugged in your sleep and we would let my butterfly enter your body. If only you hadn't been so curious and stolen the manuscript as soon as you arrived, you wouldn't have had to wait this long and learn everything. I guess this…pain… it is all your fault, now. But don't you worry! We are almost there. In a bit, my last butterfly, a symbol of my transformation, will come alive as I die. Guided by Maurizio, the butterfly will find its way to you. This will mark the beginning of our metamorphosis, a transfer of essence. You will wake up after the exchange has occurred, but you don't have your own butterfly, so you won't inhabit a new body. My soul will overpower yours, and you will be stuck with me in there, for years to come. You will probably perish slowly, unfortunately. I extend my deepest gratitude to you, Riccardo. Thank you for coming back home to me."

Riccardo's scream reached an ear-piercing pitch, his physical struggle causing Licia to momentarily release his arm. Seizing the opportunity, he swiftly used his free hand to deliver a swift slap to Maurizio's face. The abrupt jolt caused Maurizio to lose his balance briefly, eliciting shouts from Perihan.

In that chaotic moment, Riccardo managed to turn the doorknob, thrusting himself outside and fleeing into the obscurity of the garden. His sole objective was to create distance between himself and the enigmatic individuals inside the house. Suppressing any thoughts, he focused on keeping his mind clear. The weight of his grandmother's last words threatened to overwhelm him emotionally, but he pushed those thoughts aside.

Sprinting toward the garden door, Riccardo understood that his challenges would only intensify once he was outside. Despite the circumstances, the lack of a vehicle and anywhere to go meant that, no matter how fast he ran, Maurizio or others would likely catch up and pull him back to the villa. The haunting images of Perihan and the peculiar butterfly dome in Licia's possession left him traumatized, regretting the loss of the manuscript.

Riccardo swung open the garden door, fully aware of the risks, yet realizing the absence of better options. Stepping onto the street, he collided with another figure attempting to enter the garden.

"You can't… Riccardo, no, not like this. Go back inside," Lorenzo pleaded.

"No, they're searching for me. They are all after me!" Riccardo exclaimed frantically. "We have to run," he insisted, pulling Lorenzo into his plan.

Lorenzo reached into his pocket, producing a set of rusty keys that he dangled in the dimly lit air. "We can hide in the greenhouse," he suggested, without waiting for confirmation. Taking hold of Riccardo's arm, Lorenzo led him back into the garden and directly to the greenhouse. Silently, Lorenzo unlocked its door, guiding Riccardo inside before securing it. Maurizio exited the house, headed toward his car to look for Riccardo.

"Shh. Don't make a sound. Let them leave the house in search of you," Lorenzo whispered, his breath brushing against Riccardo's ear as he placed a gentle kiss.

"Lorenzo, my grandmother is alive! She wants to take over my body," Riccardo whispered. Fear gripped him. He closed his eyes, crouching against the back of the door, and waited. The sound of Maurizio's car receded as it departed the garden, leaving a sinister calm in its wake. Riccardo surmised that the others had either departed with him or returned to the house, anticipating his eventual return for the ritual.

Lorenzo turned around, cautiously peering outside. "It appears safe," he whispered. "But for now, we should remain here. Follow me," he added, crawling on all fours beneath a long metallic table in the center of the greenhouse. Riccardo mimicked Lorenzo's movements, their hands grazing against the cold floor as they made their way to the other side. Once they reached their destination, a nauseating stench permeated the air, causing Riccardo to retch on the side.

"What is that smell? It's unbearable," Riccardo complained in a hushed tone, disguised by the green buckets nearby. They contained chunks of meaty substances, swarmed by buzzing flies and emitting a putrid odor. Drawing nearer, he shone the light of his phone onto the buckets, revealing slimy, iridescent flesh. As he focused his attention on the space behind the container, he saw an otherworldly sight: a monstrous creature's lifeless, staring eyes, its body dismembered and confined to the buckets.

Overwhelmed by terror, Riccardo spewed more vomit. "So it's all true," he uttered to himself.

"What's true?" Lorenzo asked, his voice trembling.

"The book, what my grandmother wrote... Look at this." Riccardo pointed to the grotesque remains of the unearthly monster, tears of horror streaming down his face. "This is... abominable," he said. Lorenzo let out a horrified shriek, mirroring Riccardo's shock, his entire body quivering. The remains of the revolting creature were surrounded by a ghastly pool of gooey paste, a murky, dark-cherry-jam color that seeped out in every direction. Riccardo understood this was what the maids had been trying to clean for days now, bringing its blood back home in those green plastic buckets and probably pouring it down the toilet upstairs. The repugnant stench hung thick in the air, attacking their sense of smell with an overpowering odor of decay and putrefaction. It was a smell that clung to the back of Riccardo's throat, refusing to be ignored. Little flies, bearing the sheen of death's feast, swarmed voraciously around the disfigured cadaver. They performed a macabre ballet, their wings buzzing in a relentless, discordant chorus. The scene was nothing short of a sickening banquet, as the repulsive insects gorged themselves upon the decaying flesh of the nightmarish creature.

"Please, we need to find a way out," Riccardo begged to his only friend in the world.

Lorenzo hesitated, unsure of how to comfort his friend

amid the unfolding turmoil. With the objective of finding escape, he reached for his phone and dialed his mother's number. Riccardo briefly glanced at Lorenzo but remained silent as Lorenzo pleaded into the phone, urging his mother to come and rescue them from Perihan's house. "Don't park, just stay outside. Text me when you're here, and we'll run to you. It's a matter of life and death," he pleaded, hastily ending the call. The putrid stench of the decaying monster in the room made Lorenzo nauseous, and he covered his nose within his sweater once again.

Riccardo seemed to be in a trance. Lorenzo didn't understand if he was talking to him or to himself.

"When someone possesses another's body, their identity is erased. They wake up with no memory of their past self... She wants to take over my body. No," he corrected himself, "she wants to resume her life in my body. With the monster dead and teardrops finished, her time is running out." Riccardo wiped the mucus from his nose and dried his tears with the back of his arm. Lorenzo regarded him with concern, but Riccardo seemed oblivious to his presence. He spoke aloud, trying to process the situation. "She has one butterfly left. It must be the butterfly Licia was carrying... This book isn't meant for me, it's meant for her, for when she wakes up in my body. This whole book is her autobiography to regain her memories. But it means hell for me," he muttered, shuddering involuntarily.

"Riccardo, calm down. My mom is on her way. She'll save us," Lorenzo said softly, attempting to soothe his friend by gently brushing his arm.

But Riccardo couldn't calm down. "My life is in danger. They brought me back here to use me as her vessel. She's not dead. Not yet. I thought I saw her at the funeral, but I kept my distance from the casket. She could have just been lying there. She's not dead… She explained everything to me her-self! God, she started writing this thing a long time ago, but when she found out the monster was dead, she completed the rest of it… Probably why the handwriting is very precise at the beginning and becomes harder to read toward the end," he said. "We have to go now," he concluded urgently.

"Go where? They might already be back or waiting outside the villa to catch us. We can't just escape on foot. We need a car," Lorenzo insisted, dialing his mother's number once more.

"Okay," Riccardo said.

"She'll be here in three minutes. Come on," Lorenzo said after Barbara answered the call, crawling back toward the main door, which he had locked earlier. As soon as Riccardo caught up with him, he pushed the keys into the lock and slowly turned it, preparing to make their escape.

Lorenzo cautiously peered out into the garden, his eyes scanning the surroundings for any signs of danger. Satisfied that it was clear, he closed the door without locking it, his mind focused on their escape plan. "There's nobody in the garden. Mom should be in the car outside. I'll count to three, and we go," he whispered to Riccardo, certainty in his words. Taking a deep breath, he counted silently, then on the count of three, they moved with deliberate and silent steps toward the entrance.

Lorenzo, his heart heavy with both fear and hope, leaned forward and pressed a gentle kiss on Riccardo's forehead, a silent reassurance of their bond. With a firm resolve, Lo-renzo turned the doorknob, and together they stepped out into the night.

Relief washed over both boys as they spotted Barbara's car parked across the street, its headlights illuminating their path. Barbara waved from the driver's seat, urging them to hurry. Lorenzo took two quick steps forward, but just as they were about to reach the safety of the car, their hopes shattered. Maurizio and a burly stranger emerged from both sides of the pavement and grabbed the fugitives. Their strong grips tightened around Lorenzo and Riccardo, immobilizing them. Barbara switched off the car lights and stepped out, a sad smile playing on her lips. "I'm sorry… I couldn't let you go. Perihan gave my son his life back years ago. I owe her this," she explained, her words heavy with regret. She turned to Lorenzo, her eyes filled with a mother's love. "I know you're angry now, but you will understand me eventually. We need Perihan to continue living. We can't let her die."

Despite their desperate struggles and futile attempts to break free, they were overpowered and forced back into the garden, their captors leading them into the dimly lit greenhouse. Once inside, Licia stood there, clutching the butterfly dome, flanked by the blind twins, Eva in her widow's attire with spider brooches adorning her veil, and others. Riccardo found himself ensnared in their midst, helpless prey, while Lorenzo was held firmly in the arms of the hulking stranger, unable to move.

Barbara spoke, her voice laden with the weight of her guilt. "Lorenzo suffered from cancer as a child. There was no cure. When I met Perihan, my son was living his final days. She gave him the first drop, ended his life, and brought him back, renewing every cell within him." Her words hung in the air, a confession mixed with a need for desperate justification.

Eva, her voice a seductive whisper that slithered through the room, interjected with a hint of bitterness. "Tears were more potent back then. They possessed healing and rejuvenating powers. That was before their strength waned, leaving only the ability to resurrect lives. And even that has its limits, as you know," she hissed, her words intertwining with the stifling air.

Barbara turned to Lorenzo, a question burning in her eyes. "She was so generous. She even gave him an extra drop. Did you tell him that, Lorenzo?" she asked. Lorenzo remained silent, devoid of emotions. Riccardo noticed just then that the charm necklace around Lorenzo's neck had a pendant holding the last remaining tear of the monster, a gift given to him by Perihan years ago.

Suddenly, the room fell silent, interrupted only by the smell of Fracas, Perihan's signature scent. Her magnetic presence filled the space as the stunning Perihan, in her seventy-year-old form exuding an aura of timeless beauty, approached the group. Clad in the flowing red gown that matched her long crimson nails, her expression devoid of a smile but brimming with intensity, she locked eyes with Riccardo, gripping his face firmly in her hand.

"Nobody runs away from fate, my dear," she declared. "The ritual can finally begin."

24

Perihan locked her gaze onto Riccardo, their eyes meeting with an intensity that sent shivers down his spine. "The true freedom," she began, her voice firm, "lies in leaving ourselves behind, transcending the boundaries of our limited world to embrace the vastness of the universe. And that is why we are here, Riccardo." She was flipping through the pages of the manuscript, satisfaction radiating from her.

"I started writing this right after Maurizio told me about metempsychosis," Perihan continued, her tone tinged with urgency, "but I had to rush to complete it when I learned, on my birthday, that my fallen angel had finally perished. No more tears, no more resurrection, no more playing God for me." Her eyes remained fixed on Riccardo, her plan of possessing him with her soul now apparent.

Licia approached with the butterfly dome, holding it close to Perihan. Eva handed Perihan a small, sharp knife, and she knelt, her eyes fixated on the delicate light blue, almost lilac wings of the phengaris arion. She touched the glass dome with the sharp edge of the blade. "What exquisite beauty," she remarked, her voice laced with a touch of admiration. "An illusionist of sorts. This butterfly is incredibly devious. It's a blood parasite feeding on another insect, the myrmica ant. A master of disguise, it pretends to be an ant larva to trick them. Sometimes it even copies the queen ant's special sounds to control other ones. The myrmicas, thinking it's one of their own, carry it to their nest. Once inside, the caterpillar either eats the ant babies or begs for food. It's like a sneaky houseguest. After being well-fed and staying warm through the winter, it transforms into a beautiful butterfly with a fresh start. After I end my own life, my friends will guide this butterfly into your mouth, instead of this aging vessel of mine, and I shall awaken within you. There will be much reading to be done until I find myself again." She chuckled, her laughter filling the room like effervescent champagne, though the tension in the air did not go unnoticed by her companions.

Lorenzo's voice erupted from behind, breaking the suffocating silence. "Let him go!" he shouted, his desperation evident. Perihan's attention shifted to Lorenzo, her intense stare sweeping over him, a powerful interest in her eyes. "Greed does not suit a man," she scoffed, her voice dripping with condescension. "Not only have I saved you once before but I have given you a second chance at a long life. Look at your neck. You are the sole bearer of a teardrop here. Be grateful and remain silent."

Riccardo felt the pang of betrayal: probably his only friend, the only person he trusted in all this, had failed to disclose his prior encounter with Perihan. Now it seemed as if he were complicit in trapping Riccardo within this nightmarish scenario. Yet Lorenzo's eyes told him there was more to the story, a misunderstanding, perhaps. Riccardo summoned every ounce of strength within him, exerting force on his arms and legs, struggling against Maurizio's hold. With a burst of energy, he managed to break free, delivering a powerful kick to the butterfly dome. The glass shattered, the wooden stand splintered, and the phengaris arion tumbled onto the soil. Chaos erupted as everyone recoiled in shock at the act of violence against something delicate and precious. Maurizio and the other man released their grips on Riccardo and Lorenzo, their attention consumed by rescuing the fallen butterfly from potential harm.

Seizing the opportunity, Riccardo swiftly snatched the book from his distracted grandmother. She screamed in frustration as she lost her grip on the manuscript, but he wasted no time. He dashed out of the circle. "Lorenzo! Run!" he shouted, urging his friend to find the car outside. As Lorenzo made a frantic move toward the greenhouse exit, his heart pounding with fear, an abrupt pain struck him right beneath his Adam's apple. He stumbled, his breath trapped in his throat, gasping for comprehension. A warmth dripped down his neck, and as he turned around, he locked eyes with the piercing stare of Perihan.

In her right hand, she held the small, sharp knife. She thrust the blade directly into Lorenzo's throat, and a river of blood flowed down his neck. The blood trickled down the cold steel edge of the weapon, descending in a steady rhythm, each drop echoing as it splattered onto the greenhouse floor, mixing with the dark cherry-red gooey substance from the monster.

Lorenzo's body went cold as the inevitability of his fate washed over him. Perihan, unrelenting, released her grip on him, the deed done. Riccardo, bearing witness to this horrifying scene, unleashed a scream that pierced the very heavens: "No. No! Lorenzo can't die, no!" His cries joined the cries of Barbara. They both raced toward Lorenzo's fallen form, desperate to save him from the clutches of impending death.

But Perihan, her will unwavering, issued a sharp command to Maurizio, her voice laced with a sinister authority. Maurizio seized Riccardo, preventing him from reaching his friend. They fought as Riccardo tried to free himself once more, but the position he was in did not help. The manuscript fell to the floor.

In her final act of chilling defiance, Perihan screamed, thick veins throbbing in her wrinkly neck. "Do you honestly believe that, between the two of us, *you* are the one who truly deserves to inhabit this world? There's an overwhelming quantity of bodies wandering this earth, yet regrettably, not all these souls truly embrace life. They possess these robust, healthy vessels and do nothing because, more often than not, they waste their potential in indolence. They pass their days before glowing screens, passively watching others' lives, constantly complaining about life's challenges without summoning the necessary resilience and tenacity needed to excel. If they truly aimed to elevate their existence and that of those around them, they'd recognize that lethargy is their worst enemy. Most, much like you, are constantly weary and obstinately lazy. I began my journey in hell's mouth and persevered until I made a miracle out of it. Who are you to withhold your body from me now? What purpose does it serve? Who in Paris eagerly awaits your return? No one! What grand projects lie on your horizon? None! Whose life depends on your presence and companionship? The resounding answer is *no one*! Twenty years in this world and you have achieved nothing! Stop wasting my precious time, Riccardo. You've never been more than just a vessel. Your time is up, and there is no way to prevent what I am here for."

With cold determination, Perihan took the knife and deliberately severed her own throat, the blade slicing through her flesh with grim precision. A red cascade erupted from her ruptured artery, splashing out like a frenzied fountain. Amid this gruesome downpour, Riccardo fought relentlessly to free himself from Maurizio's unyielding grip. As the blood from Perihan's throat gradually lost its vigor, the blue butterfly on the floor began to stir back to life.

Sensing a momentary distraction in Maurizio as the butterfly reawakened, Riccardo summoned every ounce of strength for one last desperate attempt at freedom. He lunged forward, managing to break free from Maurizio's hold, his body soaked in the macabre rain of Perihan's lifeblood.

Before he could fully regain his footing, a brutal punch from Maurizio's clenched fist found its mark, sending Riccardo sprawling to the floor. The chilling image of Perihan's blood smeared upon his clothing and the resurrected blue butterfly now flapping its wings through the air marked the nightmarish tableau that closed in as he lost consciousness.

25

As Riccardo left the greenhouse, bathed in the eerie moonlight that cast a spotlight upon him, he kept crying. It was unclear whether these tears were of grief or of joy. Clutched tightly under his arm, the manuscript traveled with him on his way to the house through the desolate garden.

Upon entering the house, he made a futile attempt to dry his tears as he ascended the stairs toward the guest bedroom. Yet, a sudden and savage force erupted within him, making him pause before the door. An unexplainable impulse found life within him, compelling him toward Perihan's room. Before he dared to open the door, he hesitated, inhaling the scent of his own clothes. The nauseating blend of blood and sweat clung to him, causing his face to twist in revulsion.

Inside the room, he placed the manuscript on Perihan's bed and took off his dirty shirt. He opened the wardrobe, selected an embroidered sweater that, although too small, seemed to fit his mood. In one of the dressing table's drawers, he uncovered a bottle of Fracas perfume. He doused himself with

the scent, savoring the noxious aroma as it clung to the flam-
boyant sweater. With curiosity, he examined his reflection
in the mirror. His fingers drew closer to the sides of his eyes,
scrutinizing the skin intently. "At least no more wrinkles,"
he muttered, his voice laced with a tone of accomplishment.

After taking his shoes off, he settled comfortably on the
bed and opened the manuscript to the first page. He smiled as
he recognized his handwriting. Just like the phengaris arion
inside him, he had left the ants' nest as a wonderful butterfly after a long winter and was finally ready to start his next
chapter.

★ ★ ★ ★ ★

AUTHOR NOTE

Despite my mother's interest in horror films during her pregnancy with me, and for whatever reason, her many viewings of *Jaws* before my birth, I was not allowed to watch horror movies until I turned five. One of my earliest memories takes place in a city in eastern Turkey, at my grandparents' house. One night, my grandmother tucked both me and my sister into bed, kissed us goodnight, and instructed my mom to switch off all the house lights, as we had plans for an early picnic the next day. "Time for bed, everyone!" she shouted in the dark.

Knowing my love for horror films and our shared passion for them, my grandmother whispered under the covers as she laid me down, her long red pointy nails lightly caressing my cheek. She suggested I wait until my sister fell asleep before sneaking out to meet her in the living room. My sister, Gizem, who is only a year and a half younger than me, and who typically loved late-night chats in the dark, fell asleep quickly that night. Heart pounding in my chest, I quietly crossed the icy tile floor to meet my grandmother, bathed in the bluish glow of the television. She was wearing one of her pink nightgowns with elaborate embroidery and feathers, lounging comfortably on the oversized sofa.

"I've made some popcorn for us!" she whispered cheerfully. "They're showing Freddy's Nightmares tonight!" I jumped onto the sofa, snuggling into her warm embrace infused with the scent of tuberose. When questioned about her heavy perfume before bedtime, she'd reply, "Who knows who I'll dream about tonight! I'd rather be prepared..."

And so, we watched those Freddy episodes until the early hours of the morning. One scene, where Freddy transformed someone's fingers into hotdogs, haunted me for years, preventing me from ever ordering hotdogs again. My mother eventually discovered us asleep in front of the still-running TV, furious at my grandmother for exposing a five-year-old to a horror series all night. Consequently, we had to cancel our picnic plans due to having been up so late.

Following that night, my grandmother and I secretly continued our horror movie club, which only deepened our bond. My grandfather on the other hand, more reserved but passionate about lepidopterology, filled his studio with butterfly illustrations from ancient books and would often discuss them with me.

When I lost my grandparents, grief overwhelmed me. To cope, I transformed my emotions into a fictional world where, in a parallel universe, my grandmother would stop at nothing to keep watching horror films with me. Grief, like a soundproof room, drowns out all other noises of life, trapping you in a seemingly inescapable space. It was in these imagined parallel worlds that I found comfort, creating secret passages that, though imaginary, could transport me back to happier times.

May Perihan leave you with the lingering scent of tuberose flowers and build you an imaginary corridor to any destination you desire.

Yiğit, Milan, 05.2024

ACKNOWLEDGMENTS

I want to express my heartfelt thanks to my mum,

Reflecting on my childhood, I'm filled with deep gratitude for your nurturing love and boundless creativity. Every weekend, you whisked me off to bookstores, letting me choose new books that ignited my lifelong passion for stories. And then, you made our own book club, where we laughed and shared our thoughts over those very books. You turned ordinary days into something extraordinary, shaping my interests and strengthening our bond. Thank you for infusing my childhood with such warmth and creativity, transforming who I am today.

To my grandmother,

You lived life boldly and proudly, and I cherish the attention and love you showered on me. From our late-night horror movie marathons to your comforting hugs scented with tuberose, you taught me to embrace life with courage and passion.

To my teachers Didem Babacan, Leslie Moore, and Barış Sayber,

You have dedicated your lives to shaping the next generations. I was in middle school when Didem discovered she had a terminal illness but continued teaching us English with un-wavering dedication. She went the extra mile by simplifying complex English books into accessible stories for her Turk-ish students, and she taught us colors by changing her scarf daily during chemotherapy. Her final days were spent in the hospital, where we gathered to present her with a book filled with our fondest memories, illustrated together. Didem, I have never forgotten you.

If I've ever been a teacher's favorite, it was undoubtedly Leslie. I always wanted to impress her, so I worked tirelessly to complete tasks ahead of schedule and in the most excep-tional manner possible. Leslie encouraged me to start writing short stories, generously providing feedback on each one. I still treasure those stories, adorned with her insightful com-ments, as my talismans.

And then there's Barış—charismatic, open-minded, and endlessly enthusiastic. She possesses a unique ability to under-stand my imagination instantly, diving into imaginary worlds without needing much explanation. Whenever I begin craft-ing a new story, I reach out to Barış to gauge her enthusiasm and gather her feedback. If her voice carries that distinct edge of excitement, that's when I embark on the drafting process.

To Giuliano,

You are my greatest gift, and a never-ending source of in-spiration. Thank you for walking by my side through all of life's journeys, even the imaginary ones.

To my supportive agent Lane Heymont,

Thank you for believing in me and my work right from the start.

To my wonderful editor Emma Cole,

Your feedback and support have been invaluable in shaping my story. I couldn't have done it without you.

To my dear friend Dua,

You are a true polymath, effortlessly juggling music, book clubs, movies, and more with such passion and grace. Your multifaceted creativity is a constant source for pushing the boundaries.

To the people who have filled my heart with affection, respect and gratitude for their support: Antonio Buatti, Amina Muaddi, Andrew Sean Greer, Aurora Foschi, Blair Trader, dad, Donna Tartt, Douglas Coupland, Emma Roberts, Georg Wilson, Giordano, Hanya Yanagihara, Helen Downie, Sandra Nikoko, Janet Mock, JV, Karah Preiss, Lisa Taddeo, Nadia Lee Cohen, Mr. Rachid, Romy Blanga, RT, Sahibe Karaca.

To everyone at Mira, HTP Books, and HarperCollins,

Thank you for trusting in my story and giving it a chance to reach readers.

Thank you to my precious sister, Gizem, who will always be my Gizmo since the day we watched *Gremlins* together.